DA

THE IMPOSSIBLE
LIVES OF
GRETA WELLS

Center Point
Large Print

**This Large Print Book carries the
Seal of Approval of N.A.V.H.**

THE
IMPOSSIBLE LIVES
OF
GRETA WELLS

Andrew Sean Greer

CENTER POINT LARGE PRINT
THORNDIKE, MAINE

This Center Point Large Print edition
is published in the year 2013 by arrangement with
Ecco, an imprint of HarperCollins Publishers.

This book is a work of fiction. The characters, incidents, and dialogue are drawn from the author's imagination and are not to be construed as real. Any resemblance to actual events or persons, living or dead, is entirely coincidental.

The text of this Large Print edition is unabridged.
In other aspects, this book may vary
from the original edition.
Printed in the United States of America
on permanent paper.
Set in 16-point Times New Roman type.

ISBN: 978-1-61173-917-6

Library of Congress Cataloging-in-Publication Data

Greer, Andrew Sean.
The Impossible Lives of Greta Wells / Andrew Sean Greer.
pages cm
ISBN 978-1-61173-917-6 (library binding : alk. paper)
1. Identity (Psychology)—Fiction. 2. Reincarnation—Fiction.
3. Depression in women—Fiction. 4. Large type books. I. Title.
PS3557.R3987I57 2013
813'.54—dc23
                                                    2013024167

For my mothers, grandmothers,
and all the women in my life

Endless thanks to Lynn Nesbit; Lee Boudreaux; Walter Donohue; Cullen Stanley; Frances Coady; Michael Chabon; Beatrice Della Monte von Rezzori; Brandon Cleary; Carmiel Banasky; the Cullman Center at the New York Public Library, especially Jean Strouse and Alice Hudson; the San Francisco History Center; Chapin's 1917 *Greenwich Village*; Miller's 1990 *Greenwich Village and How It Got That Way*; the Macdowell Colony; the Yaddo Corporation; Santa Maddalena; the Aspen Writer's Foundation; and the Cattos—but most especially to Daniel Handler, my best reader; and to David Ross, my best companion.

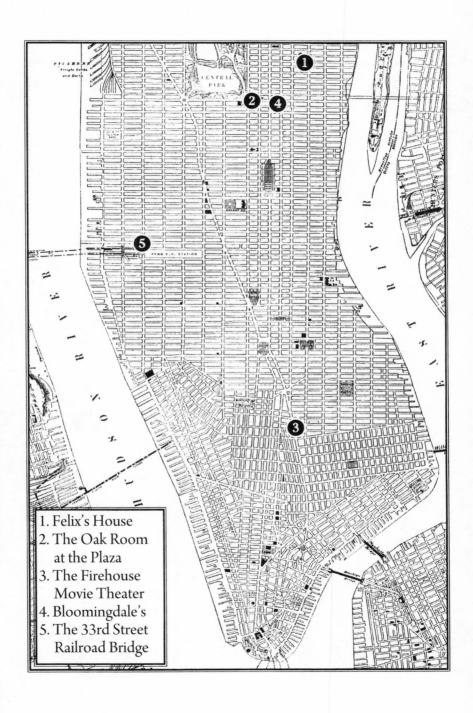

1. Felix's House
2. The Oak Room at the Plaza
3. The Firehouse Movie Theater
4. Bloomingdale's
5. The 33rd Street Railroad Bridge

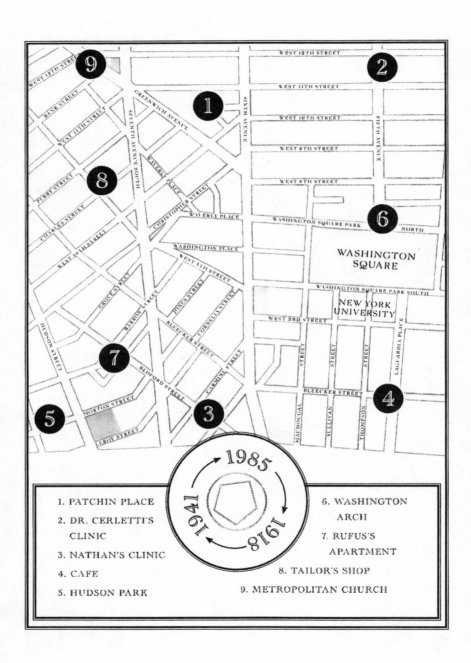

1. PATCHIN PLACE
2. DR. CERLETTI'S CLINIC
3. NATHAN'S CLINIC
4. CAFE
5. HUDSON PARK
6. WASHINGTON ARCH
7. RUFUS'S APARTMENT
8. TAILOR'S SHOP
9. METROPOLITAN CHURCH

Part One

OCTOBER
TO
NOVEMBER

OCTOBER 30, 1985

The impossible happens once to each of us.

For me, it was near Halloween in 1985, at my home in Patchin Place. Even New Yorkers find it hard to spot: a little alley west of Sixth Avenue where the city tilts drunkenly into an eighteenth-century pattern, allowing for such fanciful moments as West Fourth crossing West Eighth and Waverly Place crossing itself. There is West Twelfth and Little West Twelfth. There is Greenwich Street and Greenwich Avenue, the last of which takes a diagonal route along the old Indian trail. If any ghosts still walk there, carrying their corn, no one sees them, or perhaps they are unrecognizable among the freaks and tourists out at all hours, drunk and laughing by my doorstep. They say the tourists are ruining everything. They say they have always said that.

But I will tell you: Stand on West Tenth where it meets Sixth Avenue, in the turreted shadow of the old Jefferson Market Courthouse with its tall tower. Turn until you see a set of iron gates, so easy to miss, peer through the bars and there: no more than half a city block, lined with thin maples, dead-ending half a dozen doorways down, nothing glamorous, just a little broken alley of brick three-story apartment buildings, built long ago to house the Basque waiters at the Brevoort, and there at the end, on the right, just past the last tree, our door. Scrape your shoes on the old shoe brush embedded in the concrete. Walk through the green front door, and you might turn left to knock on my aunt Ruth's apartment, or walk upstairs and knock on mine. And at the turn of the staircase, you might stop and read the heights of two children, mine in red grease pencil and, high above in blue, that of my twin brother, Felix.

Patchin Place. The gates locked and painted black. The houses crouched in solitude. The ivy growing, torn down, growing again; the stones cracked and weedy; not even a borough president would look left on his hurrying way to dinner. Who would ever guess? Behind the gates, the doors, the ivy. Where only a child would look. As you know: That is how magic works. It takes the least likely of us, without foreshadowing, at the hour of its own choosing. It makes a thimblerig of time. And this is exactly how, one Thursday morning, I woke up in another world.

Let me start nine months before it happened, in January, when I was out with Felix to walk Alan's dog. We had locked the green door behind us, and were making our way past the ice-covered gates of Patchin Place while the dog, Lady, sniffed each barren patch of dirt. Cold, cold, cold. The wool collars of our coats were pulled up and we shared Felix's scarf, wound once around each of our necks, connecting us, my hand in his pocket and his in mine. He was my twin, but not my double, so while he shared my flushed cheeks and bent nose, my red hair and pale complexion, my squinting blue eyes—"fox faced," our aunt Ruth called us—he was taller, greater somehow. I had to steady Felix on the ice, but he insisted on going out that night without his cane; it was one of his good nights. I still found him so ridiculous in his new mustache. So thin in his new over-coat. It was our thirty-first birthday.

I said, "It was such a lovely party."

Everywhere the shivering hush of a New York winter: the glimpses of high apartments, the shimmer of the frozen streets, the muted glow of restaurants late at night, pyramids of snow at corners hiding trash and coins and keys. The sound of our steps on the sidewalk.

"I was thinking," he said. "After I die, I want you to have a birthday party where everyone comes dressed as me." Always thinking of a party. I remember him as bossy and self-righteously moral as a child, the kind who assigned himself as "fire captain" and forced the rest of the family through ridiculous drills. After our parents' death, however, and especially after he escaped our shared scrawny adolescence, all that ice melted at once—he became almost a convert to the side of fire itself. He grew restless if a day had no great event in store; he planned many of them himself, and would throw anyone a party if it meant drinks and costumes. Our aunt Ruth approved.

"Oh hush," I said. "I'm sorry Nathan had to leave early. But he's been working, you know."

"Did you hear me?"

I looked at him, his freckled face, that red mustache. Dark commas beneath his eyes. Thin and scared and quiet, all the fire burnt away inside him. Instead of answering, I said, "Look at the ice on all the trees!"

He let Lady sniff at a fence. "You'll make Nathan dress up in my old Halloween costume."

"The cowgirl."

He laughed. "No, Ethel Mermaid. You can sit him in an armchair and feed him drinks. He'll like that."

"You didn't like our birthday?" I said. "I know it wasn't much. Could you please teach Alan to bake a cake?"

"Our birthday cheers me up." We walked along, looking up at silhouettes in windows. "Don't neglect Nathan."

The light caught the ice on the trees, electrifying them.

"It's been ten years. Maybe he could use a little neglect," I said, holding his arm to steady him.

On the cold winter street, I heard Felix whisper, "Look there's another one."

He nodded in the direction of a hair salon that had always graced the corner. In the window, a sign: CLOSED FOR BUSINESS. My brother stood for a moment while Lady considered the tree. Felix said simply, "Gone home."

That was the phrase: journal of a plague year. The dog-grooming salon. The bead shop. The bartender and the tailor and the waiter down at the Gate. All of the CLOSED FOR BUSINESS signs. And if you asked about that waiter they'd say: "He's gone home." The bartender with the bird tattoo: "Gone home." The boy who lived upstairs and set off the fire alarm: "Gone home." Danny. Samuel. Patrick. So many ghosts you couldn't make out the Indians even if they wailed for lost Manahatta.

A loud bang; a woman had come out of the building: frizzy dyed black hair, trench coat. "You assholes are killing the trees!"

"Hi," said Felix sweetly. "We're your neighbors, it's nice to meet you."

She shook her head, staring at Lady, who was preparing to squat in the frosted grass. "You're ruining my city," she said. "Get your dog out of here."

Her tone was so harsh we were both shaken; I

15

could feel my brother's hand clenched in my pocket. I tried to think of something to do or say other than just turning to go. She crossed her arms, defiant.

Felix said, "I'm sorry, but . . . I don't think girl dogs hurt the trees."

"Get your dog out of here."

I watched my brother's face. So gaunt, barely a reminder of the strong, grinning twin I'd always known, the flushed pink face now worn away. I gripped his arm and began to pull him away; he didn't need this, not on our birthday. But he would not budge. I saw him building up the courage to say something. I had assumed he had used up all his reserves of courage in the past year.

"All right," he said at last, reining in Lady, who stumbled. "But I have one question."

The woman smiled smugly and raised an eyebrow.

He managed a grin. And then he said something that made her take a single step back as we disappeared around the corner and began our nervous laughter together on that cold night of our last birthday. I carried what he said through the tough weeks that followed, then the awful months, the half a year of hell that drove me deeper into sadness than I had ever known. Standing there firmly, calmly, asking that woman a question:

"When you were a little girl, madam," he said, gesturing to her, "was *this* the woman you dreamed of becoming?"

It all came faster than we could plan for. One day Felix was talking cheerfully about the books I had brought him. And then the next morning I was getting a call from Alan saying, "He's going, it's too fast now, I think we have to—" And I was rushing over to their apartment to find Felix going in and out of lucidity. Apparently his joints were so swollen it hurt to move, and the pain was beyond reckoning; the headaches had returned with severity, and the last bout of antibiotics had done no good. We stood on either side of him asking over and over, "Do you want to go?" and it was over twenty minutes later that my brother was able to open his eyes and hear us. He could not speak, but he nodded. I could tell from his eyes he was there, and knew.

Patchin Place, alone with Nathan, mourning my brother. The snow fell heavily upon the gates that winter, and weighed down the maples outside my window. Ruth took Felix's bird, and I listened to it chirping in the apartment below, staring out, as I did, at a birdless winter day. Felix was wrong about so many things, but he was right about Nathan: I should not have neglected him.

The man I lived with but never married, my

Dr. Michelson, a smart and gentle man, smiling in a red-brown beard and glasses. Long, narrow face, lined with worry at the eyes below a receding heart-shaped hairline. When we first met, I had always thought of Nathan as an "older man," but after I turned thirty the truth dawned on me that he was only eight years older, and that as time went on the gap would close, until we were both equally old, and the revelation came with a sadness that I would lose something I "had" on him. At forty, he had a slightly sad, pleasantly smiling demeanor that led people to say, "But you're so young!" What they meant was that he had not grown bitter. He always closed his eyes and smiled at that remark. I suppose it's because he was what he'd always said he would be. He was a doctor, loved by a woman. He lived in Greenwich Village. Despite the gray in his beard, what I felt kept him young were the childhood hobgoblins he retained as pets: his fear of sharks, even in a swimming pool; his fear of mispronouncing "dour." He laughed each time he caught himself, and told me so. Who knows how many others went untold? But I grew to love them as intimates, and when after years I heard him saying "dour" correctly on a few separate occasions, it was as if an old one-eyed cat had died.

You could sum up his personality by the phrase he spoke so soothingly, at every difficult occasion in our courtship: "I leave it to you." Somehow, it was the antidote to all my fears. Was I spending too much time with Felix, and not enough with him? "I leave it to you." Should I stay late at work or attend his mother's party? "I leave it to you." That phrase drained me of worry; I loved him for it. He became my companion, for ten years. In those last months of Felix's life, however, Nathan was a ghost I could not see. I ignored him and brushed him aside, and for a while he understood. And then he did not understand. He was so kind, but when crossed could just as easily be cold. And then I lost him.

Just a few months after Felix's death, I discovered he had taken a lover. I followed Nathan one evening and found myself before a brick building, the zigzag smile of a fire escape, seeing the silhouettes of my lover and his young woman. Who knows how long I stood there? How long does one stand before a scene of dread? It had begun to snow, in tiny dust flakes, and this lengthened how the light fell from the window onto the street.

I will always wonder if I did the right thing. I stepped away from the building and I walked back home, and warmed myself within the solitary bed, and never mentioned it to him. With everything going on, with all the grief I had plugged up, I could easily understand his need for ease and attention, for playing husband to this play wife—trying out another life, in a way—and I said to myself, "He will come home to me, not her." After all, we had shared so many things, including the years before gray hair. Who else would ever fit him so neatly?

He did come home to me. He did leave her. I know it because one night a few weeks later, when I sat in Patchin Place reading a book while white-bean soup simmered on the stove, still an hour away from being ready, he came home streaked with rain, his face very red and puffy, and something distant in his eyes, as if he'd witnessed a murder. Beard gleaming with droplets. He said hello and kissed my cheek. "I'll take off these wet things," he said, and went into the other room and closed the door.

I heard a violin quartet, not what he usually listened to, but he must have tuned the radio to anything loud enough. But it was not loud enough. I heard it beneath the music, as he sat hidden from me in the other room, the sound he could not control and yet desperately wanted to hide: the sobs of a broken heart.

In some scene I can barely imagine, he had said some final farewell and kissed her, made love some final time, and pushed his way out the door as she sought for the right thing to say, the thing that would make him stay there. Make him leave me instead of her. He held the doorknob with one shaking hand; they stared at each other. Did he cry yet? For she did not find the words—and here he was. Sitting in the other room, sobbing like a boy. Violins dervishing around him. And here I was, in my chair with my book and the big brass lamp casting a hoop of gold across my lap. Knowing what he had done. Wanting to tell him that I was angry and hurt and grateful. The violins made their bumpy way down the octave. And, after a while, Nathan came out of that room and asked, "Do you want a drink? I'm making one for myself, a whiskey." There with the grief so plain on his face. How many weeks, months had it been? How many phone calls, letters, nights had he given to her? Over like that, like breaking a neck. "Yes," I said, putting down my book, "the soup will be ready soon," and we drank and fed ourselves and did not talk about the great thing that had just happened.

The real surprise was that, a few months later, he left me after all. In a rental car, parked outside the gates, me in the driver's seat.

"Stay with me, Nathan."

"No, Greta, I can't anymore."

His hand on the car door, choosing the words that would end our lives together. It did not really matter what they were. I picture myself at that dire moment: pale in the streetlight, tears caught in my nearly invisible lashes, red hair recently cut short in a last bid for change, lips parted as I tried to think of anything left to say.

Door handle open, wind rushing in, the last few minutes—I realized the flash of his glasses in the streetlight might be the last I ever saw of him.

"What am I supposed to do?" I shouted from the car.

He stared at me coldly for a moment, then touched the door and said, before he shut it, "I leave it to you."

"Try hypnosis," my aunt Ruth counseled me, rubbing my temples with oil. "Try est. Try anything but shrinks, darling." She was my sole companion in those months. I'm sure my father would not have approved of her visits; he always found his sister flighty, selfish, uncontrolled, the dangerous artist who had to be stopped. The kind of woman, he once told me, who would yell "theater" in a crowded fire. A comfort, an ally, but she knew nothing of my mind.

Everybody had advice. Try acupuncture, they would tell me when I roused myself for a party. Try acupressure. Try yoga, try running, try pot. Try oats, try bran, try colonics. Quit smoking, quit dairy, quit meat. Quit drinking, quit TV, quit being self-centered. The psychiatrist I found at last, Dr. Gilleo, talked to me endlessly about my dead parents, my childhood memories of golden dogs running on golden afternoons with my brother, and found the ordinary thorns of an ordinary life. Was it so bad, I asked him, to be sad because sad things happened? "There are a number of new antidepressants," he said. "And we will try them." I did try them, from Ambivalon to zimelidine. And still they could not shake the nightmare: of answering my door and seeing Felix there, in his absurd mustache, asking to come in, and me telling him he couldn't. "Why not?" he asked. Nightly I told him, "Because you're dead."

Ruth rubbing my temples, kissing my forehead. "There there, darling. It will pass. It will pass." Adding, unhelpfully as always, "I think what you need is a lover."

It is almost impossible to capture true sadness; it is a deep-sea creature that can never be brought into view. I say that I remember being sad, but in truth I only remember mornings when that person in the bed—the person in which I was contained—could not wake up, could not go to work, could not even do the things that she knew would save her, and instead did only what was bound to destroy her: alcohol, and forbidden cigarettes, and endless lost black hours of loneliness. I'm tempted to distance myself from her, to say, "Oh, that wasn't me." But that was me, staring at the wall and longing to crayon-draw all over it and not even having the will for that. Not even the will for suicide. That was me in my room, looking out the window on Patchin Place as the maples turned yellow into autumn.

You could already make out my neighborhood heightening its mood in preparation for Halloween. Store windows were filled with silver-painted nude fauns, great glowing puppets, skeletons and witches of every type. Hollowed-out pumpkins lined the gate of Patchin Place; I felt you could lay my head down among them. The streets looked lonely. I looked lonely as I made my way each morning to work, and each evening home to a slighter, darker twilight, my street trading all its colors for blue, while from the west came the bright, streaming lavender sunset on the Hudson. It lit up all the sky, the tall apartment towers black and jagged against it. That is where I lived. In the fall of 1985. How I longed to live in any time but this one. It seemed cursed with sorrow and death.

How clearly I could hear my brother asking me from the grave, Was this the woman you dreamed of becoming? Was this the woman?

And then, one day, tapping his pencil on his pad, my dear old Dr. Gilleo: "There is one more thing we can try."

The doctor's office was not quite what I expected. Perhaps because it was Halloween, I thought it would look something like Dr. Frankenstein's laboratory, carved out from the side of a cliff. Instead, it was an ordinary brownstone that shared a courtyard with what I remembered as an old grammar school; now, it had become part of the medical suite, and nurses stood in the courtyard, smoking. I sat for a few minutes in a plaid chair, across from an old lady with a bright green shawl and a knitting bag, and then was told Dr. Cerletti would see me now. The sign on the door: CERLETTI, ELECTROCONVULSIVE THERAPY.

"Miss Wells, I see here we have informed consent from Dr. Gilleo, is that right?" said a short, bald man with large half-rimmed glasses and a gentle expression.

"Yes, Doctor." I looked around the room for the device that would cure me.

"He did a pretreatment evaluation for us, is that right?"

"I've been depressed," I told him. "We've tried pills. Nothing seems to work."

"That is the only reason you would be here, Miss Wells."

Dr. Cerletti looked at his clipboard. "Do you mind if I ask a few questions?"

"Only if I get to ask a few. I'm terrified about electroshock—"

"We call it electroconvulsive these days. I'm sure Dr. Gilleo went through it all with you. No data suggests any kind of damage to the brain."

"Electroconvulsive doesn't sound much better."

He smiled, and the smile on his bland, kind face was reassuring. "Things are very different

25

from what they used to be. For instance, I'm going to give you thiopental, an anesthetic, and a muscle relaxant. It will be much nicer than going to the dentist."

"That's Sodium Pentathol? Will I tell you the truth, Doctor?"

"Were you planning not to? It doesn't actually induce truth telling. It just lowers the patient's resolve."

"Sounds like the last thing I need."

"For right now, it's just what you need," he said, writing something down and frowning. "We'll do this twice a week except the last, a course of twelve weeks. Twenty-five procedures. We will be finished by February. It will help you make it through a hard time. I understand your brother died recently."

"Among other things," I said, staring out the window and watching the nurses. "Will it change me?" I asked the doctor.

Dr. Cerletti considered this very carefully. "Not at all, Miss Wells. What has changed you is your depression. What we're trying to do is bring you back."

"Bring me back."

He smiled again and took a deep breath. "You can go about your normal life. Tell me if you're trying to get pregnant."

"That's not likely, Doctor."

"ECT is harmless for pregnant women, but it's

something we like to know. You might experience some disorientation afterward. That's perfectly normal."

"What kind of disorientation?"

"Please lie down. A slight dizziness. Possibly, just possibly, hallucinations. Not knowing where you are, quite who you are for a moment. Some people have auditory hallucinations, bells ringing, that sort of thing."

"Wait. That sounds serious."

"Lie down, please. It isn't. Patients say it's like waking up in a hotel room. At first, you're not sure where you are. But then you're yourself again. Lie down, there you go. First the anesthetic. You won't feel anything electrical at all."

The nurse arrived with two syringes—the anesthetic and a muscle relaxant. I lay down on the crackling paper and looked at the constellations in the acoustic ceiling tiles. I closed my eyes. The doctor said that I would feel the first injection, but not the second, and that it would last only a minute while he administered the procedure, which would be one and a half times the seizure threshold for a woman my age. We needed to tip me into a seizure to reset my brain, was how I understood it. Cerletti nattered on about medical history, perhaps to calm me, saying how much better this was than the old days. Long ago, they had used static electricity capacitors, can you believe it? I felt something metal attached to each of my temples, then the cold swab of alcohol on my inner arm, then the awful pinch of a needle going in. I held my breath. Almost immediately an unpleasant smell filled the room—rotting onions—my mind unlatched, and then I found myself elsewhere. *Don't bring me back,* I remember thinking: *Take me away.*

As for what I felt—later, I would come to think of it as being cut out of the world. The sensation —not unpleasant, but more like the shock of cold limbs immersed in hot water—of the draft being removed from my skin, the crackling paper cot from my back, the air from my lungs, so that I hung for a moment utterly separate from my surroundings. Cut out of the world, as a gingerbread man is cut out of dough. Cut out, and taken who knows where?

What do you call the time when we are missing? The time, for instance, when we've had so much to drink that minutes stutter by with blanks inserted, or whole hours are lost to us— and yet we were there, said and did things, and are held responsible for what occurred? Or even the little lost moment when we awaken to find ourselves partway through a phone conversation, and have to bluff our way through? What is that gap time called? What part of us is functioning? Are we to blame for what we do? And finally: Who are we when we're not ourselves?

"There."

I opened my eyes. The doctor was smiling down at me, and I noticed a drop of perspiration between his eyebrows. "You may feel a little hangover for the rest of the day."

I looked around at the same room, unchanged, just slightly underwater. And then I said something very odd, which made him smile: "Where are the *what*, Miss Wells?"

"I'm sorry, I must be coming out of it."

"Do you think you can walk home?"

I told him yes, of course.

He nodded and said, "I think you'll notice a shift. We're trying these procedures back-to-back, so I'll see you tomorrow and then next week; just set it up with Marcia on your way out." He smiled at his nurse and, as she left the room, he gave her a little pat on the behind. The nurse, a blond permed creature with blue eye shadow and a sideways nose, brought out my clothes and waited for me to change, a little grin on her face. Perhaps it was from the doctor's pat. Or perhaps it was from my funny little question, while still under the anesthesia:

"Doctor, where are all the children?"

"I saw something," I told my aunt Ruth later that day. "I mean, when I closed my eyes, when they . . . I thought I was somewhere else." We sat in my apartment pouring tea; rather, she sat,

29

and I lay in my bed with my hand on my forehead, fighting the "hangover" the doctor had predicted. A small, simple room with one large window to the north and the bed placed beside it, but what had once been my childhood bedroom was now starkly modern: white walls, huge framed prints of my own photographs, red blinds, a plain low bed piled with white pillows. No furniture, no girlish touches at all except one wooden chair draped with the day's black trousers. A bed, a view. Not so much a room as a statement of purpose.

"Are you still dizzy?" she asked. She wore steel necklaces and a black cotton dress and, though she was only in her fifties, she dyed her hair stark white, on her private theory that it would make her ageless. "More tea, more tea. You know I hate what they're doing to you."

"Aunt Ruth, this isn't what I need right now. I need clarity. I'm seeing Alan in an hour."

"Well, don't listen to me," she said. "You sure you're up to seeing Alan?"

"You're not throwing your Halloween party this year, Ruth?"

"Don't change the subject. Of course I'm not. How could I without him?"

"He'd want you to hold one."

"Well, then he shouldn't have died," she said briskly. "Don't tell me it's not extreme, electric shock."

"Electroconvulsive. It's a last resort. They tell me it's a seizure to break a pattern in my mind, but I know what it really is. They think I should be someone else. This Greta isn't working, obviously. She's worked for over thirty years, but it's time for an update. Replace all the parts."

"Just one part."

"Just one part. Just me. I hate it, but I don't know what else to do. I can't . . . I can hardly get up in the morning. And yet . . ."

"What exactly did you see?"

It came just after the odor of rotting onions, I told her. After the sensation of being cut out of the world—I never felt what I thought of as electricity—I opened my eyes and thought the procedure was over. But I found myself in a different room. Or that's wrong—it was exactly the same room, but changed. The walls were mint green and not white; where the ECT device had stood there was a larger enameled machine, and a tray with wads of white cotton; a chart on the wall marked the parts of the brain. But the shock was what I saw out the window. Where before was a gravel yard of smoking nurses, now it was a paved square painted with lines and numbers. And full of running, panting, laughing, screaming children.

"And then I opened my eyes again."

"You mean you closed your eyes and opened them again?"

"I mean, as if I had two sets of eyelids. And I opened the second set. And I saw the children again, this time in knickers and . . . old-fashioned dresses, standing in a line. And then it ended— there was the doctor's face above me, and I . . ." I began to laugh, and put down my tea. "I asked him, 'Where are all the children?' I guess he already thinks I'm crazy anyway. I can't explain it. It felt exactly as real as the doctor's office. I heard the noise of traffic outside, through an open window. I could smell fresh paint."

"Are you sure? I heard only dogs can smell in dreams."

"It wasn't a dream. He said there would be . . . disorientation, is how he put it."

My aunt sat very still and regarded me with the simplicity of someone who is deciding whether to take you either very seriously, or not seriously at all; there is no halfway anymore. From her apartment below came the sound of a bird in its cage, Felix's old parakeet, warbling away as it always did—singing, my brother claimed, to the birds beyond the window glass and never knowing it could not be heard. It sang and sang as my aunt looked at me; even her ever clattering jewelry was silent for a moment, and in her black, shining, staring eyes I saw a fascination and interest she had not shown in me for months.

"How could it not be a dream?"

"Well," I said, drawing back slightly in my bed.

"Well, maybe it was a spark in my brain, some-how, you know, connecting various old memories, my old classroom and old movies, a spark that made them seem real for an instant."

"You are sure it wasn't real?"

"How could it possibly be real?"

Her eyes roamed over my face like someone reading a book; I must have been that open and obvious in the hours after my procedure. She picked up the cup and saucer. "There are two kinds of people, I think," she said, and the bird sang through the pause she placed there. The apostrophe between her eyes deepened, then softened. "There are the ones who wake up in the middle of the night and see a woman in a wedding dress sitting by the window, and they think to themselves, 'Oh my God, it's a ghost!' That's the first. Someone who feels something real, and believes it is real. And there are the ones who see the phantom and think, 'I don't know what I've seen, but it's not a ghost because ghosts don't exist.' In my life, I've learned those are the two kinds."

She took a sip from her teacup, then simply set it on its saucer, smiling. "And nobody is the second kind."

"Alan, you seem wonderful," I said before I embraced him. Alan, my brother's lover until the end, in his forties when they met and now approaching fifty. We had made a date for a quick drink, and though I nearly called to cancel, I found my dizziness clearing. We had not seen each other for months, and before that very little after Felix's death. It was another sadness in my life, but I think we avoided each other, as criminals avoid the scene of a crime.

Alan stood a foot above the crowd, dressed in a snap-button cowboy shirt and jeans, a braided belt, an oiled leather coat. I watched as his smile made all the lines in his face come alive. Lines from sunny childhood summers in Iowa, and weekends with Felix and me in the Hamptons. Silver hair cut close, silver stubble on his big chin, with its pale scar from a gardening accident he played off as "mountain lion attack," and yet—I had to make an adjustment for his illness. Here: a smaller version of the Alan I'd known. A narrower embrace. Felix's big broad man now had a boy's figure, and his coat only barely kept me from feeling his ribs. I said nothing but that he looked wonderful.

"Thank you, Greta." He smiled, and put his hand on my cheek. "You've gone missing."

"I've had a hard time," I said. It was one of those old touristy cafes on Bleecker that have never lost their charm for me. We took an uncomfortable wooden booth in the corner, near a rusty Russian samovar, and he removed his coat. The cowboy shirt no longer bulged with his

34

muscles, and, thinner, he somehow also looked younger. Beside us, a young man with a wide, clever face was beginning a house of cards. He had a tourist map beside him, and he looked up and caught my curious gaze. He raised an eyebrow and I turned away.

"How's Nathan?" Alan asked, stroking his chin as if feeling for the old scar.

My sigh had a little laughter in it and I signaled for a coffee. "He left me, Alan. No, it's all right. Well, it's not, but it was a while ago, and . . . I'm dealing with it in my own way. It's too long a story for now. Have you met anyone?" He smiled shyly, that grown man! Sitting with his square jaw and midwestern expression of plain concern, and then that smile! I put my hand on his rough one. "Don't worry, Alan, Felix was never jealous, and I'd be worried for you if you hadn't. Though I'd understand that, too."

"Nobody, really," he said, picking up the salt shaker and balancing it on its side. "There's a guy who wants to take care of me. I don't want anyone to take care of me."

"You never did."

"I miss him," he said solemnly, spinning the salt shaker. I think the truth was, Alan was always much softer than Felix, easier to hurt; his quiet was half contentment and half unspoken suffering. There had been a wife, and children, before Felix. There had been a whole forty years of some other Alan. Perhaps that's why he had loved my brother; Felix's greed for life made up for lost time. Alan never loved to dress up, or to dance, but he had loved to watch it play out before him. In his worn jeans, wearing a slight smile.

"I miss him, too," I said. I watched Alan spin the shaker on the table, watched it gather light and throw it on the walls like shards of glass. He stopped the shaker with his fist. I said, "You know what I wish? I don't wish I could get over it. I wish something impossible: I wish it not to have happened."

"Well," he said.

"I wish it not to have happened. I've lost my mind, Alan. They're giving me ECT."

He took my hand and squeezed it.

"I had the first procedure today. It's making me hallucinate."

He grimaced. "My drugs do that. It fades. It comes again. I'm so sorry."

"Let this guy take care of you, Alan."

He took my gaze very seriously, narrowing his eyes, causing those lines around them to deepen, then after a moment he shook his head and let go of my hand. "I'm too old and sick for all that." He sipped his coffee and shrugged; his hair was haloed in silver. "This young man, he thinks it would be romantic to be there at the end. To be the widow at the funeral. I told him

I've been that widow. It doesn't feel like any-thing at all."

"You're not going to die, Alan."

It is a foolish thing to say to anyone, but it was especially foolish at that moment. He raised his eyes from his coffee cup and they were the same cracked green glaze, shining with pain and amuse-ment at me; the dying have a way of looking at the rest of us in this strange way, as if we were the ones merely mortal. From far off, a siren wailed and wailed. A sigh beside us; the house of cards had fallen and lay everywhere.

"Of course not," he said with a chuckle. "None of us are."

I stayed up very late that night, looking through contact sheets of photographs, trying not to think of Alan or especially of Felix. Perhaps I was afraid of my dreams, that my brother would arrive in them again. It was not until four or so in the morning that I found myself in bed, staring at the bland white walls, the photographic prints, the red blinds pulled up to show a midnight Greenwich Village and that constant view: the houses of Patchin Place, the Jefferson Market tower, the garden beside it. The yellow heads of gingko trees decorating everything in between. *I wish it not to have happened.* I recall closing my eyes and seeing one bright blue star floating there in the darkness, pulsing with light. *Any time but this one.* How it split in two, and those split, and so on and so on, the throbbing blue stars dividing until they formed a circular cluster of light, and there was a kind of thunder as I fell into it—and that is the last thing I remember.

October 31, 1918

Late afternoon; I must have slept through an entire day. A slow, soft awakening, like pulling one's way out of a web—the distant sound of ringing bells. I could feel the sunlight playing on my lids, the shadows of the trees outside, and for a moment I felt as I did as a girl, at a friend's country house, when Felix and I would swim in the river and feign sleep on the shore so our father would have to carry us one by one to the car, whispering to our mother, "Isn't it wonderful to be a child?" I took a few long breaths, thinking of summer and of Felix, before I had the strength to open my eyes.

I lay there for a long time trying to make sense of what I saw. Sunlight and shadow. Striped satin and lace. A piece of fabric hanging over me, dappled by the sun and leaves, billowing slightly from the open window. The sound of a steam whistle, and the clatter of hooves. Striped satin and lace; it was quite beautiful, moving in slow waves above me, just as my mind had been moving in waves as I awoke: a canopy bed. My eyes moved down to take in the rest of the room, which was lit with the same watery refracted light. My breath began to quicken. Because the bed I had fallen asleep in had no posters, no fabric. And the room I saw before me was not my room.

Here it was, what Dr. Cerletti had warned me about: the "disorientation."

For I knew that it was my room; the shape and size of it were the same, the placement of the window and the door. But instead of my white walls, I saw pale lilac wallpaper patterned in ball and thistle. Gold-framed paintings placed along it, and sooty gaslight back plates. A little table with a Japanese tableau of porcelain chopsticks and a painted fan. Long green heavy drapes hung beside the window, pleated and tasseled, and before me a great oval looking glass was set in a tilting frame, reflecting the striped fabric of the bed. Curious, fascinated by the effects of Cerletti's procedure, almost sure of what I would find, I pulled myself up before the mirror and watched as, inch by inch, my own shape came into view. . . .

What else can we call it but beautiful when we are someone new? I marveled at the long red hair falling in waves over the delicate yellow nightgown I had never owned before, trimmed with little useless ribbons. I touched my face and wondered: What trick was this? How could this be me?

I laughed a little, letting my fingers run through my long hair. Dr. Cerletti had said this phase would pass, and I decided to enjoy it while it lasted. Soon enough, I would be shorn-haired little Greta Wells, in slacks and a jacket, wandering from room to room. Until then: I would be this beautiful creature my doctor had made.

A knock on my bedroom door. "Greta?"

A relief. At least something familiar here. It was Ruth's voice.

I blinked at the woman in the mirror before I climbed out of bed and saw how the yellow nightdress fell to my feet. What an elaborate hallucination this was.

"You've slept the day away," Ruth said as she opened the door and entered. "You foolish girl."

I laughed again; my "disorientation" seemed to include Ruth as well: She wore an outrageous black cloak, breastbone beads, a tight turban with a great black trembling feather. I sighed when I remembered it was Halloween. Surely she was in costume. Surely I was as well; the procedure had merely erased some long part of the day. As for the room, the steam whistle, the horse— well, it would all soon fall into place.

"We have to get more hooch before the party starts, which is very soon," she was

41

saying. "Get yourself together and come along."

I said nothing. A little voice in my mind was saying, *Pay attention, you're not yourself,* but I waved it away. I smiled at the little white curls that poked out from her odd turban.

"We have to get back before him, he's lost his key," she said, then looked me up and down. "You're not even dressed. Let's get you into your costume." Ruth walked herself around my bedroom, chattering the whole time, poking through my scattered things, until she came upon a mirrored gilt armoire—sized, perhaps, for hiding illicit lovers—and flung it open with a bleat of delight. "Aha!" I was handed a white blouse and dirndl and slowly put them on. I sat very still as Ruth quickly did my hair. A letter lay on the dresser, unopened, and something bade me to pick it up and put it in my pocket. *Pay attention.*

"There you are. My little Gretel!"

I stood at the mirror looking at the fairy-tale girl before me. A dirndl, hair in two long braids, done up in green ribbon. *You're not yourself.*

"And look at me, darling," she said, fiddling with a device attached to her belt so that her costume revealed itself: all along her skirt, candy canes lit up in bold electric light. "I'm your witch! Now let's go fatten you up! Ready?"

I knew that a step outside would take me further still. So, like Alice before the looking glass, I took one more look at my reflection before I said:

"I'm ready."

For all of my life, beside the tower of the Jefferson Market, down at the end of Patchin Place where Felix and I used to swing on the iron gates, there had been nothing but an empty fenced garden. And now, in its place, there had suddenly sprung up a huge brick building, lit by the setting sun. From one barred window, I saw what I thought was a twisted sheet, but soon realized was a woman's arm, as white as a feather; it did not stir the whole time I watched. I was mesmerized, smiling at the dream I was in.

"What is it, darling?"

I laughed and pointed. "Look!" I said. "What is that?"

She squeezed my hand. "The prison. Now come along."

"A prison? You see it, too?" I asked, but she could not hear me in the noise of the crowd making its Halloween way along Tenth Street. Something was coming together in me. The change in my city, the change in my room. My long hair, my long nightdress. "Ruth, I thought you weren't throwing a party."

"What are you talking about?" she asked me, pulling me along. "I always throw one."

"But you said—"

"He'd kill me if I didn't! Be careful, dear, you seem unstable."

"I'm not myself," I said, smiling, and she seemed to accept that.

We stepped out the gates of Patchin Place, and, very calmly, I pulled out the envelope from my pocket. "Greta Michelson," it read. "Patchin Place." My last name had never been Michelson. But it was the postmark that made me stand still in the moving crowd.

I began to laugh. It overcame me, what had happened. *You make a wish*. The postmark explained it all.

NEW YORK, N.Y.
OCT 20
9³⁰-AM
1918

They say there are many worlds. All around our own, packed tight as the cells of your heart. Each with its own logic, its own physics, moons, and stars. We cannot go there—we would not survive in most. But there are some, as I have seen, almost exactly like our own—like the fairy worlds my aunt used to tease us with. *You make a wish, and another world is formed in which that wish comes true, though you may never see it*. And in those other worlds, the places you love are there, the people you love are there. Perhaps in one of them, all rights are wronged and life is as you wish it. So what if you found the door? And what if you had the key? Because everyone knows this:

That the impossible happens once to each of us.

Another world.

With fascination, I looked around this version of my life in 1918. Nothing was different from my 1985 Patchin Place except the prison beside the tower. The Northern Dispensary, visible down Waverly, was the same as ever (a slice of brick cake), though at Seventh Avenue rubble was piled everywhere, with some recent, violent construction, and women in high-buttoned shoes and costumed like gypsies or pirate queens made their delicate way. Many were wearing gauze masks to cover the lower halves of their faces, tied behind their heads. Below: scattered ancient cobblestones. Above: silver fishhook moon. Between: a bustling crowd of strangers calling to one another from windows, carriages, balconies, and doorways. Just one small thing had changed, such a small thing really.

What difference could it make, the era in which we are born?

"It's beautiful," was all I said, almost to myself.

Two people began to sing along with a phonograph, a man's voice and a woman's. Ruth said, "We have to get going. He hates to wait. And take that ring off, don't be so ridiculous."

I removed my ring to look at the engraving inside: NATHAN AND GRETA, 1909. In this world, he had married me.

Ruth's hands emerged magically from her long sleeves and fluttered frustratedly in the air, then one snatched the ring from me.

"It's Halloween, and you're young! And he's far away at war, up to his own pleasures, bless him. Leo will be looking for you at the party." Then she leaned in close and I could smell violets and cigars and the sweet cinnamony oil she must have used to dress her hair. "Free love, darling," she said, patting my cheek.

So, in this world, Nathan was at war.

"Watch out, ma'am!" Heedless of the world around me, I had bumped into someone.

"I'm sorry, I—"

It was a young man dressed for Halloween as a genie. He smiled and touched my shoulder before moving on. His touch made me gasp. I tried to catch my breath as he made his way into the crowd.

Ruth took my hand. "Come now, darling."

But I could not move, watching him walking away from me, chatting with his companion and laughing, disappearing into the crowd.

I felt her tight grip on me. Her concerned whisper: "Greta? Are you all right?"

"I know that man," I said, pointing where he had been, a shimmer in the moonlight. I felt tears well in my eyes. "They're alive," was all I could say. "They didn't die."

"Darling—"

"That man," I said, gesturing to the genie disappearing into the crowd. "His name was Howard."

How could I explain it? That the year before, I had seen him every day selling me half-price baguettes at the bakery. Same short blond hair, same pale beard, same ivory smile. Just as he used to look standing behind the counter, months before. And waving at me late at night on the street, in tight jeans and with his buddies. And on the photograph taped to his coffin.

Laughing again, turning, looking around at me: familiar young men appearing in this unfamiliar world. Men who had died months or years before from the plague miraculously revived! There, in an army uniform, was the boy who made jewelry from papier-mâché beads; he died in the spring. And that one soldier, the stark blond Swede jumping from the streetcar, once sold magazines; he'd died two years before, one of the first: the cave's canary. Who knows how many more were off to war? Alive, each one, alive and more than alive—shouting, laughing, running down the street!

Of course: 1918, a world set long before the plague. A world in which they had not died.

• • •

Twilight had descended when we returned, carrying growlers of beer, to Ruth's apartment—decorated, in this world, as a fairy-tale land. The ceiling was pasted with silver stars, and a cardboard gingerbread house stood at the entrance to the dining room, dotted with peppermint candies, some of which had already fallen to the floor. On the wall was a paper castle, and from it fell a waterfall of Rapunzel hair.

I had been lost in thought amid the crowds of revelers. "Ruth," I said. "I'm going to tell you something impossible."

"Not now, darling," she said, leading me back outside. Yellow leaves blew in a spiral behind her. "Later, when we're drunk."

"I'm not who you think I am. You told me once—"

"Who is? I'm going to make the punch," she said, squeezing my hand. "It has to be strong, to beat the flu. And last us through these insane times. You stay here, I'm sure we've kept him waiting."

She disappeared into the house, the bright electric lights of her dress burning into my eyes.

Another world. My life if I had been born in another time. Ruth was the same, but what else would have changed? I looked down at my hand, empty now but still bearing the pink pinch of my wedding ring. Married. I should have guessed

Nathan might be at war. Of course I would not find him here, waiting for me in this world.

I looked around and saw, all along the path of Patchin Place, leading right up to my aunt's door, a peculiar thing: a trail of bread crumbs scattered on the stones. I felt the strange magic contraction of the worlds. I stared at those bread crumbs a long time before I began to follow them, one every few feet, back down Patchin Place toward the gate. It never occurred to me to look up, to see who might have left them, not until I reached out my hand to touch one, to be sure it was real, and a voice yanked me back: "Gretel!" I looked up and felt a black bolt in my brain.

For there at the gates stood a fairy-tale man, removing his feathered cap. "I've been pacing the block. You took so long!" he shouted. There is the thing you hope for, and then, beyond it . . .

As fox faced as ever, smiling, with skin and muscle and blood and all the spinning, churning apparatus of life: "Why did you take so long?"

I can barely write the words. It was my brother, Felix.

"You can't be here," I said. "You can't."

He asked me, laughing, why not?

I stared at him a long time before I answered, "Because you're dead."

● ● ●

"Sorry to disappoint you, bubs. I'm still kicking."
A well-remembered laugh. Red hair cut close on
the sides, those few freckles still haunting his
skin, pale eyes flashing. "No," I said, bracing
myself against the wall. "I was there, I watched
you, I held your hand."

That smile again. "Well, it's Halloween! The
dead walk the earth! Let's go inside and have
Ruth make us a drink." A shout from inside, and
the sound of shattered glass and laughter.

But as he turned I gripped his arm, tight. His
arm, solid and strong and alive. Not gaunt anymore, not thin or weak. He looked at me seriously
now. I thought of the last time I had seen him,
trying to swallow a spoon of poison, the wire-
work of tendons shifting in that arm. And here.
Alive. How does the heart keep beating?

"Greta?" he asked, his face focused on mine
now. We stood, regarding each other, and I'm
sure it was only face-to-face that you could recognize our similarity. The lashless eyes that hid so
much, the full red lips that gave away everything, the coloring of skin and hair that were
mere variations, as if a passing shadow had
briefly fallen over me.

"Felix, something's happened," I said firmly.
"I'm not myself."

He stood quietly for a moment and I watched
his smile tense in the streetlight. I held his hand

50

tightly and would not let my eyes leave him. Tall in his lederhosen, neck bare to the night wind. Here was the old nightmare, arriving on schedule as it had every night, this time brought on not by my sleeping mind but by Dr. Cerletti's magic wand.

Some partygoers arrived, looked at us, and smiled; I smoothed my apron over my dirndl. I saw that, together, we were characters wandering far from their storybook.

"I know you've been sad," Felix was saying to me after they went inside. "I know it's been hard with Nathan gone. I know that's why you went to the doctor; I'm sure he didn't expect these side effects."

I looked up and saw the moon had risen between the buildings, but then realized it was dangling from a window, on a fishing line, lit from within by a candle, and I saw in that window a pretty female Harlequin making it swing above the crowd. From behind her a man dressed as a black cat kissed the nape of her neck.

Felix squeezed my hand. He pulled some of my hair back from my face. "I know you've been lonely."

"Yes," I said at last. "I've been lonely."

"I'm sorry I was away so long. Ingrid's father wanted me to meet my future family. But now I'm back." The lights of a passing cab shone across his face. "I'm back for a while." An arrogant little smile beneath that arrogant little mustache.

And then I realized that I could say the thing I had been whispering to myself all these months, lying in my bed and staring out the window with lashes sticky from tears. I could say it at last to the person I was always addressing, the person I thought would never hear it. There before me in his costume. I held him close again and said: "I missed you."

He laughed a little, accepting my embrace.

"I missed you. I missed you," I repeated.

"I missed you, too, Gretel."

I pulled back and kept his hand in mine. He was smiling. Above us, the moon swung from its line as Columbine began to sing to the crowd below. I asked him who Ingrid was and he squeezed my hand again.

"Ingrid," he said distinctly. "You've met her. You'll remember. She's lovely, a girl in Washington, a senator's daughter. You'll remember." He laughed but I saw his concern working away in there. "I'm marrying her in January."

"Marrying her?"

The careful smile and shake of his head. "Hard to believe anyone would marry me, right? Well, I'm one of the few eligible men in town. There's some luck in being German."

To my relief I found myself laughing. My brother? Hanging from a lamppost in his boyish costume, rolling his eyes and his wrists, winking at me—couldn't everybody see it? Not girlish, exactly, not the way he had been as an adolescent, trying on my shoes and necklaces; he had trained himself in certain ways, and grown in others, and was man enough. But anyone could tell. Anyone who cared to look, who knew a thing about life. "Felix!" I said. "Felix, you can't be serious! I may be dreaming, but you can't be marrying her."

He stiffened, lowered his eyebrows, and let go of the lamppost. "Yes, I am. You've always said you like her; don't change your mind now."

"Well, I'm sure I do, but what about Alan?"

"What?"

"This is my dream. If you marry anyone, it should be Alan."

Quickly, without hesitation, "Marry him to whom?"

It was the swift response of a man who is not really lying, but has constructed a careful world —like an acoustic chamber—that swallows the lie before he even knows he has said it. For the mind knows what the man does not.

"Oh, I see," I said to him.

We stared at each other for one second. Moonlight made its way over the roofs onto the street, in a small strip, creeping along like an alley cat, lighting up the antique version of my old life. The monkey's paw. I had been given a world in which my brother was alive, one in which he would not even go to this war, but I had not dreamed precisely enough; this world was a trap.

"Greta," he started to say, but stopped.

There is a truth that everyone knows but you. Each of us has it; no one is immune. Not a secret, not a scandal, but something simple and obvious to everyone else. It can be as simple as losing weight, or as difficult as leaving a husband. How awful, to sense that everybody knows the thing that would change your life, and yet no one is friend enough to tell you! You are left to guess, all by yourself. Until the moment comes when it reveals itself to you, and of course this revelation always comes a moment too late.

"Furlough papers," came a gruff voice behind us. A big snub-nosed officer in a deep blue uniform. It took a moment for me to understand this was not a man in costume.

"I'm excused from service, Officer," said my brother. "I'm German."

"Papers."

"Yes," he said, and I could see Felix suppressing his rage. "Yes, right here."

I seemed not to have brought any kind of purse. I wondered if I had papers. I wondered what those papers would be.

What Felix produced was a little card, which went immediately into the officer's hands; the pink-faced man examined it with a frown. I could see, at the top of the card, in bold copperplate, the words: ALIEN ENEMY REGISTRATION.

"Who is your employer?" the officer asked.

"I'm a freelance journalist."

"I need an employer."

Felix turned to me and said very calmly and quietly, "Go into the party. I'll find you later."

"No!" I shouted.

The officer pulled him back: "Talk with me, Fritz, not your girl." He asked who Felix's associates were in this neighborhood and if he was a member of any German organizations.

"No!" I insisted to Felix. "I can't lose you again!"

"Go, Greta," Felix hissed as the officer barked again for his attention, asking if he was a member of the Communist Party. I watched the policeman pull my brother out of sight. Red hair, long legs, lederhosen: gone. Standing there in Patchin Place, I cried out for my Hansel—as if my bones had all been broken.

I did not last long in that world, on that first visit. Ruth found me there, crumpled at her doorstep, and took me up to my apartment. "He's gone!" I kept saying. "I lost him again!" Passing her door, I saw only fairy-tale costumes and heard only laughter and the chandelier sounds of a party. She whispered, "He'll be fine, he'll be fine. But, darling, you should have told me your doctor was coming."

She took me into my bedroom, and there stood Dr. Cerletti.

Small wire-framed glasses, in this world, but bald as ever, in a neat brown suit. He carried a wooden box by its brass handle. "I tried to call, Mrs. Michelson. I apologize, I should have guessed you would forget after yesterday. We're going to do these at home. It's as easy to do here as at the hospital."

"I'm sorry," Ruth said to the doctor, sitting me on the bed. "She didn't tell me. I didn't know."

He said nothing, but put the box on a little table, unfolding the lid down the middle like a tackle box. Inside, nested in green velvet, was a glass jar, half coated in foil, from whose lid emerged a brass knob. Sunk in the velvet, around it, lay a silver circlet. A wire led from it to the device. He lifted out the jar and set it before me, then carefully removed the circlet with both hands. "We do these twice a week, Greta," he said softly, holding it before him. "You remember. I'll see you again next Wednesday. Eventually, you may be able to do them yourself."

"I don't remember this . . . ," I said.

He said it was a capacitor. A Leyden jar. I had only to touch my hand to the knob. I looked up at Ruth and she seemed to be close to tears. Her electric dress glowed in the dim room, making our faces pink above the device. "Go on," said Dr. Cerletti. "You did it yesterday." Was this what Alice felt, when she saw the bottle that said DRINK ME? She knew this would help her get there, to the place she desired. That beautiful garden behind the little door.

He placed the circlet gently on my head. I looked down at the strange jar; there seemed to be water inside. Did I imagine it glowing? And, after a moment, I put out the index finger of my right hand and brought it to the bright brass knob. . . .

When he was gone, Ruth undressed me and gave me a sleeping pill the doctor had left, although my body wanted nothing but sleep. I recalled the bright spark that leapt from the device to my finger, the blue spark that lit my brain. I kept telling her he was dead, Felix was dead, and she kept trying to hush me, calm me down, when a shout came from the street—"Greta!"—and in my daze I moved to the window, thinking it was Felix escaped from the police. But it was a stranger. Was the device already working? A young man in a Civil War costume below my window, flowers in his hand. Wide clever face, small eyes, an eyebrow raised. An enormous, drunken smile. In the moonlight, his hair gleamed in bolts of brilliantine.

"Look there, a boy outside my window. He just blew me a kiss," I said.

"Oh, darling," she said, "that's just Leo. Now sleep, please, go to sleep for me. I didn't know, Greta." I looked down and he waved at me, this Leo, before she pulled me back to bed.

I recall how the flash of her glowing dress against my closing eyelids was like the neon glow of hotels flashing VACANCY VACANCY on a long night ride. I felt the weight of my mind hanging from a branch, pulling, pulling, and before I knew it the stem had snapped and I was falling, blind, into the void.

There almost has to be a heaven. If other worlds surround us, just a lightning bolt away, then what would stop us from slipping there? If love has left us, well, then there is a world where it has not. If death has come, then there is a world where it has been kept at bay. Surely it exists, the place where all the wrongs are righted, and so why had I not found that place? Instead, I had been given this: a life in which I had been born in another century, and grew up in corsets and ribbons alongside my twin, and married my Nathan and sent him off to war. A life in which my brother lived, but did not live well.

So why this one? Why not a perfect world in which nothing slipped from my fingers? For surely, there has to be a heaven. Perhaps it was my job to make one.

November 1, 1941

What a strange sleep it was! I woke: bright sun, and light flickering gaily on the ceiling, and the fading sound of bells ringing in the air. The sheets were soft and warm; I felt refreshed, as if I had slept a hundred years. The sound of whispering voices, footsteps, creaking floorboards. But it was the smell that alerted me, even before I opened my eyes. Gone was the gaslight, soot, and manure, the cinnamon and violets of that other world. Here: dust and aftershave. Why aftershave? My eyes opened to a different scene entirely. I could not help but smile. *I'm not back at all, not yet,* I thought to myself. *I'm somewhere else again.*

Golden curtains hung on my bedroom window where green ones had been, and landscape photographs instead of paintings, and yet it was still my room, still my home. Outside: the same low brick buildings of Patchin Place, the yellowed gingko leaves of an autumn in my Village. But where had the prison gone? I looked with interest on an unfamiliar lady's vanity below a folding mirror: the canisters of creams and powders, the long-handled brush, the hairpins all neat in a tin box. They were all strangers to me, and yet, that was my own red hair snagged in the brush. A mirrored wastepaper basket caught the morning light and sent streamers around the room. It was quite beautiful. Dust and aftershave. It seemed so possible that I could be somewhere else, again, that each morning would unfold anew like a pop-up book of possible lives. So was it any surprise when I heard a knock on the door? Two people talking, but one particular voice—"Mrs. Green!"—one particular phrase before he walked into the room:

"I leave it to you!"

Nathan, turning to smile at me from the doorway. But he was changed, as everything was changed: clean shaven as he stood above me, with wire-rimmed glasses, khaki uniform. How strange to see him without a beard! He looked so young: same long narrow face, lined with worry at the eyes, same heart-shaped hairline. His hand on my cheek, his smile unforced and kind, his brown eyes darting thoughtfully to a glass of water beside me, which, a moment later, he tilted to my lips and from which I drank. I swallowed and he got up to leave but I found myself grabbing his sleeve with my right hand. My left seemed to be weighed down.

"Nathan," I said.

"Shh," he said, pressing my arm down by my side again and kneading my hand. "Be quiet and rest. Dr. Cerletti said the first few procedures can be hard."

"Everything is changed."

"The doctor said you might not remember. Don't worry about that now."

"All right," I said. I am not one to spoil an enchantment. I looked down at my left arm and saw it was in a plaster cast. With my other hand I touched the cool surface. I could feel the break inside it, and let out a gasp of pain.

"What is it?"

I looked into his face, so altered by this clean, smooth jaw and close haircut and whatever life he'd had in this world, and yet instantly him, instantly the headstrong Nathan. I said the obvious: "I've broken my arm."

"Yes," he said. "There was an accident." I tried to lift my body. "Don't try getting up," he said, taking my shoulders in his hands to place me back in bed, but I flinched from his touch; I felt I would die if he touched me like that, after all this time.

"Don't," I said. "Something's changed."

"What do you mean?"

"I'm not from here. I'm not who you think I am."

"Darling, I know you're confused," he said, sitting down.

But I was no longer listening. For out the window I saw there was a change to my view. A billboard, set on a rooftop, whose message never existed in my world.

"What year is it?"

He tried to keep the concern from his face as he squeezed my hand. "I have a sleeping pill in the other room, the doctor said it would be harmless—"

"Nathan, what year is it?"

"It's nineteen forty-one, darling. November first, nineteen forty-one."

"Of course," I said. "It's all coming back to me." And as he stroked my hair I tried to smile. I looked out at the billboard with its man-high, looping mint green letters:

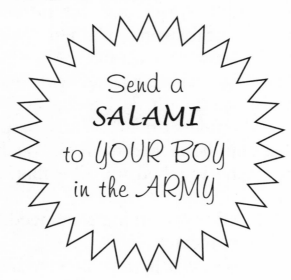

• • •

Nineteen forty-one—a world of other choices, other chances! With antique taxis honking in the streets, and brass-buttoned policemen shouting from Sixth Avenue, and giant women's hats floating by the gate of Patchin Place like jelly-fish, army boys shouting at girls, the smell of cigarettes and roasted chestnuts, with factory smoke thickening the air—here it was, Manhattan of another time, and not only had my Nathan never left me in this world. Here, he had married me.

So there were at least three lives to lead. A life in 1918, with a husband away at war. A life in 1941, with him here by my side. There was no question it was the procedure that had brought this impossibility about, but how could I get back? And would it last only as long as the electricity did? Or would I leap every night, from star to star, until I reached a beginning? Or an end?

"It's all coming back to me," I said. And as he stroked my hair I tried to smile. I struggled to right myself: 1941. *Be here,* I told myself. *Be this Greta.*

There had been a car accident, he told me. Almost three weeks before. This Greta I was inhabiting, she had broken more than her arm; she had broken her mind as well, I understood, had become a sad and hysterical wife to this

Nathan, dressed in his army doctor uniform. A psychiatrist had been called in, a friend of Nathan's—a Dr. Cerletti, of course—and with hushed tones and drawn curtains had administered a "procedure" to help me back from the darkness. Of course this was how it went. Of course this was how our minds had connected, in that blue electric flash of madness, across the membrane of three worlds so we switched places, two Gretas and myself, and awoke to different lives.

"The doctor said your memories would come back, but slowly." He reached to the table beside me and produced a flat engraved silver case, which he clicked open like a compact to reveal a row of cigarettes as white as teeth. He took one and lit it.

"You're a smoker," I said.

Nathan squinted at me queerly and stroked my forehead again. "You just rest." As he moved, its lavender smoke wrote in cursive all around his body. His whole body tilted over me and—dear God!—I could smell some old-new-fashioned cologne, and the crisp starch of his shirt, and the faint leathery grease of whatever was in his hair, but underneath it all I recognized the scent of my old lover. And it was awful, awful to be brought back so thoroughly, nearly as awful as what he next said, breathing into my ear: "Just remember I love you."

I had not ever thought that I would cry in front of him again. Not after what he had put me through in my world. There is the thing you hope for and then, beyond it, like a prize kept locked and out of reach behind the counter, there is the thing you dare not hope for. To win it without expectation, without warning and—worst of all —without earning it in any way, is for the world to become a magical place. One in which prayers are not answered, and wrongs are not righted, nor anything kept in balance, but punishments and rewards are given at random, as if by a drunk or insane king. Which is to say: a hurtful place to live. I had to look away so he would not see my absurd tears.

"Your brother has been by, but Mrs. Green was strict, and our Felix—"

"Can I see Felix?" I interrupted.

He laughed. "Well, he's right outside, waiting for you! He's asking for you constantly."

So he was alive. And what would my brother be like this time? As headstrong and foolish as ever, emotionally overwrought over some new love or another, whatever form that might take in this strange world? Surely times had changed enough since the last time I saw him. There would be no ridiculous fiancée in Washington, no coded look there in his eyes. Surely this time my Felix would be himself, and if that were so —I swore to myself—then I would never close my eyes again, never leave this land that I had traveled to.

"Send him in! Send him in!" I shouted.

"At least you remember *him*. You know, yesterday," Nathan said, a little mischievously, "you thought you were from the past. Or something like that."

"Aren't we all from the past?" I said, smiling. "Did I say what it was like?"

"No, but I guess you thought it wasn't anything like this!" He laughed. "But now you're back. Really, you feel up to seeing him? We didn't want to wake you."

"Yes," I told him. "Of course, I'm longing to."

This seemed to thrill Nathan. His long, still shockingly beardless face bent in a smile beneath his glasses and vanished into the hall, talking to someone there. The door gleamed in a square of white varnish.

Left alone, I looked around the room with the sensitive eyes of a detective inspecting a murder scene, looking for clues to this world. It was fairly tidy for a sickroom, though a pair of laddered stockings had been snake-shed onto the vanity beside a bottle of nail polish. On a nearby roll-up secretary lay a pile of envelopes, stationery, and a marbled fountain pen. Gold dust floated everywhere. I tried to take it all in anew. A strange metal machine sat in the corner, something like a sunlamp. That was when I caught sight of my triptych reflection in the vanity's hinged mirrors.

It was not me there. The one I had grown so used to seeing, in my own cracked mirror in that other-room-like-this-one: tall and short haired, hips too wide in jeans, breasts too small in blouses, misshapen and flawed, sometimes better, sometimes worse. It was me, of course. Except this woman was beautiful. Her red hair was brushed high in the front and curled in thick waves on the sides, so carefully and artfully done I could not imagine how she achieved it. And below this, somehow enhanced by the nightgown I wore, was a body flowing in cream satin like a dressmaker's form, despite the heavy cast. Never had I looked like this. I touched myself with my free hand, unbelieving. For it had not occurred to me that I did not merely shift into another self. I shifted into another body.

So this, too, was something I would learn to adjust to: the strange sensation of a body not my own. To lift an arm and find it smoother, paler than the one I remembered. To feel the other so broken. Mine, and yet not mine. To touch my face and have my fingers come away with peach foundation, and to put on a string of pearls and find my hands caught in the masses of hair I had not worn since I was a girl. The sharp face I had seen in every mirror: blurred, softened like the rest of me. What another person would have made of the body we were born with.

"Greta?" came Nathan's voice from the door, and I was confronted with a new, spectacular tableau. Of course, I thought to myself, why didn't I expect this?

There, framed by the white-painted wood, I saw Nathan holding a little boy of about three or four who koala-clung to him. He had small green eyes and sleek waves of brown hair. "Felix," he was saying to the child. "Hush now. Look, Fee. Your mommy's here." Then he set the boy on the floor and, sailor hat falling behind, my son ran joyfully toward me.

I had never considered children. No, that's not true. I had considered them as people consider moving to a foreign country; they know it would change them forever, but it is a change they never see. We had talked about it, Nathan and I, throughout our relationship. Even at the very beginning, we had a way of checking in with each other. "I just want to see," he would ask after half a bottle of wine, "how you're feeling about children? Any change?" And, smiling at his long bearded face, pulled tight in concern, as if by a drawstring, I would say I hadn't thought about them at all in the time since he'd last asked. "How about you?" I'd counter, leaning back in the couch and hugging a child-cushion, waiting to see if his question were really a statement, but he always shook his head and answered, "No, no change yet." A pause, then a smile from both of us.

So it was a shock, of course, after he had left me, when I heard he and Anna were trying to get pregnant. All of our semiannual examinations, in which we probed each other for a sign of that disease, the little tumor of desire, and he had always said that he felt nothing, that he loved our life and did not wish to trade it for another, those nights finishing the bottle and toasting our barren home. It was untrue, or at least partially untrue. Nathan had wanted a child after all. He had simply never wanted one with me.

He came to me, the little boy, on tiny sheep-white socks. He threw himself into my arms, and I was overcome by the softness of him, the scent of sour milk and jam, the slight crackle of his ironed green romper, embroidered in a wigwam pattern across the front, with its stiff white collar and sleeves so that he was Pilgrim and Indian all in one. He embraced me as completely as his small arms could handle, then wriggled in a playacting of joy. "Careful of Mommy's arm!" When Daddy said he was already late for work, but that Mrs. Green was here to help Mommy, his face looked as if he had been slapped; a freak thunderstorm of tears commenced; Nathan looked to me and I understood that I was to take over now. He had been the good husband for long enough, and carried this extra burden, but I understood that the parenting belonged to this Mrs. Green and to me. I felt this world attaching itself to me, merging me with the Greta who had lived in it so long. I held him in my arms, that little squirming stranger. My son.

"I'll be back a little later than usual," Nathan told me, though he needn't have said that because I had no idea what it might mean. A kiss on my brow and one on Felix's, then it was on with his hat and trench coat (military hat and coat, doctor's insignia), and out the door. I watched his departure with a shiver of regret, for I knew something he did not: that in my world, he did not love me anymore.

For our first game as mother and son, we played hide-and-seek. "Go hide!" I told Felix, and off he went in a flash as if he knew precisely where was best. This was my chance to examine how this 1941 apartment differed from my own, and from the one I had visited the night before. The hallway, with its silhouettes of strangers and madcap shelves of pottery horses, had to be the doing of my husband, not my forties self; I could not believe I would have chosen each bland little item so carefully, and assembled them like the statues buried with the pharaohs. The bedroom I had already examined. The little nursery, off the hall, was a surprise; in my ordinary life, the wall had been plowed through to expand the master bath, but here was a tiny prefecture that was my son's own. A trunk in the corner revealed a set of worn tin soldiers (swords bent into plow-shares). In a small drawer of the trunk, a crow's cache: pebbles, scraps of silvered paper, and torn use- less dollar bills. Most touching of all were a few baby teeth, tinged with dried blood. A box labeled FROM UNCLE X contained a bottle of talcum powder that had been relabeled INVISIBILITY POWDER.

In the living room: a ghost—no, once the cigarette smoke cleared, I saw a fiftyish woman in a dark green dress putting something into her purse. She had a small face that grew pinker toward the center, an astounding bosom glistening in velvet, and a round topknotted hairdo whose blond had been salted with white. This must be Mrs. Green. "Good morning, Mrs. Michelson, how are you feeling?"

"Better, thank you." Mrs. Michelson!

"Dr. Michelson said you had a bad couple of days." Her accent was distinctly Swedish. Her manner was old world, friendly; she had the distant helpfulness of a stewardess.

"Yes, yes, but I've recovered."

"Very good, madam."

As she talked, she pointed with her smoking cigarette. She had a look of efficiency and kind-ness and I somehow felt very sorry for her. I could not tell if she was regular help or someone brought in just for this emergency, this "accident" that had broken my arm and mind. Mrs. Green and my son would be of no help; I had to find my aunt Ruth.

"I've given Fee his breakfast," she went on, "and was about to take him to the park. I thought maybe you still needed rest." She told me a few details about my son, which I had trouble understanding, but nodded at anyway, and information about a half-baked chicken pot pie in the icebox that I might want to put in the oven.

"Yes, perhaps that's best."

"So I'll do the groceries and speak to the laundress; do you have any errands?"

"No, no I—," I began, glancing at the bedroom. And yet there, in fact, just at my bedside table sat an appointment book such as a doctor's wife would keep.

"Madam?"

"Yes, I'll rest. I'm still dizzy and forgetful, you'll forgive me."

"I understand, you've been under strain. Leave it all to me. What would you like me to get for dinner?"

"Whatever you think best."

"I was thinking lamb chops, potatoes, and a jellied salad."

"Very good."

"And is your son dressed?" she asked.

"No, no. In fact, he's hiding somewhere."

"Hiding?"

"We were playing hide-and-seek."

At last she allowed an expression to play over her face, and instantly I felt I had done everything wrong. She said nothing, perhaps because it was beyond her imagining that a mother would play hide-and-seek in the hour when a child should be dressed for the cold and the park. Perhaps the earth might now split in two.

"I'll find him," I told her. She smiled as if I had accidentally rung her "call" button, nodded her head, and went to the kitchen. I could not tell if I admired or hated her.

I found my son in the bathroom, shrieking with real terror when I pulled back the shower curtain to find him squatting there, then collapsing in hilarity at his own cleverness. I delivered him to Mrs. Green, who had brought out the pie herself, and whose gray eyes took in first his soiled clothing, and then his delinquent mother. She led him away to change him. It was then that I crept over to the appointment book.

"Mrs. Green," I shouted, running into the nursery. "I've changed my mind."

She was in the midst of pulling a struggling Fee into a pair of woolen knickers. He seemed as forlorn as an animal made to wear human clothing. Mrs. Green stared at me with those eyes, and I nearly crept back, but I was determined. "I'm going to take Fee to the park. You do my errands, and heat the pie; we'll be back for lunch."

"I see," she said plainly. "But are you sure? It isn't our habit to—"

"I'm sure. Get him dressed, we'll be off in a minute."

"I see."

Then I headed to the bedroom, my ridiculous robe falling in anemone ruffles around me. I glanced at the clock: nine thirty. Just enough time. The open page of the appointment book read, in my own handwriting:

Felix at Hudson Park at ten.

buy Victory Bonds

Gone was the prison of 1918, and the desperately ugly el line on Sixth, but war bonds posters still effaced every shop window and the men in uniforms smoking everywhere were hardly different from that other world. "Flowers!" an old Italian lady shouted from the sidewalk, bent over from the weight of her basket of violets and sweet peas. "Flowers! Flowers!" A blond chorus-girl type, in long, red Chinese trousers, was walking her Pekingese and throwing her smile everywhere when she tripped and one of her slippers fell off into a puddle. I retrieved it for her; she flashed me a smile and a wild look: "Geez, now I can't take these back, can I?" A Pekingese bark of a laugh.

She fit her little foot back in and went off, once more, among the hot-blooded sailors, behind twitching.

And then we were west of Seventh Avenue, at Hudson Park, on a block I didn't recognize; I certainly didn't recognize the park with its strange sunken garden and memorial to firemen. It didn't exist in my 1985 world. It looked like a drained fountain, and not particularly made for children; it seemed made more for a Victorian mourning set. I let Fee race into the playground, suddenly unleashed from his love of me, toward some more immediate desire among the boys in short pants and caps.

My mind went back to the house, mentally climbing the stairs, heading to the living room, parting the veil of cigarette smoke to find Mrs. Green still standing there gazing upon me with a look of efficiency and kindness. I wonder—no, I know for sure, that she saw, to the very core of me, the thing that everybody knew. Of course, it had to exist in this world as well as any other. The thing that everybody knew. I thought: *Perhaps if I fix this, it all will end; the curtain will fall in a dustheap and life will be restored, and sanity.* Perhaps that was my purpose here.

Then something rash and ridiculous occurred to me. I put my purse on my lap—a funny lumpy piece of leather—found the catch, searched through its handkerchiefs and lipsticks, and there it was. A pack of Pall Malls. I pulled one out and lit it with a match, and enjoyed the taste of death that no one here suspected. Oh, I deserved that little pleasure. What a wonderful world I had entered!

My little Fee sat talking with a blond boy, trying to get him to wear his knit cap; he seemed willing but big headed. I made out whom I assumed to be his mother from how she stared at me. Scandinavian, youngish and leggy despite the length of her shadow-plaid coat. I wondered how she did it: managed her life in this strange age. I knew there would be a war, but that we were not in it yet. I knew women would soon go to work by the masses, and man the machinery, and build the nation rivet by rivet while our hems rose to save cloth for uniforms, and our nylons went to parachutes for young men falling into the Pacific. But none of this had happened; it was about to happen; could this woman feel it?

"Hey, bubs, here you are, what's hoppin'?"

And there he was. Alive, again. In ridiculous shamus hat and coat—another world, another Felix.

"Tell Green I'm coming over for her chicken pot pie," my brother said, sitting beside me and bumming a drag from my cigarette. I had already held him for a minute, and at last released him, seeing the baffled expression on his face.

All I could do was say, as always, "I missed you."

"I'm kidding, kiddo! I know, no visitors. Green would shoot me." He laughed, this third version of my brother. Dressed so unlike himself, in a baggy brown suit and tie, with a knot as big as a peach, and a dented fedora on the back of his head. His red hair was combed with pomade, and his classic nose was marred by a small cut. The mustache was gone, but the few freckles were there; the bright blue eyes were also there, some of their mischief diluted in the gray light of the day.

"Why no visitors?"

"Doctor's orders," he said.

"My old friend Dr. Cerletti," I said. I noticed the wedding ring on his hand. I stared at it for a long strange moment. Felix Wells, married man.

"If you say so." A radio from a parked car played brash swing music and the wind carried a woman's laugh to us. He shook his head: "The tourists are ruining everything."

"How's Ingrid?" I asked boldly.

"Ingrid? Busy with the baby. Busy with me; I'm a poor husband." Another laugh.

"The baby," I repeated. The sky above us opened its coat and flashed a patch of blue, showed the shape of its clouds.

"I came to check on you, bubs." His voice was softer now, which in Felix meant he was not kidding, kiddo. I felt a warmth of recognition; he kept giving me the things I missed, the things I'd lost.

"What did the doctor say? They didn't tell me."

"The doctor? That you'd healed but were . . ." His whole face crinkled in worry. "Well, that you'd been very sad and were getting . . . help. A procedure. I wish you'd told me, bubs." He reached over to take another drag, closing his eyes, and I heard the tobacco smolder in its minor fire.

"I don't remember," I said. "I don't remember anything. What happened to me?"

His eyes went from me, to my son, to the woman sitting across the way watching us. Then returned to me with that look I knew so well. The crackling music played from the car window, where the driver drummed his fingers. What was the thing that everybody knew? "Are you all right, baby?"

Where was my ally in this particular dream? Where was Ruth? "Felix, I need your help."

"What did they do to you?"

"What happened? There was an accident."

"We don't have to—"

"Jesus, just tell me, they won't tell me."

He looked at me with the intense pain of someone watching something burn to the ground. I suppose it was watching his sister, who had always been stable, normal, ordinary, and good, fall apart in front of him.

"There was a car accident, you and Ruth. It wasn't your fault. You were badly hurt and shaken . . ."

"Where is Ruth?" I asked him.

We sat there on the bench, each regarding the other with such pity and envy, the way that siblings do. "Greta," he began.

"She died, didn't she? In the accident," I said. "She's dead."

He nodded slowly. Golden leaves turned in the wind around us.

"Oh, Ruth," I said, letting my head fall into my hands. I felt the tears starting and I let myself sob a few times; I felt my brother's hand on my back. That was when I felt it again: the sensation that I was not merely visiting these worlds. For I felt her death keenly, though I could picture her in turban and beads, alive in other worlds. I wept and wept into my white gloves. I was not borrowing these other Gretas; I was becoming them.

"I'm so sorry, Greta. I thought you remembered."

"No, no," I said. "Oh God. And I need her here so much. Poor Ruth. What am I going to tell—" But here I stopped myself.

"That's why Nathan found a doctor. You fell apart, Greta." He leaned over and put his hand on my knee. "I shouldn't have said anything."

I sniffed and wiped away my tears, then drew myself up tall. "I have to tell you," I said. "I'm not myself."

He winced in pain once again. I felt my hand begin to shake with some surge of emotion; I dropped my cigarette. I was not used to it. Surely in this life, like the last, I was always playing the sober sister. And now—to be the one to break down. It was unbearable. I was reminded of a scene I had once passed on the highway, of a small sports car with a chain attached, slowly and carefully pulling an old truck out of a ditch.

The thing that everybody knows. For Felix, it was of course that his sister had lost her mind.

"There are things," I said, "that you might be shocked if I told you. That you wouldn't understand. I've seen things . . . I've gone places that—"

"It's okay, it's okay."

He took my hand and we were both so cold.

"Felix," I said. "I'm not who you think I am."

He looked at me for a long time, taking in the words that I had said. The light changed all around us, glowing on each person in the park, my son, the woman, as if lighting a cast of characters. Then at last he spoke: "Me neither, baby."

And in those words I heard my dead brother at last.

Then Felix stood up, shaking off the moment. "I have to go," he said, gathering his coat, then turning. "I want you to meet someone. I want you to come over for lunch next week, Ingrid will be off at her parents'. I have to go." He looked up with a halfhearted smile, his cheeks flushed with color. "Bubs, I would understand anything you told me," he said. "Anything." Then he slipped on the coat, turned back. "Plant you now," he said, winking. "Dig you later."

What is it to lose a twin? My brother was not just the boy I grew up with; he was my entire youth. I have no memory without him. From the get-go we were allies in the world, with our own language (a combination of family German and babysitter's Spanish), our own monsters and deities and doors to other worlds. I understood everything he did, and why. I knew his body and his bravery and his foolishness. Older and older, and nothing was different, no parting, no change. When he said he liked boys, it made so much more sense—after all, *I* liked boys. So should Felix. We liked everything together. Spaghetti and bratwurst and ketchup. That we could now talk about boys was an enormous relief. And to lose him.

I watched my brother as he walked away through the park, tipping his hat to an old woman in a bright green shawl. Lost to me, again, lost in a brand-new way. But I remembered his words. And, as in a drop of water, within that "anything" a world revolved.

• • •

That night, I assumed that I was saying good-bye to that second world, and treated myself to the possibility that I would awaken in yet a third! And so I held each moment with tenderness. My son kissing me a sloppy good night. Mrs. Green packing yarn into a purse. Nathan brushing his teeth. Strange to see people going about the daily motions of life, when you are the only one who knows it is good-bye.

That night, for instance, as I watched Nathan undress. Undoing the buttons of his trousers—an old-fashioned gesture—and hanging them on a wooden valet as he stood in his high-waisted underwear. Sitting there, nearly naked now, unaware that he should not be doing this, should not be with me, and yet I could do nothing to stop it that would not seem insane. I could not say, "Stop, this is wrong, in my world you don't love me." I could not say, "Please don't torture me." So I sat there as he removed his undershirt, his undershorts, and stood nude until a pair of striped pants covered him and he slipped into bed beside me, yawning as if nothing had happened at all. A good-night kiss, a "Good-night, love." And as I closed my eyes, I felt as guilty as a Peeping Tom.

And yet, I awoke the next day to that same narrow face—"Good morning, love"—and saw the same billboard out the window. No shift, no travel. Of course it was the procedures that sent me traveling at night, and I had to wait a week until the next one, but at the time I considered I might be trapped there forever. Waking each morning to have a little boy peeking in at the door, running to me. Sleeping each night with Nathan beside me. And would it be so bad?

What was most wonderful about my journeys, I now believe, was that I alone could appreciate the beauty of those worlds. None of the ordinary people in 1918 found flickering gaslight quaint or beautiful, or saw the old Dutch market houses as anything but eyesores; to them, the world was both falling apart and coming together all too much. In 1941, as well, for those people it was all too modern and too old. The old billboards and funny metal sounds of life, the way that women flounced their skirts, and how men were always removing and replacing their hats, things that are gone forever; it was nothing to them. I was that visitor who comes to a country and finds it charming and ridiculous all at once. Why would anyone wear those hats? Those skirts? And why have we lost the simple decency of saying hello to strangers on the street? But to those who lived in those times, of course, none of it seemed strange. It was ordinary life, with all its troubles, and only when they were jolted off the rails for an instant did they see how odd, how beautiful, everything around them was. Jolted by love or death. They would never consider that it might disappear, or that they might one day miss the quiet Fifth Avenue snowfall that slowed their Model T, or the awful smell of oyster shells and horse manure, or the green el trains that blocked their window view. I was the only one who knew what would be lost.

"Your brother is on the phone at the moment, but Mrs. Wells is in the parlor with Baby."

I never thought I would hear that sentence in my life. But I had ceased wondering at the impossible; I suppose your eyes adjust in a looking-glass world.

"Thank you," I said to the maid, a short blond girl with a bent nose and a Coke bottle in her hand, filled with water, that I mused must be for ironing. "Show me in." And she did, bottle sloshing, leading me through what appeared to be my brother's home, though without his stark sense of style. Here it was striped wallpaper and old tatted upholstery. Of course it was decorated by a woman, this wife who waited for me in some pink parlor with "Baby."

To my surprise, I stayed in that 1941 world for nearly a week; I had to wait for Dr. Cerletti in order to travel, which meant I awoke in a new world only every Thursday and Friday. As I would later discover, this gave me just a day in some worlds, an entire week in others: a day in 1918, this week in 1941, followed by a day in 1985, a week in 1918, and so on. All of my travels would follow this pattern—or nearly all.

And so here I was, at my brother's house. Mrs. Green had given me the address without any questions and took little Felix into her care. Out the door, of course, into a world I had learned to navigate. Soldiers and sailors and children with pennywhistles silenced by mothers wielding anvil-size handbags. The subway was a bit of a puzzle, as I had nearly forgotten the difference among the IRT, IND, and BMT lines, and how one bought a ticket, but I was no more mystified than the excitable French couple fumbling with coins that, with their Indian heads and Mercurys, were as exotic to me as to them. On the dark green–painted train I sat beside a tired shopgirl, her best peacock dress faded from too much washing and pressing, her feather boa limp as an eel, removing her shoes in the car with an audible sigh. And navy men everywhere, red faced, eager eyed, and watchful, rolling with the turns of the car as with the roll of their ships, resting powerful farm-boy hands on their clean white pants. When the pretty shopgirl looked their way, they seemed as scared as of a bank robber.

Felix's house was in the East Eighties, in what they called Yorkville. I was surprised to learn it was a German neighborhood, and the street provided evidence: German bakeries and cafeterias, coffeehouses and men's societies. We were Germans, of course, brought over by our father as children. Later, I would learn our nationality excused Felix from service, in both worlds, but not from complications in a nation at war with our country of birth. On a stoop two boys stood talking, one still straddling his bicycle (his pants leg bound by a gleaming bicycle clip), yelling, "*Tote mich!*" until the other pulled out a very realistic gun and said, "Bang!" —a little cork popped out of its mouth, then dangled from its invisible string as they both cracked up. Only in one bakery window did I see a notice about a meeting; my German was rusty, but still it was impossible to escape its message. At the top, printed in black, was a swastika. And next door was my brother's house.

In the pink-toned parlor, sitting sideways in a slipper chair, I found a slight brown-haired woman in a frilled milkmaid dress holding a newborn child. The maid said my name, and the young woman looked up very peacefully—and then her face flickered, briefly, with the most astounding expression! I would say it was fear, almost as if she was doing something wrong, and I might punish her, but mixed in there was something complicated, subtle. In an instant it dropped below, and her surface was serene again, her smile very bright as she stood, holding the baby close in its swaddling clothes, and sweetly said, "Greta! Well, now I'm glad I stayed in town." I walked forward to embrace her and she smelled of lilacs and powder.

"Oh, the baby's so beautiful!" I exclaimed (not knowing the sex) and she smiled proudly and tucked the blanket under the creature's chin. "Can I . . . ?" I said, holding out my hands. I saw her mouth purse in concern, looking down at my cast. I understood: We were not friends.

"Do you want some tea?" she offered, sitting down again with her baby and smiling at it. "Or something to eat? No, you're going out to lunch with Felix."

"That's right," I said carelessly. "He wanted me to meet a friend."

"Oh? He didn't mention it to me. What friend?"

Her face shifted to me, eyes sparkling, and a voice came from the hall: "Ingrid, you remember I told you my sister and I were lunching . . . Oh hi, Greta!"

Later, as we made our way to the restaurant in a cab, I told him I had misstepped slightly in my conversation with his wife, and Felix glared at me with his lower lip pressed out. He was thinking something through. "What do you mean?" he asked. "Of course that's fine, I just forgot to tell her. She knows Alan, he did my will. Don't make her think my life is so mysterious, bubs." He laughed, then looked out the window the way you do in cabs, finger to his chin, and I understood how deep he must be in.

How strange. To step into the Oak Room in my velvet dress and feathered explosion of a hat, purse under my arm like a baguette, chandelier glitter on everyone's shoulders, and see Alan there!

Sitting at the table, waiter beside him, with his hands forming a tepee, his silver hair cut military-style, a wide-shouldered suit, but the same square, lined face as ever! Same cracked-green-glaze eyes! Big and broad and healthy, as he had been when I'd first met him, years before. I wanted to run up and tell some old Felix joke only we knew and see his midwestern countenance turn red with pleasure. Then he would pat my arm to comfort me. Over the beloved dead.

But I couldn't. Because Felix was not dead. He was here beside me, talking to the maître d'. And I couldn't run up to Alan because he didn't know me. I was only now—as he stood up and visibly, nervously swallowed—meeting him for the first time.

"Hello," I said, smiling and taking his hand, "so you're my brother's lover?"

Of course I said nothing of the sort! Would you have every banker drop his martini in his lap? The whole of Manhattan would short-circuit. Instead, I took his firm hand limply and said, "So you're my brother's lawyer?"

He said he was, and he had heard a great deal about me. He and Felix exchanged glances several times, like actors who have forgotten whose line comes next.

They fought over who should pull out my chair—the waiter did it, arriving magically at the right moment, then vanishing—and who should order for us all.

"I will," I said. "Felix, you'll have the pork chop and onions. Alan, you look like a man who likes a rare rib eye, with spinach. I'll have the same. And martinis," I said to the waiter, handing him the menu. "Gin for the men, vodka for me." Oliver Twist? asked the waiter. "Olives," I said, then sat back and smiled at the small bright room.

Both men stared at me in astonishment. "Well, a woman has certain talents," I admitted, arranging my napkin.

"But how did you know how I liked my steak?"

"Felix has said so much about you," I explained, watching Felix and seeing his cheeks redden. "So I feel I know you. You look like a rare-rib-eye man. A man who shaves without a mirror." A jolt of alarm from Felix; I saw my game had gone too far. Now Alan was looking into his lap.

"Greta is going to work," Felix offered, and this time it was my turn to be shocked.

"Is she?" Alan asked, leaning toward me. "What jobs are they giving women these days?"

"Oh, let Felix tell you," I said.

My brother smiled. "Women are getting all kinds of work. It's fascinating, really. Greta's job, you sure you want me to tell?"

I shrugged. "You're so much more charming with words."

"She's photographing great buildings, inside and out. In case we go to war, and the Germans bomb New York. So we can rebuild them just the way they were, isn't that interesting?"

Alan raised his eyebrows. "You're like an African griot. You're preserving our civilization for us."

"Hardly," Felix said. "All photographers think about is light and shadow. They don't give a damn what the subject is."

I grinned. "Sad to say, he's right. Oh, martinis!"

My twin brother tapped his hand on the table in time with the piano and looked around the room as if not interested in me or in his wife or anything but some appointment he was missing. It was so odd. It was infuriating, and so like my brother, but not in any of the ways I'd hoped. I had longed for this Felix to be the one, to be more like my brother than the 1918 version (all slogans and Diamond Jim smiles), and yet of course we forget that when the dead come back to life, they come back with all the things we didn't miss. The bad cooking and the late arrival and the habit of hanging up the phone without saying, "I love you." They aren't fixed; they're just back. And here he was, adolescently pursing his lips as if bored out of his mind. I could have hit him with a dinner roll. Bored? Here we were! The three of us, alive, together! So what if I was the only one who knew the lines, who knew how things should go? At least sit here and stop fidgeting, Felix, I wanted to say.

But then I saw that Alan was the same. To the unaccustomed eye, they looked like two men bored to death by a chattering woman. Nodding their copper and silver heads, playing with the mixed nuts on the table, gulping down their drinks like medicine (the olives submerging with terror). But I knew. That they were not bored; they were robbers who have hidden their cache somewhere in the room and were giving it all away, not by staring at the spot, but by staring at everything else, eyes roaming the ceiling, the floor, the tabletop. They were giving it all away. Any detective would have found the hiding place instantly, lifted up the floorboard, pulled out the diamonds and said, Here! You fools! I could see it in these nervous men, tapping and fiddling with rings and topics of conversation and forks and knives. Not even brushing against each other. I had gotten it all wrong. If you had silenced the clatter of dishes and silver, the noise and hubbub of a crowd two drinks into lunch, the sounds of the street and the kitchen, you would have heard the water ice clinking on the table from how their hearts pounded away. How simple: They were two men in love.

"Where is the food?" Felix asked, looking into his drink and finding nothing left. "I'm starved, aren't you?" He looked up with a halfhearted smile, his cheeks flushed with color.

Men in love. I wanted to reach across the table and thrust their hands together. But of course I could not do it; I could not even let on that I knew.

"Oh, they want us to get good and drunk," I said.

"Then I'm ready!" Alan said gamely.

So it had already begun. I was prepared to meet the man, a lover of a later time, who, like tropical plants that never bloom out of their climate, would be no more than a platonic friend my brother yearned for. But here, it was so obvious! They needed no prompting. For they were already lovers.

"Alan, tell me again how you two met."

He looked at me very professionally. "Well, let me remember, it was at a party, right?"

"I think it was one of Ingrid's playwrights," my brother broke in, leaning back in his chair and glancing out the window. "He had an opening, of course we missed the show, I think it was all

Irish ghosts and family drama, but the party was in a rich lady's place up on Park Avenue. The elevator man wouldn't let you in unless you could name the hostess and the playwright, thank God Ingrid was there, I didn't know either!"

"It was Amanda Gilbert, I handled her divorce," Alan informed us. "Baffling crowd. There was no one to talk to but your brother."

"Either longhairs, lesbians, or bagatelle matrons."

How did it work? Did they each take long lunches and meet in a hotel known for such things? Did they go on working weekends to the country, have late-night drinks with clients? What were the lies they told their wives or girlfriends or secretaries? What were the lies they told themselves?

"Oh, now I remember!" Alan said, laughing inwardly. "One old lady in feathers yelled at a waiter for bringing her lime instead of lemon, and I saw this young man turn to her and say . . . Oh, what was it?"

Felix pretended he didn't know and picked at a Brazil nut.

"You remember!" Alan insisted, appealing to me. "He turned to her and said, 'Madam, when you were a little girl, is this the woman you dreamed of becoming?' I knew I had to meet him."

And then they looked at each other at last and

laughed. Anyone could have told then; they nearly touched each other at the memory, but withdrew their hands to their drinks instead. Surely their eyes had locked at that party and each had seen, in that moment, the "tell" they must have learned over the years, the flash of interest that part of the mind understands completely for one brilliant instant—then silences with a bullet like a witness who will say too much, so that it is forgotten and one can walk over and introduce oneself to the young red-haired man flushed with drink, with no more guile than a lawyer with a possible client, producing clever conversation and a business card. No one watching would have noticed except a wary wife, and I wonder if Ingrid had been across the room, seeing every move as a spy sees a brief-case handed over at a train station. For their eyes must have revealed it all. Never leaving each other's gaze. It didn't matter what they said. Surely words are just the background music when passion pounces on a soul.

"I am so glad to meet you, Alan," I said. "You seem like best friends already."

They didn't know what to say to that, and luckily at that moment the food arrived. They smiled at their plates as if they read there a great fortune.

It was only afterward, as Felix and I were waiting for taxis (Alan had already left, down the block), that I got up the nerve to say, "Alan seems wonderful."

Felix smiled warmly and said, "I thought you would like him." The porter opened the taxi door and we stood there for a moment on the brink of speaking. Starlings or somethings were whirling overhead. A screech of tires, and a woman in a bright green shawl jumped back, shouting, causing a scene, but we did not look there. We looked at each other, lips open. How to say it? Phrases were whirling in our minds, like the starlings or swallows or somethings, possible ways to say it. *I want you to know* was one way to begin. Or: *I understand everything*. We looked at each other. The woman shouted, the cabbie shouted. "Felix . . ."

"Later," he said, and slipped into the cab. Slam, whistle from the doorman, and he was off again down Fifth Avenue. Of all the ridiculous things, tears came to my eyes and I turned away. He was alive here, carelessly, effortlessly alive, with all the petty troubles and worries that the living have. A wife, a child, a lover; such troubles. But there he went, again. And the feeling came, again. He did not know, not him or Nathan or little Fee, that my prolonged stay here had ended; the procedure was mere hours away. Today: the taxi leaving. Tomorrow: home. It was a little death, each time, I would come to feel. Less like a traveler than a mayfly, living for a day, a week, then gone. Reincarnated as myself, again, struggling at the screen door, again. Two procedures: over. Twenty-three to go.

I soon discovered how the procedure in this world differed from the others. I came home and found my son engaged in some Swedish game of Green's, in which he was made to hide behind the sofa while she knitted on the couch. I was too much a novice mother to protest, and Green's raised eyebrow (her knitting, like the weaving of a spider, never ceased) silenced me. Fee's head popped up—a puppet show—and he rolled his eyes and grinned mechanically before running from his counting place and embracing my knees. "Momma, Mrs. Green told me a story about a ghost, a woman who used to live here, did you know about that? Did you know she darns socks in the hall at night? Can I stay up tonight and watch her, Momma? Can I?" Knit and purl went the old girl's web, that eyebrow still on high, and who was I to argue? Perhaps the ghost she meant was just a shimmer of myself, slipping between the worlds in sleep.

"Mommy needs a nap, darling. I'll be out later to take you to the park."

"Not now! I've been inside all day!"

"Just a little while. I need to change."

"Madam," came Mrs. Green's voice and I turned, my hat dangling from my hand. Her eyes seemed to be encoding something. What could it possibly be? "Perhaps you forgot," she said gently. "The doctor is in the bedroom. He has been waiting, and the nurse is here as well."

"I see." I stood there for a moment feeling the weight of my hat in my hand, the coarse weave of its cloth, the irritating little feathers that stroked my dress with an audible sound. My gaze went all over the room, like a bird in search of a window. Yet there was nothing to do but go into that bedroom, nothing to say but what I said. "Thank you, Mrs. Green."

I wondered what on earth she made of this madwoman walking the halls.

They were there waiting for me, and their conversation broke off immediately as I entered the room with as much dignity as I could muster. Bald Dr. Cerletti smiled professionally as he nodded; he was in a navy suit and silver glasses, his demeanor somehow diminished from his contemporary self. "Mrs. Michelson, here you are." He did not wear a doctor's white coat, nor did the nurse (the same girl, her hair a different blond from a different bottle) wear a uniform. They were in civilian dress; I later found this was a courtesy to my husband, as was this house visit for a procedure typically done in the hospital. I looked around and saw the sun-lamp had been rolled across the room and was beside my bed, which had been unmade to just a sheet. The machine was plugged into the wall.

"Would you lie down, please, Mrs. Michelson?"

A commotion started on the street—a soldier's fight, it sounded like—so the nurse closed the window and drew the curtains, dimming the room except for a bright vertical bar of gold that shone between the drapes and cast its duplicate on the wall across from me. I removed my shoes and dress, placing the hat on the vanity where the birds seemed to watch me from its brim. In my slip, I lay down on the sheet and took a deep breath.

"We're trying a little more today. You shouldn't notice any difference. Now lie back and relax. Same as always." The nurse rubbed gel on my skin, just on the right side. The doctor took two metal disks and put them against my temple.

"Wait. I'm not ready."

"Relax. It will be over in a moment, you'll feel so much better. No more daydreams."

"Wait."

But he did not wait. The nurse sat beside me on the bed and there was something gentler about her in this form, more pitying and kind, a sad daughter at a deathbed, as she placed the cotton wand in my mouth and held my free hand tightly. She squeezed twice, as if to comfort me, but I realized it was a signal to the doctor, for on the second I felt the charge going through me— briefer than in the other worlds, but moving like a wave within my mind. I moaned audibly and hoped my son never heard these cries, these unmotherly sounds coming from the bedroom; what did Mrs. Green say they were? Was this the ghost she spoke of? Would he remember them, or just the story she made up about them? I felt my face tighten into an animal's snarl and I was shifting. Something like a wire moved through my veins until I was all metal, bending for them, and then the blue fantastic vision filled the room, a web of light, and I wept to see my thoughts blow off, in groups, like dandelion seeds. I watched them float off and away. There was my son. And my husband. And, of all surprising things, there was the young man Leo. Off and away. What was so wrong with daydreams?

NOVEMBER 7, 1985

The light falling through the metal blinds, striping my body in the bed, should have told me everything. And yet I woke with delight at the thought of what new miracles Dr. Cerletti had given me, even found myself calling out Nathan's name. But no one appeared. The wind blew through the open sash and rattled the blinds, and the sound was too familiar. Throwing away the gauze of dreams, I saw the three abstract photos in their frames, and the chair piled with clothes, and recognized my old life waiting for me, schoolmarm-tsking me for ever thinking life could be perfected. That life could be anywhere but here and now.

"My theory," said my aunt Ruth, pouring me champagne in a teacup and gesturing wildly with her free hand, "is that you are experiencing the Buddhist transmigration of souls!" I had of course told her everything. I had no other ally to confide in, after all.

That afternoon in 1985, she was dressed in her

black-and-white kimono. Her white hair was messily uncombed and she stood perfectly still while some hidden radio was braying through the wall, causing the glasses in the highboy to clink ominously on each downbeat. *I can't get no,* it said in a muffled voice. *Satisfaction.*

"Transmigration of souls?" I asked.

She gestured wildly in the air. "Well, the Buddhists believe in thousands of worlds outside our own, with their own boddhisattvas, arranged like the petals of a lotus."

"Ruth, do you ever drink tea in your teacups?"

"And physicists have the same theory," she told me. "Mathematically their formulas make more sense if, instead of an atom going left or right, it goes both ways. It forms two worlds, a left world and a right world. And that these other worlds are being formed constantly. Like the petals of a lotus!"

"I don't know anything about it. I only know what I saw."

"Well, I know about it," she said, raising an eyebrow. "Married to Nathan. And Felix, alive!" I watched as she removed the cover from the parakeet's cage and it hopped along on its twig toward her. "So many worlds."

"Ruth, maybe I should talk to Dr. Cerletti."

I can't get no, said the wall. *Satisfaction.*

She put a little seed into the bird's tray, all the while talking: "Well, of course, baby, if you want. But you know what he'll say. That it's all in your head." She walked over and pounded on the wall.

"I suppose."

Ruth sat back down on the sofa, scratching behind her ear and looking out at the last autumn colors of the garden; clouds must have been passing over the sun, because the yellow gingko leaves slowly pulsed with brightness, as if someone were working a switch. She absently removed a thread from a cushion. "It's easy to say something is all in your head. It's like saying a sunset is all in your eyes," she said, gesturing, pursing her mouth in small furies. "It's stupid, it's nonsense. It has no brain for beauty."

"But he might keep me from this paranoia—"

"Well, you knew what he would say. And you knew what I would say." *I can't get no.* She stood up and pounded on the wall. "It's just interesting that you came to me. Imagine what Felix would say."

"I have my procedure again today. I'll be back in nineteen eighteen for a week. I can ask him then."

She smiled.

"Ruth," I said quietly. "I'm so lonely here." She put her hand on mine. The music stopped at last, and in the silence we could hear Felix's parakeet singing longingly from its cage.

NOVEMBER 8, 1918

I awoke the next morning to the whinnying of a horse, the echoing chimes in my brain, and knew at once where I was.

"Madam?" I heard outside the door. "Do you want coffee?"

For it was as I had hoped: My trips made a logical pattern. From 1918, to 1941, to my world, and back again. Like scales on a piano. *You asked to be back,* I thought to myself. *And here you are.*

"Yes, Millie," I found myself saying as I looked out the window on the chill November of 1918. "I'm going down to see my aunt."

That morning in 1918, I was treated to a strange mirror of the conversation I had had with another Ruth, in another world.

"Perfect them?" Ruth was saying to me as she poured champagne into a teacup. "What do you mean perfect them?"

Apparently, the 1918 Greta had confided her

own travels to other worlds, and Ruth had greeted me with the twinkling eye of someone who knows all your secrets. And indeed she did. I sat on her daybed, with pillows behind my back and chrysanthemums bristling from a green vase beside me. The silver trelliswork of the wallpaper—so garish, so like my aunt—reminded me strangely of the light effects I had witnessed as I slept, when the world disappeared from my skin and an electric lattice, like the accordion gate of an old-time elevator, unfolded behind my lids while presumably some unseen porter worked the lever—and down I would go. First floor: flu. Second floor: war. And there Ruth sat, directly opposite, in a pink kimono and small wire-rimmed glasses that magnified her eyes into objects of wonder. Champagne in teacups, white hair, kimono.

"You did this before," I told her. "Yesterday, you gave me champagne in a teacup. In your kimono."

"It's my last champagne," was all she said. "I missed you this week. Another Greta was here, not as charming."

I laughed at the idea. "Really? How funny to think of that, but of course another would be here. Is she sad, too?"

"Not as charming," she repeated. "She thought I was a hallucination."

"At least she told you everything."

A flash of anger in her face. "No one likes to be called a hallucination. Then my own came back, to this world. She's the one who told me. You want to perfect them, you were saying. That's what she said, too."

Her cat materialized on my arm and began its tightrope walk, vibrating deliriously through the pads of its feet, mesmerist eyes affixed. I wondered about the other Gretas, how they would differ from me. Was it possible? "I just thought maybe that's the purpose. Three women who wanted to escape their lives, and so we did. We just happen to all be the same woman. So maybe I can perfect their lives. And maybe, while I'm missing, they can perfect mine."

Ruth picked up the cat and carried the suddenly powerless creature to a pink armchair in the corner, all the while talking. "What would you have them change?"

"Maybe they see things I don't. Maybe they can fix me."

"And what would you change about the other Gretas?"

"What happened to Felix? Is he in jail?"

"No, no," she said. "The police were just harassing him. It's not a popular thing to be German, you know. Or to be a young man not fighting in the war."

"I don't think he's happy here," I told her. "He's not like the brother I knew."

"So you want to change other people, too."

"Well," I said with confidence, "I know how they *could* be if things were different. If they were born in a different time." I watched the cat as it considered its armchair, and then, with one claw and after some thought, as it absently removed a thread from a cushion.

Ruth stood up very straight. "I hope you're not trying to perfect *me!*"

The image came to me of her grave in 1941.

"No, no, Ruth, I couldn't change you if I tried. Now will you tell me," I said, "what brought on my procedures here. What happened?"

Sudden sunlight drew a bright box on the counterpane, containing the cat, who stretched in an ecstasy of fur. Ruth thought a moment, then said, "It was a very hard time. But you got through it." Then she looked up at me. "Nathan became very close to another woman. It was a small thing. It was months ago."

Brick building, zigzag smile, two silhouettes.

There came the shrill sound of a mechanical bell. She tapped my knee and said, "He's here!"

The creak of Ruth's old door called out (did she never oil her hinges, not in any time?) and I heard a male voice talking from the hall. Then the sound of footsteps. I stood up from the daybed, touched my hair (it was in some huge brioche formation), and shared a glance with Ruth, whose eyes and hands sparkled back at me with all their gems. "Maybe it makes things clearer for you," she said. She tightened the turban around her head, shooing away the cat, who glared at the flowers with a look of mischief. Laughter from the hall.

"Felix!" I shouted.

He smiled in confusion. For it was not Felix there.

The perplexed young man stood there with a bouquet of roses in one hand and a hat in the other.

"Leo!" Ruth exclaimed, and to my surprise she walked forward to kiss him! "Oh, you're as adorable as ever! Isn't he, Greta?" A magnificent wink, and I recognized him: the young man from the street on Halloween. He raised an eyebrow and smiled slyly at me, raising a dimple on one side of his wide, handsome face, the cheeks shining from a fresh shave, though he looked as if he could not keep a shave for long; his chin was already blue with a new beard. "But we need to get you a new suit and a better barber. Look, I'm treating you like a nephew. I've got a package I can't get down from the study and you promised to help! Just in the study, you'll see its brown paper."

Two Felixes, two Ruths, a new Nathan, and now this Leo person. I was someone switching television channels, trying to keep all the characters straight.

"Happy to do it," he said. He had a surprisingly

low voice for a young man. "But only for a moment. I just wanted to leave the tickets, I have to be at the theater. Here they are. Oh, and these are for you." He did a little juggling act with his hat, the flowers, and his pockets to produce an envelope. He nearly handed the hat to Ruth, but she took the other two very smoothly.

"You darling boy. The study, brown paper." Leo nodded and looked at me.

Shorter than I remembered, but upright and confident in his worn blue serge suit. His large brown eyes, long lashed, bright with intelligence, took in everything about me, everything about the room. His thick brown hair seemed ready to spring from its pomade back to the wild state it must see every morning. I would later learn he was an intense young man, more likely to wander Washington Square, retracing scenes from Wharton and James, than to sit smoking cannabis in the Mad Hatter and talking nonsense. This perhaps was why he was drawn to an older woman. Another smile. "I'll be right back." As he left, I noticed a slight limp: I would learn it was from a childhood accident, and sometimes, when he misstepped, he would laughingly turn it into a kind of dance. This was what had kept him from the war.

Ruth pivoted on one shoe and turned to me.

"I saw him outside my window that first night," I said.

"She met him a while back. At a play in the alley," she said. "You understand, don't you? Because of Nathan, what he did. She is so lonely."

"I understand. But I don't know what I'm supposed to do," I said. "How old is he, anyway?"

"I think she said twenty-five."

"Twenty-five?"

She held a finger to her lips to quiet me. "Just tell Leo you can't wait to see the show tonight. Oh, there are two letters for you."

"The show?"

"His show, darling. We're going to the theater." She threw off her kimono and I saw that, underneath, she wore an elaborately pin-tucked dress in black silk, a black rose blooming from her breast. "I'm your elderly chaperone."

The Playhouse was, to my surprise, not in the Village at all but in an almost unrecognizable Lower East Side, on Grand Street. There, between the pickles and the pushcarts, I found myself hobbling down a street that seemed paved with tar-stained wooden blocks, and everywhere impoverished Jewish women stared at me with babies in their arms. Peddlers on all sides sold bananas, buttons, blankets, anything the heart could dread or imagine. Two young women stood in front of one cart, trying out eyeglasses by reading a newspaper the peddler had nailed to a post. "Cloth for cash," another old man said to us, his eyes red as embers, "cash for cloth," as if he didn't believe it himself. Almost immediately we were in the theater.

Or, rather, firehouse. Apparently the old firehouse had been converted into a theater, and a little turnstile had been installed within the great red engine door. A man in a suit sat on a pickle barrel inside, collecting dimes. He bit each one in his back teeth before dropping it in the barrel; the process was interminable. The smell of pickles clung to us even when we sought out a seat near the front. "You want Leo to see you're here," Ruth whispered. She had told me we were going to see *The House of Mirth*. I had read the book in college, but could remember barely anything except a vision of Lily Bart's exceptionally white skin, made whiter still by the overdose she took. I wondered what role Leo would take, and recalled a rather handsome platonic friend as well as a ne'er-do-well married man. I could not picture him in any role. But I could not picture him in my life, in any role, either.

It was at that moment I remembered the letters. Among the beaded fringes of my purse I found the snap, and tore open the first letter with a military stamp. What a strange sensation, in that other world, to see that old familiar handwriting I used to see every day on grocery lists, and bills to mail, and the little love notes I once found in books I was reading:

October 20, 1918

Dearest Greta,

It has been a hard month here in - - - - - but I fear the hardest is yet to come. People talk of peace, but where I am there seems no end to young boys brought in wounded, suffering, crying for their mothers. But we have suffered nothing compared to the locals. A small trip and one only enters towns of widows, all in black and clawing at you for a piece of bread or comfort. Whole trenches fill with flu victims. We cannot treat them or cure them. God knows what would happen if our staff got sick! It is a small bit of hope that some boys survive, and are well in days, though only to head into battle the next.

But I don't want to depress you with these thoughts. Peace will come, perhaps soon, if the Huns are routed as the generals say they will be. Your letters have been a great comfort to me. My mind is only on you, and on the child we will have on my return, God willing! The war will end. I will return. The smoke will clear, and we will see each other as we once did when we were young. And I will be home.

With love forever,

Nathan

The old history lessons of public school made their way out of the rubbish heap of youth. Armistice. Today was the eighth of November. The Germans would be routed; the kaiser would soon abandon his post and flee the country; the war was nearly over, and yet it astounded me, looking around, that none of them knew! Surely the papers were full of negotiations and concessions; surely the war had ended weeks before and the famous November eleventh date —the eleventh hour of the eleventh day of the eleventh month!—was merely a formality. But no; overhearing conversations and remembering Liberty Bonds posters in windows, I realized that being this close to peace, to the end of all that horror, was not like being close to the end of a novel; you could not weigh the final pages in your hand. They did not know. They lived in fear, not knowing that the last days were upon them. And 1918 Greta, receiving letters such as this from her husband, did not know. That very soon the war would end.

I was making my way through these thoughts, barely paying attention as I opened the second letter and read it through.

"Ruth," I whispered loudly, but did not manage to extract her from her conversation. "Ruth!"

"Darling, yes."

"How long have I known Leo?"

"I think a month or so. I started getting flowers

sent to me around then. I knew they were meant for you." She added that he had been seen in Patchin Place, staring up at my window. "I'm afraid to tell you," Ruth said quietly as a gong was struck somewhere backstage. "That the boy's rather attached."

"Is he my . . . ?"

"Your sweetheart, is what I would say," she said. "Your admirer. Nothing serious has happened yet."

I showed her the letter. The message was brief, and I managed to see the thrill in her eyes before the lights dropped and audience noise fell to a hush. She put her hand on mine and squeezed. Things had suddenly become more complicated than expected. First a loving husband with allusions to sorrow. And now this. *Greta,* it had begun.

I will never forget the night you said you loved me . . .

The theater now was dark as a forest. A piano began to play an antique waltz. In the twilight we could see the curtain opening on something square and white, and then, a moment later, the bedsheet glowed with the miraculous words *The House of Mirth*. It turned out I had completely misunderstood the performance we were seeing, and Leo's role. It was not a play at all. It was a moving-picture show.

Small footlights came up left and right,

revealing two young people on stools: a kohl-eyed girl in even more old-fashioned dress than the crowd, and Leo, wearing a tight wool suit, bowler, and eye shadow. Both held megaphones, and Leo immediately lifted his and read the title aloud, along with the names of the performers, one of whom was a female Barrymore I had not heard of. Then the scene opened on a silent picture of a beautiful woman walking down a New York City street of brownstones, smiling at a sunny day. The girl in the bustle dress read the words that appeared on the screen: "Lily Bart had missed the three fifteen to Rhinebeck." They were to read the title cards of this movie, while the piano changed tunes according to the action; the girl read the female parts, and Leo the male ones. At first I assumed it was a theatricalization of the moving picture, but after a long time I understood the real reason, and then I was ashamed. It was not for any theatrical purpose. It was because most of the audience could not read.

A man appeared on the screen, a wry man in an ascot, and Leo read the card: "Oh, I'm not dangerous." A few in the audience laughed. But I sat and looked at my young man with the painted mustache.

So funny to sit and see a stranger and be told: "That's your lover." The one in the chair? No, on the stool, in the hat. Aha, thank you, Doctor. It seemed curious that another me loved that young

114

man, staring boldly at me in the alley; in my aunt's hall; five-foot-something of headstrong youth.

I would do anything for you, the letter went on to say. *So be kind to me.*

It took me a moment to realize that he saw me. Of course; unlike the theater, here the audience was lit by the glow of the film; he could see us almost as well as we could see him. Who knows how long I had been staring at him? Or he at me? But the moment caught us both out of character. Eyes locked in the white light of the projector, hiding nothing. So tell me: Who were we then?

"Well, wasn't that fun!" Ruth said, rushing forward as Leo came out of the stage door. "They should do that with all books! Have you standing over my shoulder reading all the men's parts would be so much more fun, don't you think?"

"As long as you pick a short book," Leo replied, and as she cast me a look that said: *I envy your youth, if I had your luck and your figure, I wouldn't hesitate for an instant, life is too short,* and he chuckled knowingly and shot me a look that said: *See how well I fit into your life, see how nice I would be to have around, try me for a while.* They chattered and flirted, and were all want, want, want. And all for a girl who wasn't me.

It was agreed that Leo should accompany us

home, and on the way we discussed the book and the movie, which Ruth seemed to know by heart. I watched the pushcarts and barrels of pickles and schmaltz herring and men standing around. I felt people's eyes on me, now in the darkness more than before. I wondered where my brother could be. Sitting with his fiancée? Waiting for me somewhere? At least I knew he was out of jail.

"Excuse me," I heard Leo say, interrupting my aunt's flow of words. "I wanted to show you both something I thought you'd like."

"What's that?" she asked.

"It's a secret," he said, raising a roguish eyebrow. "My friend's a gardener here."

I was going to ask "Where?" because I had lost my way (the streets seemed to have changed—or rather, not yet have changed) but realized we were standing just at the edge of Washington Square Park. My heart could have leaped like a fish from a bowl: I saw it as it used to be. No bright glare of lamps on the fountain; no gathered crowds of roller skaters, visiting youths, old hippies spending a chilly night. Only the old elms from which supposedly they used to hang criminals for public viewing. A startling thought: Someone alive remembered those days. And there was the arch, shockingly white, of course, cleaner by sixty-seven years, yet still the same pale open mouth on Fifth Avenue, and it took me a moment to realize it was missing one of its George Washington statues. I supposed some sculptor was still chiseling away at a deadline.

Leo looked under a nearby white stone for a while. "Found it!" he said, smiling, and boldly took my hand, leading me to the east side of the arch. Ruth followed, lifting her skirts in the wet grass. I had never noticed before the little door cut into the stone there, or the tiny keyhole; it had never occurred to me the arch could be anything but solid marble. Leo slid the key in the lock and, with a satisfying creak, the door slid open to darkness. All we could see were the first steps of some stairs. A smile from Leo, full of daring:

"Nobody comes up here. Nobody even knows it exists."

Three glasses of wine stood, now empty, on the stone ledge of the arch, beside Leo's hat. He had apparently prepared; the glasses and a bottle of wine had been hidden in the staircase below. The lantern was out—"Too risky," Leo whispered. "Last year some artists got the key for a party and there was hell to pay"—so for our visit we were treated to darkness, silence, and a view that was not my New York: gasworks billowing gilded steam, the black Hudson littered with a jeweler's shop of boat lights, the few lamps flickering in servant attics north of us, the vagrant fires glowing south.

Leo stood beside me, and Ruth had stationed herself farther away. I saw her, hands clutched together, looking out on the city, oddly silent.

"Look," Leo said, and she turned to where he pointed. "There's the courthouse. And there's Patchin Place."

You could more imagine it than see it, but there was in the darkness perhaps the gleam of the gates, just between the courthouse and the prison. The lamplight of our little alley.

We stood looking without saying a word. In the darkness, I could feel the young man's eyes on me.

Suddenly I heard Ruth's voice. "I heard a story," she said. "About a Chinese sorcerer who wanted to live forever. So he cut his own heart out and put it in a box and hid it where no one would ever find it." I looked over to see the light catching her jewelry. "Now where do you think he hid it?"

From behind me, I heard Leo say, "I don't know."

"Take a guess," she said. "A castle with a dragon? A mountaintop?"

"I'd hide it down a well," I said.

She laughed. "Yes. Something like that. In a flour sack. The least likely place some young hero would look for it."

"Very clever," Leo said, closer to me now.

Ruth's voice grew quieter. "I wonder where New York has hidden its heart."

The silence of the park sat in the space she left there.

"I wonder," Leo said softly.

I looked at him and he smiled broadly. Those eyes watching me so closely. He was indeed handsome.

They talked for a while, the two of them, in hushed tones while I leaned out over the edge to see the city. Its flickering lights. I thought of that other Greta, who endured what I had endured—a straying husband—but who had not lost him. Her Nathan had returned, and stayed, but I understood her need for comfort. For someone, perhaps someone very young, who would remind her she was alive. A young actor, his eyebrow raised, so clearly in love. Why not? She had chosen lightning, after all, like me. Was it so impossible to choose passion as well?

A rustle from Ruth: "I'm cold, I think my moment has come. Take your time, this is going to take a while in these skirts . . ."

She made her way down through the trapdoor with a little laugh, into the small brick chamber below that no one in New York suspected. I looked at the lights one last time before turning to go.

Leo touched my arm and began in an insistent whisper: "Greta—"

"We should help Ruth—"

"I need to ask you," he said. "Who am I to you? When you think about me."

The city lights gave a softness to his features. His lips were slightly parted, his eyes worried. I could feel my face and chest getting warmer from his look, his touch. I thought of Nathan in 1941 and said, "Let's not talk about this now—"

His voice grew quieter, his eyes lowered. "I want to know. What's the word you use in your mind?"

"Don't ask me now," I said, trying not to look at those eyes. I understood her attraction. But what he wanted was not me; it was another version of me. "Later, ask me later."

"I mean, when you think, Oh, I'm going to meet Leo. He's my . . . what?"

"Don't ask me this now, I'm . . ." I fell back on that old phrase: "I'm not myself."

"Who am I to you, Greta?" he asked.

The darkness had drained all color, so we were in silent-movie tones, his face a mottled moth-wing gray. I could see him breathing as heavily as a machine with a load it was not built to carry; I could tell he had suffered quietly for long enough, had promised himself both that he would be quiet, not spoil the night, and that if he got me alone he would not be quiet, he would risk everything. In all my travels, in my anxieties, I had thought only about the troubles of my life. A brother resurrected, a husband returned, a child born, mystery after mystery darting around corners, things restored and taken away again;

the whole horrible beautiful magic act of my life. I had not yet thought of this. That someone else's life depended on me.

"Leo," I said. I found myself touching his cheek. He flinched; his whole cheek caught fire.

I had not yet thought of this. That I had arrived in this era with a gun my other self had bought and cleaned and loaded for me and placed in my hand, the safety off. Twenty-five years old. Handsome, clever, those eyes. Who was he to me? I thought of the only kind thing I could say, the only thing I knew:

"You're my sweetheart."

He took the word as a suffering man takes medicine, hoping it will work.

"You're my sweetheart," I repeated, and then he took me in his arms and quickly kissed me. I did not resist him.

In a moment he pulled back and looked at me as if searching for the latch that would open me. Breathing hard, cheeks spotted with red, closing his eyes, and who knows what he saw there? I only know he held me away from him and opened his eyes.

He nodded and said, "Ah. Your sweetheart." It was almost enough. But not enough, I could tell. The medicine had not done its job. He released me, stepping away to the railing. "Let's find your aunt, the steps are hard to manage." He laughed at himself.

"What is it?"

His hand went to the trapdoor.

"Isn't that what I am to *you?*" I asked.

"No, Greta," he said, looking away, to the east where those steam clouds, lit by gaslight, rose like spirits into the night sky, up to stars I had never seen from light-crowded New York, and had to travel all the way to Saratoga, one summer, to view, looking up from a late walk with my mother and asking what the starry cloud was up there. And her saying: *It's the Milky Way, darling, it's the galaxy we're floating in, haven't you seen it before?* There it was, above us, as it would never be seen in the city again. Spectral, silvery, the backbone of night. It did not belong here; I did not belong here. This young man who was not mine, standing by the ledge with his back to me, thinking so hard about what I had asked him, waiting a long time before he took a breath and said, laughing a little: "Greta. You're my first love."

Felix came by to visit, but wouldn't tell me much about his encounter with the police, though I could tell it had shaken him. He stayed only briefly and sat at the window the entire time, smoking, staring at the birds. "I didn't tell Ingrid about it," he said. "I didn't want her to worry. Just police mischief, but she's so delicate. She's such a good chance for me." The autumn light caught his long freckled face and I wondered what to do with him. If I could even talk to him about his life. In a moment, he smiled the old smile I remembered and kissed me good-bye. "See you later, bubs. Don't look so worried. The war has to end soon."

And it did. It was later that week that I heard the trumpets on the streets. I heard the crowds shouting, "It's over!" and went out to see them hugging one another with joy. What a strange and magical scene to have been summoned for. I came home, where Millie handed me a folded note— Leo wanted to meet me at eight, under the arch— then informed me meekly that folks were gathering at my aunt's. It was already packed with people when I went down there. Ragtime was playing somewhere—*"C'mon and hear! C'mon and hear!"*—competing with military marches playing somewhere else, and of course no conversation could be heard above the racket of talk and laughter. On the sofa, a dark-featured man in a toga sat speaking to a group of well-dressed girls gathered at his feet; as I passed by, he kissed each one on the forehead and they swooned. Around the corner, I did at last recognize my aunt, standing under a ridiculous lamp of Prometheus bringing fire to the mortals (the fire was an electric bulb), her jet-beaded back to me, shimmering like a fall of rain. In a moment she turned around and saw me. Her expression was a fireworks of joy. She shouted something at me I couldn't hear. She shouted again. Only on the third try did I make out:

"It's happened! The war is ending just when you said it would!"

"Did I?" It must have been that tattletale: 1941.

"You said November eleventh. At the eleventh hour."

We think we have a rippling effect on life, and perhaps we do. But perhaps, at least for me, not on history itself. Not on the big events, the wars, elections, and diseases. How could I have thought so? Such a small person as I was in the world. Someone in this room, surely, would make it into books, be studied and written about. If they had traveled to other worlds, in other times, things might have shifted like an earthquake. Some people were like that. Aunt Ruth, perhaps. But not little red-haired Greta Wells.

Aunt Ruth leaned in; I could smell she had been drinking something stronger than red wine. "My dear, you're a prophetess."

I was that, at least. I wondered what else I could tell her, what could be of use to her or anyone I knew. That yes the war would end, but another one would start in barely twenty years—twenty years!—and this time there would be new horrors to contemplate? That her plague would end as well, and it, too, would be replaced in sixty years by something just as deadly? Why hadn't some future Greta, some prophetess or angel, come to my time to tell us it would end, our own trouble, that the boys would stop dying by the thousands? That the world would care, and cure it? Instead of sneering at the bodies lined up for burial? Where was that woman? Why had I been chosen as the last, the final version of myself? Surely there was a better, wiser one who could show us all how it would end.

The recorded music stopped and the raucous sound of voices rose at first, then broke, like a wave, into murmurs as a piano tune began to play nearby. I saw the long-haired bartender pounding stridently at the keys, and singing. What, I could not hear. Ruth leaned in close to me again, a new gleam in her eye and her lips parted to speak. Then all at once—a common sound of joy:

Johnnie, get your gun, get your gun,
get your gun . . .

I could have wept. To see them all so drunk with wine and relief, that at last the horror had ended. That so many had died was unbearable. But no more would die. Out there in the mud, they were all saved.

Take it on the run, on the run, on the run.
Hear them calling, you and me,
Every son of Liberty.

The one who used to sell the bread, the one who groomed the dogs, the bartender, the waiter. All the ones gone off to war, surely to die as all the others had died; they were coming home! They were saved. The thought of them being saved. I had to turn away from Ruth. The sobs were uncontrollable, the shock I felt when I appeared on Halloween and saw the young men, the thought that others would come home. That it was over. The idea of a horror being over, how could they know that I understood? That I had never thought I'd see a day like this? The boys were saved.

Over there, over there,
Send the word, send the word over there,
That the Yanks are coming,
    the Yanks are coming,
The drums rum-tumming everywhere.

An old drunk man in a long Chinese robe was pounding his chest. Two young women embraced; surely they loved someone. These same soldiers would come home, never speaking of what they'd seen, and marry those girls and raise children, and they would send those children off to war again. With Germany, again. We would be here, again, in this parlor singing this same song. I stood there, in wonder, at the madness of it all.

We'll be over, we're coming over.
And we won't come back till
it's over over there!

It was only later that Felix arrived, and when I
saw him laughing in his frock coat and holding
his top hat, I felt my heart shaking inside me,
ridiculously, like a dog left alone for days—
"Felix!"—and he looked over at me curiously.
He was flushed with wine already, from his chin
up to his neatly combed hair, and he looked
more fragile than ever. A white rose wilted in its
buttonhole. I pulled him to me. But once I began
to talk to him I saw I had misunderstood; he had
not just arrived, he had been here for some time,
hidden in the thicket of people, and was just
now taking his leave. Felix said he was heading
to some other party.

"I'll go with you," I said.

"Not this time, bubs," he said, blushing deeply.
"It's not a party for married ladies." I could tell
at once it was a lie.

I laughed. "I can do as I like."

That surprised him. He had removed the rose
from his buttonhole and was pulling it apart with
his fingers, letting the petals fall into a bowl. My
comment made him stop. "I know this sounds
crazy coming from me, after how I've acted these
last years," he said, laughing, then becoming
sober. He stroked his chin. I could see him

127

deciding on his words. And then he said something really remarkable: "But I want you to think about our family reputation. I'm marrying a senator's daughter in two months. They care about these things."

I asked him what he was talking about.

"These people here are full of ideas," he said meaningfully. "Free love. Other things. Don't fall for it, trust me. For my sake, Greta."

A shift in weather, and we are a different person. The split of an atom, and we change. Why would I expect my brother to be the same one I'd known? Free spirited, bold, selfish, foolish, drinking and smoking and laughing too much with his gap teeth wide in his face? It takes so little to make us different people. Who knows what this Felix had lived through? What cloudy day, or snowfall, or shifted atom made him into this Babbitty little prude? Engaged to a senator's daughter, talking about reputations, my brother who once had sequined gowns hanging in his closet? And was it now impossible to change him? Or was it as simple as another atom turning, this way toward me?

"You've lost your mind," I said, then added boldly: "You're headed to a sex party right now."

He flushed again, this time in anger. "I'm going to a very high-level political event. It's full of very high-level men."

I laughed at that, and he grimaced at me and

without another word he was gone. Was he lying to himself, or just to me?

I stayed at the party for much longer than I expected—mostly because newcomers had completely blocked the exit—and finally succumbed to the drunken revelry by taking a few sips of the "Versailles punch" my aunt was now passing around, a hideously sweet drink made from French champagne, English gin, American lemons, and German honey liquor. More than a little of it went onto the Persian rug, and I supposed the maid would not get Armistice Day off tomorrow. I spent a good hour chatting with a handsome bearded schoolteacher, in a trim blue suit, who talked about the need for national health care. The piano was still going—this time with a girl singing a love song unknown to me—and the booze left me smiling and twinkling at everyone. I looked at the clock on the mantel.

"Ruth," I said, pushing my way toward her. There was now a very familiar smell that I associated with my own era, and I noticed the bartender with a girl in a long green dress, embroidered with daisies, passing a little cigarette. My aunt was supporting herself against a grandfather clock, and her own necklace swung in time with the pendulum. "Ruth, I'm off," I told her.

"What, now?"

"It's the actor."

"Yes? What?" she asked, then let my words penetrate the drink in her mind. She frowned. "You know he's going to be very sad."

"I'm fine, I can handle him."

She leaned back, those great eyes blinking. "The soldiers are coming home."

"Yes, yes—"

"My dear girl," she said, raising her eyebrows and cocking her head, "Nathan is coming home."

He was there, under the arch: a ragged version of the young man I'd seen there only nights before. Those eyes had seen no sleep, and his young cheeks had not seen a razor; still, Leo, always an actor, stood confidently under the arch, hands in his pockets as he looked around the park. A faint mist haloed the lights behind him. From all around came sounds of merriment, and rifles going off, and from somewhere invisible a band played marches, real or recorded, louder than was necessary. Looking at Leo under the arch, I thought perhaps he might be the only person in New York for whom the peace was misery.

I walked into the light, he saw me instantly, and I assumed he would take one step back in bitterness, like a man in a duel. Of all mad things, however, he smiled.

"Greta, you came."

I shrugged and pulled my shawl around me. "My aunt was throwing a party, the whole city's gone mad."

"I know," Leo said, raising an eyebrow. "My neighbors are throwing one plate after another against the wall."

I laughed. "It's wonderful news."

"Yes," he said, lowering his chin but keeping his gaze on me. "You knew it had to come." I said nothing. He went on: "But we pretended it never would."

The smile was gone. He put his hands back in his pockets, lifted his chin, and regarded me. "Have you heard anything from him recently?" he asked at last.

"A letter this week."

"So he's all right?"

I saw with a little horror what Leo was asking me. How selfish love is, though we never think of it that way. We think of ourselves as heroes, saving a great work of art from destruction, running into the flames, cutting it from its frame, rolling it up and fleeing through the smoke. We think we are large hearted. As if we were saving it for anyone but ourselves, and all the time we don't care what burns down, as long as this is saved. The whole gallery can fall to ashes for all we care. That love must be rescued, beyond all reason, reveals the madness at the heart of it. Look at Leo, so kind and tenderhearted. Look at him.

Forgive him for hoping my husband was dead.

"No, he's alive," I said severely. "He's coming home. Perhaps he'll tend the wounded."

Nodding. "Of course. When do they come home, do you think? The soldiers?"

"I don't know. I really don't know."

"I was asking around," he said. A visible swallow in his throat. "I heard some will be back in a few weeks. And others, maybe Christmas, maybe January."

"It could be. I'm sure he'll write me as soon as he knows."

"Of course."

There was a pause here, in which the whistling descent of a firework could be heard. As Leo turned to me, one could see how the mist had dampened his cheek. There was something angry in his eye. So dangerous, being with someone in love. Like standing beside a tiger.

"What happens?" he asked.

"I don't know."

A little flash of fury. "Your husband comes back, what happens? You said once you would always be able to see me. How can that be? Did you mean when he's gone to work? Or on a trip? Is that what you meant?"

"I . . . I suppose so, I don't know what I meant."

"Your sweetheart," he said, not bitterly but resigned. "What is wrong with your marriage that you're here with me?"

Because of Nathan, what he did. She is so lonely. "It's an emotional night. I can't tell you now."

Leo was not listening: "You don't really love him, you can't. The other night, I thought we had time, and maybe you might leave him. So I thought, The hell with it. I'll just love her."

"That's beautiful, Leo."

His head jerked up. "But you're not going to leave him."

From somewhere, a group of men began to sing some old war song.

"No, Leo," I said. "I'm not going to leave him."

Who knows what is going on in the minds of others? We stood under the arch, a foot away from each other but as distant as if a national border lay between us. And he did not move, just stared at me, his eyes taking in each aspect of me, one by one, both hands and arms, every part of my face and hair. There was no part of me he was not seeing, now. I smiled, but he did not smile. Leo just stood there and took me in. Who knows what battle raged inside him? It went on, in outward silence, for only a few seconds, but I'm sure it was a long struggle as he inventoried the woman he loved, the bits of her he could not live without, the words she said, the promises and lies and truths, the hope she gave him before one side won at last. He blinked three times and nodded.

"Then good-bye," he said and walked away into the trees.

It hadn't seemed more than misty, but by the time I got home I found I was quite damp, and my black coat and absurd hat veil had become embellished with little diamonds. All around me the crowds were starting to gather, just as on Halloween, but this time in the ordinary costumes of their daily lives. Pretty girls were everywhere, perhaps under the mistaken impression that the soldiers would magically, instantly, be home, and old men had put on their military garb to stand and smoke pipes together on corners. I wanted to shout, "Don't forget this! It's going to happen again! You're going to let it happen!" because of course they would, these young jubilant people; someday they would be the old soldiers on the corner, smoking pipes, approving of a new war. It would seem good, and just. Surely it would to me, as well. I couldn't stop it, but I wanted them to remember this, the horror they were in for. Not to cheer it.

And yet how could they not? How could I not be drawn into it myself? The girls on the streets, their dresses dampened but not their spirits, standing with bottles of whiskey to hand out to passersby who swigged as if there was no flu epidemic, the ragged young boys running every-where, unsure of what it was all about, waiting on corners with their hats out for a penny—our future soldiers—and drunks of all varieties, top hat and beat-up derby, singing songs I did not know, and leaning on every railing and lamppost in a toppling world, and then, fireworks! They spiraled sparks and made more noise than light, hissing glimmering above the village, and what vicious Cassandra could shout there was another coming? Who would even dare? Perhaps they knew. There is always another coming, as there was even now, buried in the dirt by my foot, the seed of the oak that would crack the sidewalk in two. I'm sure in my own age, when the cure came, some wicked prophetess would stand there as we cheered in the streets to shout, "You fools! Another's coming! You won't remember!" But she would be wrong. Humans remember all too well; we are made this way, and suffer for it. It is the art of living, in drink and dance and love, to forget. So let them, Greta. It was their war, not yours.

It had shocked me, what Leo did. To disappear so quickly into the black, dripping trees. But surely I had really come in at the end of a conversation, a long one he had been having with me all night—without my being there—in which he went over everything I'd said as if it were brand-new, perhaps gave speeches in his cramped room, ones where he persuaded me to leave Nathan, ones where he set up the rules to our affair once my husband returned, ones pleading and angry and forgiving. I'm sure Leo tried every delivery of those words. He was an actor, after all. And so, when he saw me, he had already gone through every possible conversation. I'm sure he didn't know it himself, but he was only waiting for one answer. And I gave it. And he saw there was no need for pleas or speeches—he had already given them, in every intonation—for they would change nothing. So Leo said good-bye, the only thing he had not practiced saying.

Well, that is that, I thought. For the best, I suppose. And yet . . . I felt a pang of loneliness. Each Greta had found someone to comfort her. What would I go back to? The same solitude? The same months without touching another soul? The only promise I had, for these few travels, was what they had made for me: a husband to hold me at night. A lover to steal a kiss on an arch. That he was not really my husband, or really my lover who left me—did that matter in the end?

I heard the party raging on at Ruth's, but didn't have the heart for it. I thought perhaps I'd lie down. It was wearying, getting everything wrong.

I opened the front door, and there was Millie, her face blurred with tears over some private worry—a boy, of course—but I wasn't up to finding out (probably the mistress never was) so asked her to make a pot of chamomile tea and I would get ready for bed. "You should take tomorrow off," I told her. "It's a holiday all round," to which she replied thank you, ma'am, it was already her day off but wasn't it grand indeed? To see the boys all coming home at last? Yes, I said, yes, stripping back down to my all-in-one with its absurd split drawers. The bed was miraculously warm—how had it been done?—and then I felt, at my feet, the hot water bottle Millie must have put there telepathically. Or, perhaps, routinely. It was delicious to have needs met I didn't even know I had.

The tea was set beside me and, beside it, two bland cookies that lingered in my mouth like sand. I flicked the gaslight and the room was violet except for my bed candle, panting like a pet. Out it went—and yet my thoughts had lit another candle in my brain. Felix was not my Felix here. And there was no Nathan. What comfort was there left? *I am so lonely,* I had told Ruth once. It seemed true in two worlds now. I felt sleep coming, the dead leaves of my thoughts gathering in piles behind my eyes, then—

A loud knocking. I heard someone stumbling down the hall. From the window: the sound of armistice joy erupting everywhere. I grabbed a robe and wandered into the hall.

In the open door to my apartment: Aunt Ruth. Shimmering in jet beads, and on her shoulder, a white parrot. Drunk as anything. Slurred speech and one sleepy eye:

"He's back. He won't have anything but you. If I were young, I'd go with him this instant, and that's what you're going to do. I won't have it any other way." To the girl behind me: "Millie, don't gossip." To me: "Let us sport us while we may, am I right? Get dressed, go now. Go now before you get a chance to think." And she staggered back downstairs, but not before the parrot chuckled twice, eyed me, and said: "Drink up! Drink up!" I heard the party roar outrageously as she reentered.

There, under the streetlight, leaning with a bottle of wine against the brick: smiling Leo. Why smiling?

The heart will hear only one sound. A "no" will pass unnoticed, and a "good-bye" will be heard only as a deferral of hope; the future is unmarred, pushed forward by events but untouched by them because the heart sees only a perfect future with its beloved, and hears only news about that future. The rest, as they say, is noise. There is only one sound it can hear. There is only "yes."

He raised the bottle in greeting, and shrugged his shoulders as if to say: What did you expect? The prisoner in the jail yelled out in favor of peace, and from one window came a snow of torn paper, which blew down our way and settled in his hair. Looking up at me, someone. *You should have waited. You would have had her, the one who loves you. Tonight: She has Nathan, and you have me.* I smiled at him from the doorway, remembering that in my world I was a single woman, and lonely. *So be it.*

Not his place, but a friend's place—a fellow named Rufus who we found at a bar—that would be empty for the night. I found I was quite drunk, but had more champagne when Rufus offered it. Then to the apartment. Up five flights of stairs, a confusing double lock that needed some pool-shark English and a nudge of the hip, and we were in, the light was on, and I began to laugh. How could I not? There, strung from every doorway and knob and cabinet pull was a web work of clothesline and, on it, surely every item Rufus owned hanging damp and drying. Long, absurd socks and sleeveless underthings, all the strange hidden men's clothing of the early twentieth century, there to amuse me. Collars were pinned in a line, free of their shirts, and cuffs as well. Long woolen garments drooped like hanged men. "Oh Lord," Leo sighed, and ducked under a clothesline, his head popping up behind it with a grimace. He offered me his hand and I ducked under as well, and we made our way to the middle of the room. "We have some time left. Let's go away. My father has a farm up north, I'll take you there, we could just cook and sleep and walk in the snow." He offered me a last swig of champagne and I took it. This room was dark, but I looked around and saw how the streetlights shone through the handkerchiefs, illuminating them like Chinese lanterns. Hanging there, glowing all around us. Strange how briefly life is worth the pain. I kissed him there with the cloth lamps on their lines, not a room at all but a pleasure park at night, hung with moons. "Oh," he said, as my hands moved naturally, a lady of the twentieth century. "Oh, wait, oh no." He struggled in my arms, then relented. I suppose it should have occurred to me that this was 1918, and he was still a virgin.

November 14, 1941

I awoke, a few days later, with a sleeping Nathan beside me, his head as still and handsome as if carved from stone, and I lay there and watched him for a long, long time. Sleeping so peacefully beside me: a husband, a father. His face bristling with the day's new beard, his nose imprinted from the glasses that lay on the nightstand, his lips parted slightly in a dream. Our heart is so elastic that it can contract to a pinpoint, allowing our hours of work and tedium, but expand almost infinitely—filling us like a balloon—for the single hour we wait for a lover to awaken.

He did at last: I saw, in the dim light, his eyes shining as they gazed on me, his lips in a smile. "Do you feel . . . ?" he asked. I said I felt wonderful. "Could we . . . ?" he asked, pushing my gown up with one hand and spreading his fingers. I kissed him and smiled and said yes.

And afterward, when he rose to go to the bathroom and I lay back in bed, prickling with pleasure, I thought of how I would awaken the next day in my world, six procedures complete. What waited for me there? No brother, no lover, no husband. I had not been able to fix that world, but I had been brought here, perhaps, to fix this one. Hearing the familiar sound of Nathan yawning and sighing from the other room. There was so little time. Already the Japanese were encoding messages, making plans, and I would lose him, too . . .

NOVEMBER 15, 1985

It happened after my 1985 appointment with Dr. Cerletti.

"You see that there are really no effects," he said, pleasantly, adjusting his half-rimmed glasses, "except a recharging of the spirit."

Again the nurse smiled down at me in her blue eye shadow and permed hairdo, and again the late-century noises of New York made themselves known from outside: the honks and shouts and boom-box beats of my life. Surely some traveler from another era would come here and find it all as quaint and backward as I had found my other worlds. As strange as I now found my own.

I said no, no effects at all. In fact, I added, I might miss our little meetings. Who else got to be struck by lightning, not twice, but twenty-five times? I saw his brow crease in concern and I left quickly.

Back in my apartment, I went through my record collection looking for something to calm my mind. Dylan, and Pink Floyd, and Blondie, and Velvet Underground until at last I found it. I started the turntable, lifted the lever that picked the needle up, and placed it in the groove.

C'mon and hear! C'mon and hear! Alexander's Ragtime Band . . .

That night, I went to sleep, as always, thinking about the life I would return to. Young Leo awaiting me in that world. Nathan in another. I smiled at the strangeness of it all. Was this the woman I dreamed of becoming?

I closed my eyes and watched as a little will-o'-the-wisp in blue ascended, winking, dividing into two and four and eight, a web began to form, a net, to haul me out of my world and back to 1918 . . .

But I did not awaken in 1918.

Part Two

NOVEMBER
TO
DECEMBER

December 4, 1985

Hello, Greta. It's Nathan.

Began the voice on the answering machine.

Three weeks had passed since my night with Leo, and I had suffered a strange glitch before finding that message in 1985. How clearly I could picture Nathan: sitting in his red armchair, in his brown sweater, smelling of pipe smoke, stroking his beard before getting up the nerve to call me. *It was nice to hear your voice the other day, I'm glad you're doing well. I'd love to meet for lunch but I'm afraid I have to do battle with Washington. Off to war! I'll give you a call when I get back. It's nice to be in touch again. Bye now.*

I stood there in my hallway, staring at the device with its blinking light. Another Greta had been tampering with my life while I was away. It was no more, of course, than I had done with each of theirs. How I longed for things to be back the way they were.

Let me back up to that first morning when I realized something had gone wrong.

147

• • •

I had awakened, three weeks before, to find something amiss. The day before had been Dr. Cerletti, peering down at me in 1985. The next: "Good morning, darling, how are you feeling?" Nathan again. Smiling, beside me again. My arm heavy in its cast, 1941 instead of 1918.

"I'm in the wrong . . . ," I began, but of course could not say the rest.

He frowned and asked, "What's wrong? Is it the procedure?"

Let's go away. My father has a farm up north. She had gone there with Leo, and Cerletti's jar sat unused.

What would happen if one of us missed a procedure? Well, here was the answer: That door would close. Our journey was like a subway line in a circle, and if one of us missed a procedure— if one station was under repair—well, the train just zipped on by. That Greta had stepped out. And so we, the other two, could only switch places until she returned. I could not explain to Nathan that the Gretas were out of sync, out of sequence: three beads misstrung on a strand.

"Nothing, darling, I'm fine. Sounds like Fee is up."

"She skipped Cerletti," I told Ruth the next day, when I awakened once more in 1985. "I can only go here and to nineteen forty-one until she's back."

148

"Tell me about your son."

My travels were an endless source of fascination to my aunt. And so I told her about Fee and how he licked his finger and would dip it in the sugar bowl when we weren't looking, leaving little divots, the Invisibility Powder that Uncle X had given him, which he still tried to use on himself, though it was long spent. "And Nathan must look funny without his beard," she said, laughing. But I have a sense, though she never asked, that, like any of us, she was really looking for clues about herself. I tactfully avoided the topic, and went on about Mrs. Green striding around the house like the housemaid in a gothic tale.

"It sounds," she said, "like you miss both worlds."

And so back and forth I went—the Wednesday procedure sending me the next morning to 1941, the Thursday procedure returning me to 1985—making a meal for my husband and son, making a path through that other lonely life, each time awakening and wondering when she would come back, when we would all return to the pattern. I did not know I would miss it so much. I did not expect I would be so envious of her life.

I have read the diary Greta left of that time spent apart from us. I have seen the train tickets, the baggage receipts between the pages. And this is how I picture it, that time she spent with Leo, whom she loved:

They took a train to Boston, the wartime signs advising against unnecessary travel still posted everywhere, then at Boston waited four hours for another train, during which they wandered into the snowy city and bought him a cheap gold ring at a pawnshop, to forestall questions later on. When they arrived at last at the station, they disembarked to a gravel yard and small shed that contained only a woodstove for the railroad workers, who stared at them begrudgingly. He blew on her cold hands and smiled until, at last, a sleigh came into view pulled by an old gray horse, like a vision from a Russian novel. Across the snow they went, bundled together, sipping coffee, feeling for each other's hands hidden in the furs and coats and gloves. The sky was gray as flannel, the trees passed in an endless etching. There were no animals. There were no houses, or people.

It was a little stone house with nothing but a stove, a fireplace, and a bed piled with cushions to make it a sofa. The house merged into a long stone wall, made from rocks farmers had been cursing for centuries, and across which could be seen another little house, with a shuttered window, in which gaped the white head of a sheepdog, staring down the road away from them. "What is he looking for?" she wondered aloud, and the driver broke his silence to answer: "His master. He cares for no one else." And then he nodded and shut them into the house. By the door was a sack of provisions he must have left earlier in the day; Leo went to it immediately and brought out a sausage he began to munch merrily. They could hear the horse stamping in the snow. She watched the quiet scene of winter. As soon as she turned around, Leo was kissing her.

She wrote in her diary that they lived, for that small period of time, in a lovers' paradise. There was nothing to do but build a fire, and stoke the stove and cook on it, and fold the little table down from the wall, and fill the soft down bed. Above the bed, one long window let in the blue meager light of winter, and as her young man lay sleeping, Greta could prop herself on her elbow and look out at the sheepdog, itself looking down the road.

"I like your eyes," he said once in a foolish moment. "I like the lines around them."

She laughed. "I'm not sure that's the best thing to say."

"Why not? I do love them."

"They're just a sign of how old I am."

"Well, what about the signs of how young I am? Don't tell me you don't love them," he said, smiling mischievously and drawing her to him.

They talked nonsense, and she allowed him to

speak of impossible things, because something about their isolation, and the snow, and the fire meant even impossible things could be mentioned. For instance, moving to Brooklyn together, to a house, with the kind of dog he liked. He said this lying on the floor before the fire, staring at the beams of the ceiling. "And a garden for you, with a path through it, and a little stage at the end for our friends to sing when they're drunk." There was no wine, but there was clear moonshine, and he was sipping it; she could not, because it gave her a headache. "We'll have an Italian charwoman and she'll steal from us! But we'll love her," he said, still staring up. She looked at his smooth face, his small lean body wrapped in a blanket, tipped in two worn black socks. "Electric light, an electric stove, and a nanny for . . . well, a charwoman at first." She looked out the window at the dog, and she could feel his glance on her naked back. Perhaps he had said a word too many.

Though I visited two worlds in those weeks, I saw only one version of the people I knew. One Nathan, tying his tie before the mirror. One Ruth, chasing the canary around the apartment. One Felix, leaving me in a taxi for a dinner with Alan. How strange—how ordinary—to flatten my worlds this way. A lunch with Felix stands out: at a German restaurant, and I was late. Felix was already seated at a stained tablecloth, chatting up the fat, happy waitress, hair braided like a glossy strudel. At other tables, men were hunkered down over their steins protectively, as if they knew that Pearl Harbor was only two weeks away, and some would be taken away for questioning. Just for being born on the wrong side. But of course they did not know. Only I knew.

Felix complained he never saw me, so busy with Fee and with Nathan. "Felix," I said, startling him. "Felix, I need you to tell me something right now, before we say anything else."

He leaned against his hand.

"I'm not here to talk about me. It's you I'm worried about. Do you love him?" I asked.

"Greta!" he said, then looked at his plate. I told him I had always known about him, and that I didn't care. It made no difference to me.

He looked up at me. "Greta, stop it," he whispered harshly. "I didn't come to hear this. I came—"

"Don't be afraid with me. Be yourself. Please, Felix. I've been through too much to lose you."

"Stop this, Greta. You're not talking like yourself."

"I know you, Felix," I said as he put down his napkin. "I know you." But then a group of German singers were upon us, waving their steins and swaying in unison, the waitress laughing. In their worn brown suits and battered hats, red faced and weary, the immigrants from our father's homeland surrounded us with their welcoming song of summer, and sun, and my brother and I could only sit and smile and listen.

Ohhh, willkommen, willkommen, willkommen Sonnenschein . . .

And, in 1985, a lunch with Alan.

We talked of autumn, and Felix, of course. We talked of my procedures, his drug schedule and taking leave from his job. How funny to see him, after another lunch where he was all business in his pressed blue suit. Here: cowboy shirt again, all in grays this time, and worn blue jeans, and veins that pulsed in his temples below the short cap of silver hair. A cane beside his chair. How handsome he must have been when he was young.

We talked of parties long ago, and laughed about them. We talked about how he relented with his new romance, and saw him oftener than he should. He was drinking wine again. But what I remember most about that time in 1985, before I took my ride again, what I recall about that lunch with Alan was a story he told me about Felix.

They had gone to an East Village theater, run-down and small, not so different from the one where Leo acted out *The House of Mirth*. "I don't remember the show, exactly. Something about war, with puppets, that god-awful kind of thing.

But there was a book at the exit where you could write your comments. Felix liked to read that kind of thing." He was smiling out the window to where a young man in a hat walked by, something familiar about him. "And he called me over to show me what a Frenchwoman had written—I assume she was French, her name seemed French—it was so funny." He chuckled to himself, pushing around his salad. "I understood nothing!" he said, with a French accent. "But it was a great show!"

I laughed and looked again, but the young man was gone.

"I should have put that on his headstone. That sums him up, don't you think?" I nodded and grinned to share another memory with him. He pushed his shoulders back and sat up straight: "I understood nothing, but it was a great show!"

And so, after three weeks, a message left that afternoon:

Hello, Greta. It's Nathan.

What a curious mystery it was, standing in my hall with my coat and hat and scarf, too warm in my warm apartment, staring at my answering machine and hearing Nathan's voice. A reminder, first, of the sad state of my life here. And, second, of the presence of these other Gretas. For that other woman had taken advantage of her time in this world to call him.

155

I had taken pains to try to fix my other lives. I wondered, what were her plans for mine?

I'll give you a call when I get back. It's nice to be back in touch. Bye now.

Standing there in my old hallway, hearing the voice of my old lover, who in two other worlds had become my husband. The other Greta took my photographs and answered the phone and met friends for drinks, much as I had in my deepest depression, when I did these daily tasks as if they were assigned by another. Back then, the world was alien because I had sunk beneath it. And now, it felt the same because I knew it could be otherwise.

Eleven procedures finished, only fourteen left for me. November had turned to December and I wondered how long that 1918 Greta could keep away from that electric jar. Wondering when she would decide to lie down again, and fall asleep, and watch the lights behind her eyes join together in a tunnel from her world. When I would see those other people, in that other world, who seemed like friends from a trip I'd taken long ago.

I made myself my dinner and ate it in front of the television. Images of the space shuttle seemed like science fiction to me now. And in my mind were two conflicting thoughts. One was that I wished to continue my travels, continue the adventure the way, it seemed, I was meant to have it. And the other, of course, was that I, too, could put a halt to things. Waking tomorrow with Nathan and telling him I was cured, that I needed no more of Dr. Cerletti. After all, any of us could stop things. Would it be so terrible, to be trapped there? Then he could stay there sleeping beside me forever. In the world where I had never lost him.

But who would want to be in my world? Which other Greta could possibly love this place, find something or someone worth sacrificing their life for?

I went to the answering machine but could not bring myself to press Erase.

And that night, at last, I traveled to that other world.

DECEMBER 5, 1918

Ringing of bells on the street, not just in my head; the sounds of a 1918 world already preparing for Christmas. The room was soft and calm, as if awaiting me, and a crack in the window let in a little cold air that turned the pages of a bedside book, one after another, at the speed a ghost might read them. Bells and salesmen and the scent of chestnuts. Italian voices. The smell of gaslight and coal-fire stoves.

I was back.

In the kitchen, to my surprise, I found my aunt rummaging in the icebox.

"Good morning," I said. "I'm back. Are you making me breakfast?"

She was in her white kimono and looked like she needed a brandy. "It's for me," she said, running a hand through her unkempt hair. "I'm out of milk. So are you it looks like, and I don't blame the maid I blame the mistress." She turned back to the icebox.

I put my hands in my gown pockets. Was she, in

fact, the same solid Ruth I had known my whole life? Because looking at her, leaning into the icebox, I could see little differences I had not noticed before. For instance: She was noticeably thinner; she could hardly keep a bracelet on her wrist. There was a common illustration in those days of two women in war. Under the picture of a fat, smiling lady with a lorgnette, it read: "Waste Makes Waist." And under the proud, thinner version of that woman: "War Develops the Spirit." I had not ever thought of my aunt, with her parties and excesses, as the latter. But I suppose she, too, had felt privation during the war; instead of moderation, like most house-wives, it was all feast or famine, and her festivals were followed by weeks of Postum and porridge. Of course she had no milk. And here she was, raiding my icebox. "I'm not good with maids," I told her. "Make me coffee. I've been gone a long time, but I'm back."

Ruth looked up and examined me, then smiled. "Are you?"

I posed in the doorway like a poster for home defense. "I'm your niece from nineteen eighty-five."

Those bracelets jangled on her meager wrist as she looked me up and down. "Oh," she sighed. "I'm so glad it's you. A lot has happened. It's ended."

"The war," I said. "I know. I was here." I looked

159

around the kitchen and saw it was in disorder; Millie must have had a day or two off, and my other self had let things go.

"Not the war," she said, shaking her head.

I walked over to her and knelt down. "Ruth, just tell me."

She blinked and said, "She ended things with Leo."

I tried to understand how this could be. When it was the desire to be with Leo that had kept her in this world. "But," I began, "I thought they went away . . ."

She took my hand and patted it. "It's good you're back. My own Greta is inconsolable. Do you really want coffee? All I have downstairs is champagne."

"What happened in the cabin?" I asked her when we got to her apartment. She said it was her last bottle of champagne, and I begged her not to open it, to save it for a better occasion, but of course she said it was so like me to think there would be some better occasion, you can't marry such hopes, they won't be faithful to you.

"She couldn't bear it," Ruth told me, standing before the silver trelliswork of her wallpaper. New flowers sat in the green vase: lilies. "Making Leo promises she couldn't keep."

I tried to imagine them in a snowy cabin, Leo sitting on the floor and talking in that low, passionate voice. Myself on the bed, shaking my head. And still it made no sense. Had I gotten it wrong? Had she not really loved him, after all?

"What promises?" I asked.

"He wanted her to leave Nathan, of course," Ruth said, pulling the champagne out of a cabinet in her bookcase. "And she wouldn't."

"I understand that," I said, looking around me in bafflement. "But it doesn't sound like her." I found myself angered by this other version of me, almost as you are angered by some drunken thing you did the night before, and which now seems senseless and stupid. Sitting in that cabin and denying herself what she wanted most.

Ruth pulled back the sleeves of her kimono as she held the bottle. "If it had been you, it might have worked. You were the one who finally took a risk, you're the one who had her go away with Leo." She smiled. "That made me so happy, with all this war and death. You made things come alive. And you're the one, I think, who could have kept him. When Nathan returned." The bottle went: pop! She looked at me under her newly painted eyebrows. "But she's not you."

I stood there silently as she poured the champagne into little glass teacups.

"She's not you," she said, sipping from hers. "She truly loves him."

"Yes," I said, somehow knowing it within me. "Yes, she does." The champagne was warm.

"She said it wasn't fair to him. And she's afraid of Nathan, what he might do to him," she said ruefully. It sounded like such an odd fear of such a gentle man. "That's not what she told Leo, though. Lovers don't leave if there's any hope at all. She just said never to come back. It broke her heart to say it."

"Oh, it's so sad."

"How awful to watch lovers part," Ruth said, "when they don't have to." She seemed absorbed in this thought, and we sat for a moment in silence. I pictured Greta leaving Leo at Grand Central Station, where he stood calling her name, walking away and forcing herself not to look back. I could so easily imagine the pain inside her; I had felt it myself with Nathan. Not similar pain, but that exact pain.

"What will happen to him?" I asked.

"He'll probably marry. That's what they do, young men. I should know." She looked out the window and I wondered what memory floated through her mind. "They marry, and in a few years you'll get a letter asking to see you once again, just for the sake of old memories," she said, looking me straight in the eye now, "and I advise you not to do it. You don't want to see the expression on his face. You'll sit there in the cafe expecting him to arrive with the same flowers and deep eyes, and he will, too, but he'll come down the street and see you and he won't be able to hide it. The shock."

"That his feelings have faded."

"No," she said sadly, "that you've grown old."

Aunt Ruth stared into her champagne, which she held with both hands. Against the trellised wallpaper, she seemed like a woman from the East. She seemed to be thinking, and then she asked, looking up with sympathy on her face:

"Do you think you could have loved him?"

I thought of that handsome young man. His touch on the arch, his kiss, that night with the clothes hanging all around us. How he looked in the morning. If my other self turned him away, then I would have to as well. "My heart is with Nathan."

A furrow in her brow. "I don't know what your other Nathans are like," she said, then gestured with one kimono-sleeved hand. "But remember, you haven't met this one."

December 6, 1941

Tomorrow would be war. Tomorrow, every radio would break into the Dodgers game and announce the Japanese attack, followed later by our own president's declaration. War was hours away. And they did not know it.

Morning shouts, and morning newspapers, and Nathan's sideways expression as he shaved, and my son so sleepy, wandering down the hall. Eggs and bacon and bright red jam. So many smiles. Send a salami to your boy in the army. Somehow I wanted to hold this moment before it broke apart forever. Mrs. Green's nutmeg-scented arrival and Nathan's peck-on-my-lips departure. A house to clean and toys to step on and put away, all with an arm in a cast. The last hours of a steady life.

"Good-bye, wife!" Nathan said in the doorway, tapping down his hat. "Have a good day!"

To be a wife with Nathan! How my old self growled at the idea. We had always rolled our eyes at marriage, knowing too well how it led to matching coffee cups, and matching children ("one for me, one for you") and soon a white-collar prison outside the city where our cars would know our bodies better than our spouses. We felt we lived above it all; we would not marry, would not contract ourselves to each other like businesses. We would be messy, and unstable. And happy.

And yet—and yet!—here I had no choice but to be a wife. I will admit, it was a pleasant sensation, walking through the Village with my purse and hat and gold wedding band, to take each step with the pride of a married lady. I was a modern woman of the eighties, but it took very little time for me to get used to the strange underthings and hems and hose of that era and treat it like a costume of dignity—an academic gown, or a WAC uniform—with the thought that here I was, a married lady. Some days I held my son's hand and took him to the park. Some days I did the shopping and searched in my purse for minuscule change. My hat was straw with roses, nothing garish. It felt so funny to be prim and proper. It felt outlandish. And to have policemen nod their heads, and men open doors, and children be pulled aside so I could pass, all for a rich doctor's wife and her wide skirts—imagine! A crook of my finger and waiters would bring wine! A hand to my forehead and a seat would open on the subway! Ridiculous. Greta Wells, who had marched for ERA. Who had gone braless in Washington Square Park. I had become the kind of woman I used to hate. How I loved it.

Straightening the antimacassars on the arm-chairs. Licking my thumb to wipe a smudge from Fee's protesting face. Watching him race two shoes across the carpet: his and mine. Touching this and that. How do you steady things before an earthquake? Nobody really knows. Even I did not know, for there was another earthquake coming I had not foreseen.

It was evening, the day done, and Mrs. Green had prepared yet another chicken pot pie and was gathering her things to leave (she had knitted at least five sweaters since I'd first met her, all for the war effort, all in hideous green) when I got the call from Nathan that he would be late at the clinic again. "Oh, what a shame," I said before hanging up the phone, and then, coiling the cord around my finger, I turned to Mrs. Green and asked if she could stay just another hour. I wanted to surprise Nathan and take him supper. The clinic was close, just around the corner, it would take no time at all and mean nothing to me. "If I may suggest, madam," she began as always. "To let Mr. Michelson get his supper on his own." I shook my head, believing her to have a tin ear for romance.

On my walk I studied the strange world I was

becoming accustomed to, the world on the brink of a war. In an odd reverse of the world of 1918 —where suddenly the fever had broken, the patient had risen, and death was banished forever—here were streets full of people who did not know that war was coming tomorrow. In the window of a bread shop, a hand-painted sign: AN INDEPENDENT DESTINY FOR AMERICA! And around the corner, at an appliance store: WESTINGHOUSE HAS AN E FOR EXCEL-LENCE! SERVING THE NAVY, READY FOR ACTION! It was as if two paths were being prepared: one for war and one for peace, and this world was trying to take both, like a bride preparing for two weddings at once, depending on who asked her. Only I knew who would ask her: Death would ask her. There were boys in uniform everywhere, and girls sat in soda-shop groups giggling and admiring them. I could see how quickly old sufferings had been forgotten; their own fathers or grandfathers had lost limbs to war, their mothers or grandmothers had wept over a son or brother. But there they were, sipping egg creams at the window, as girls in centuries past must have watched the legions pass them on some Roman road. Waving and giggling and sighing with pleasure. I had wondered earlier about the Cassandra who could prepare them. I was that Cassandra.

"He left an hour ago, as usual, Mrs. Michelson,"

I was told by the male nurse at registration. "Didn't he phone you?"

I stood examining a pot of paperwhites that sat just beside his plump left hand. The stiff green stems, the bright little petals already beginning to crisp at the edges. I leaned forward; scentless. I heard my name again and pulled my coat closer around me, then picked up the ceramic pot of dinner. Yes, I said, yes, he had phoned me; I was sorry to disturb him. I made my way out and threw the dinner in a trash can; my hands were shaking too hard to hold it.

"Where is he?" I demanded of Mrs. Green.

She stood in the kitchen, in her long, plain, rose-colored dress, arms crossed and lips pressed tight, as if to keep any flash of recognition from me. A teapot stood on a blue gas ring. My son was already put to bed, and her eyes went over and over to the shut door to his room. He was a light sleeper. Yet she said nothing at all as I shouted.

"You know exactly where he is. I know you do. You're in cahoots."

"Mrs. Michelson," she said quietly. "If I may suggest, as a friend—"

"You're not my friend! You've hidden things from me. To protect him."

"No, madam," she said. She gripped her hands before her like the clasp of a purse.

"You have!" I shouted.

Through the thin kitchen drapes, I saw a neighbor's light go on. Mrs. Green must have seen it, too, but she did not move an inch, did not undo her hands, but stood there backlit by this new light, gazing at me as if she knew that what she was about to say would change us always. Not just change me, but change the two of us. Women must be careful what we say to one another. We are almost all we have.

Mrs. Green stood, carefully considering her words. "No, madam," she said slowly, never removing her gaze. "To protect you."

I heard the teapot begin to tremble on its ring, and saw her eyes go to it. "Tell me where."

Her eyes came back to me. Her voice went quiet. "Don't go," she said. The teapot struggled against the heat. "You don't remember anything from before, do you?"

Her eyes were crinkled now in curiosity. I said, "No, no, I—"

"We used to talk about it, you and I," she told me, and at last her hand went to the stove, and saved the teapot from screaming. She placed it on a wooden block, where it shivered and hissed slightly before calming. She said, "I knew you'd have to find out all over again."

"Tell me where."

"Don't go," she said, looking up at me now. The neighbor's light went out behind her.

"Greta. Don't go." It was the first time she ever called me Greta.

I am reminded of a cocktail party in 1985, a few months after Nathan had left me, where I met a charming woman all in white who was a decorator, and after a little conversation began to relate a recent job she'd had. "You won't know the client, a Nathan somebody," she told me, which was of course my Nathan somebody, in an apartment with his new girlfriend. Without revealing my identity, I asked her about the job: the furniture, the bedroom, the bathroom; I would not let her go until I knew everything. I did this, though each detail was a fresh jab in my heart. And why? What magnetic force draws us to scenes of pain, and words that wound us? *You have seen this,* I told myself as I marched along to that apartment. *You have seen this already, you've lived through this, spare yourself.* Yet on I went. Grief will go—it always does—but not before it forces us to do these absurd things, and hurt ourselves, and bring on suffering, because grief, that parasite, above all else does not want to die, and only in these terrible moments it creates can it feel itself thrashing back to life.

And this, this time, the dread was different. As I left Patchin Place, I pictured myself before the same apartment building, low and brick, stained with rain and soot, the fire escape in a zigzag smile, knowing that it was that window there, with the light on. There beside a coal fire, in their robes with glasses of whiskey or wine, her hair spread like an octopus on a pillow. His smile happier than I knew it. It was not the pain of being cheated on; I had already suffered that, and built a callus around it so that it could not hurt again. No, that pain was over. I could not resuffer it if I wanted to. This time, it was the pain of understanding that he was no different, this Nathan. I had thought the small shift of eras had changed him, as it had changed Felix, that without my neglect, our unmarried arrangement, he would be a better man. He was a better man, in many ways: kinder, more attentive, more loving. But it was not the details of our lives. How we lived or what we said or did. It was not that the time we lived in deformed our love, with freedoms that weren't freedoms, and selfishness and modern noise or fear. It was the goddamn way of things. How could I have imagined it could change?

And yet, one difference: me. I had changed. What he had done: I had already done myself. I had felt the solitude of freedom, the pressures of war and marriage, and seized a warm embrace when it offered itself. Why not? I had thought to myself. What damage I had done, in that other world, I did not yet know. But I could gauge the damage here. I had lived through it from both sides. The mind, however, is just a figurehead above that hidden dictator: the heart. It did nothing to help the anger. Or the pain at feeling Nathan slipping away, perhaps, all over again.

I returned to my kitchen wet with rain, the paper flowers in my hat ruined, their colors bled together. I found Mrs. Green in the living room, looking out the window at the raindrops, each with a tiny streetlight tucked inside it. She turned her head to me.

"I didn't go," I said. "There was no need."

She nodded. "What will you do, Greta?"

"Nothing," I said. "That's what I did before."

"Yes it is," she said gravely. I had meant in my home world, when I had let my Nathan's affair run its course. But she meant in this world. I surprised myself by knowing something, all of a sudden.

"Was it the same woman?"

She did not say anything.

"The woman from the park? I've seen her, watching me and Fee. In a plaid coat."

She pulled out a cigarette, lit it, empluming herself in smoke. "Yes, that's her."

He came home that night very quietly, and he looked startled when he saw me—and smiled, folding his umbrella, satin-shimmering from the rain. I was sitting in my nightgown, reading a Colette novel (of all things) in the hot glow of a lamp, and he kissed me and said, "Cigarettes," so I offered him one and we sat and smoked together as the rain threw itself against the window like a naughty child. He said it was a long night, and the army was getting him prepared to stop his hours at the clinic and devote his time to inductees. A draft was all but assured. With Roosevelt in office, the talk of staying out of war had quieted a bit, but of course in army quarters there was always talk of war, never of peace. I saw no point in telling him what was coming, and I just nodded. Had Mrs. Green frightened me again? "No," I said. "No, she's become a friend." He smiled and said that was good, everyone needs an ally. I said, "I thought you were my ally." He smiled and said he was, and kissed me, then went off to get ready for bed. I stared for a long time at Mrs. Green's darning basket, the red felt tomato stuck with pins.

Better somewhere. Perfect somewhere. I thought it would be here, in this world with Nathan. I had fooled myself into thinking that, as a planet with water implies some kind of life, a world in which husbands stayed implied some kind of loyalty. But a minor miracle is needed for life, even in the best circumstances, some errant spark. And it seemed there was no miracle here. Why would there be? When he did not love me in my world?

The next day, I broke down in tears as a radio

play was interrupted with the words: "From the NBC Newsroom in New York. President Roosevelt said in a statement today that the Japanese . . ."

Who can guess what war will bring? I had barely a rest of a few weeks, and it was war, again. With Germany, again. I thought I was more prepared than anyone.

Yet I was wrong. I assumed it would be all flags and terror, like last time, but that was not what took up even a fraction of the hours. War is so much smaller than you think. It is the mind that makes it small. We would scream with horror if we could not break it into pieces: polish his shoes, and match his socks, and practice cakes without sugar, or butter, or flour. Drill with rifles, drill with gas masks. Because tomorrow is impossible, you plan today. You plan the hour. You take your cup of poison one sip at a time.

The Yanks are coming,
the Yanks are coming . . .

Who can guess who war will take? I would never have guessed Felix.

There had been a raid at a Village bar, the Paper Doll, in which twenty men were arrested for sexual misconduct. All of their names were listed in the paper, along with their addresses. Among them was my brother, Felix.

"I know how worried you must be," Alan said over the phone when I called. "But I'm sure he's fine."

"Does he need bail?"

A pause on the phone. He told me Felix hadn't been taken to jail with the other men. The FBI had separated him and kept him elsewhere.

"I don't understand."

"They've been rounding up some prominent Germans and Japanese. It's war, Greta. They weren't looking for him specifically, but they took him when they found him."

"Alan, he needs you," I said, and Alan said he knew that. He would do everything he could.

Mrs. Green was standing in the hall with me, one hand wrapped around her waist and the other searching knowingly in her apron pocket for her cigarettes. She pulled out the pack without even looking down, and lit one. I sensed that she was a good woman to have in a crisis.

"Is there any news?" asked Mrs. Green.

"It's Pearl Harbor, it's got everyone paranoid. They've been picking up Germans and . . ." But I did not know what followed that. They had found him in a gay bar, so the police would surely not treat him well. What if the other prisoners knew?

"Mr. Tandy must have been upset," I heard her

say. "I know how important your brother is to him."

I turned to study her.

"Yes," I said. "Yes."

I suppose she was a woman who saw through absolutely everything, and bore the burden of it. How frustrating it must have been, to watch the rest of us blind to it all, or pretending to be blind, when it was all so obvious if one just looked directly at each person, and listened precisely to what they said, and watched what they did, and cared enough to imagine their lives. The rest of us, throwing up our hands in defeat at ever understanding another person. When there she stood, Mrs. Green, aware of it all. And cursed to say nothing, do nothing, but simply watch the farce unfold.

"I think Mr. Tandy is one person you can count on," she said carefully.

"Mrs. Green," I said, "I believe I can also count on you."

I watched as, without any expression, merely her right hand holding her cigarette and her left venturing to her apron to return the pack, she listened to my words and said merely: "Thank you, ma'am."

With all the worries on my mind, having my brother in jail was the worst. So it was a great relief when Alan called and said he had found where they were holding Felix: of all surprising places, Ellis Island. He had pulled some strings so that I could go visit him—that afternoon, if I wanted to. I dressed as soberly as possible, in a belted collarless jacket and shirtwaist; it seemed the proper outfit for a government prison. Alan, broad and silver haired, smiled when he saw me in the doorway. "All-American girl," he murmured. "Good, very good." He himself wore a suit with a flag pin on the lapel and an armband showing a golden Statue of Liberty on a field of blue. I asked, and he said it was his division in the last war, the Seventy-Seventh, from Manhattan. I do not know why this had never occurred to me: that of course the veterans of the last war would so closely overlap the next. He took my arm.

"Shall we go?" he asked.

It was a taxi, then a ferry past the Statue of Liberty itself, green and tarnished and amazing as always, then a long process of identification at Ellis Island. We waited in the beautiful main hall until I was shown into a small anteroom with a table and Felix seated in a chair, a wry grin on his face. Dressed in a gray uniform, he looked shockingly thin. All at once, the joy of seeing him again pushed me into the room to embrace him.

"How's Ingrid?" he asked, first thing. "And Tomas?" His son.

"They're at her father's in D.C. Alan sent a

telegram that we were coming to visit you." I said this all in a hurry, and then added, "They're fine."

"Where is Alan?" he asked, looking around, though there was no one in the room but us and a red-haired guard, smoking a cigarette and staring at my legs.

"He had to stay outside, only relatives can visit," I said. The guard caught my eye and I glared, which only made him smile. "How are you? How has it been? Oh my God, I'm so glad to see you, I thought you'd been shipped to Wyoming."

Felix waved his hand. "It's fine, I'm fine. It's boring as hell, bubs." Something in his eyes said it was more than boredom, though God knows boredom is enough for men like him.

"We're going to get you out of here," I said, taking his hand. "Well, not me, I'm powerless. Alan is going to get you out."

"We'll see. They haven't even told me why they're holding me."

"It's a panic. It's to look like they're taking action. Alan says they are starting to send some men home on probation, the ones who aren't really risks. We have to persuade them that's you."

"I've been on very good behavior."

I said that would be unusual, and he laughed at last. He was not beaten down, not yet. It was not like him to be easily broken.

The guard said it was time and opened the door. I stood reluctantly. "Tell Ingrid I love her," Felix said, squeezing my hand, and we stood. "And tell Alan . . . ," he began, and met my eyes very calmly. "Tell him thank you."

"Hold tight. We love you." I made my way to the door, to the grinning guard.

"I miss you, bubs."

The guard took my arm, but I shook it off. I turned around and said, "Felix, I miss you every single day."

"He isn't any harm to anyone," I found myself fuming back home with Nathan. "He isn't a member of . . . the Bund or anything."

Nathan nodded. We sat a chair apart, the piecrust side table between us, enough to hold two thick, sweating glasses. I wore a plain wool dress and rubbed my feet in that gesture, somewhat lost, of women done with a day in heels. Nathan wore an old gray sweater, patched in suede at the elbows, rewoven by Mrs. Green's remarkable hand, leaving the faint bird prints of lost stitches across the front, and he produced a pipe to smoke. I could see he was forcing his mind and body to relax. Was he thinking of the war? Or was he thinking of the other woman? We did not talk of it. We talked of Felix.

"He's a writer," he said. "They always worry about writers."

I found a handkerchief and blew my nose. "He's a journalist. He's an American journalist for an American paper."

"He's an easy target," he said, then added, "for all kinds of reasons."

"What do you mean?"

"He should have been more discreet."

I sat in shock at what Nathan had said, and he seemed to reel himself inward from it, as well, turning to his whiskey and his pipe and not meeting my eye. I heard him mumbling about the state of America now that we were at war, and how our artistic friends had to be cautious; I heard him carefully raking his way back over the tracks he had made. Somehow I assumed, in that age, that what my brother was—it was unthinkable. Never entering the minds of ordinary people. But it was not unthinkable; it was merely unmentionable. A faggot in the family; everybody has one. Seen coming out of notorious bars, in the company of notorious men; it was not such a big town after all. Who knows how long my observant doctor husband had known this, and kept it from me? Who knows how many visits and dinners we'd had with Felix where he studied and categorized my brother like a patient with a disease? Sighing inwardly at the family secrets, as we always do with other families, pitying them for what they will not see about themselves? Smiling to himself? I wanted very much to let him know I understood. That if we were to snigger at my brother, perhaps we could open fire on every man who acted the part of a married man but hid his real heart elsewhere. If so, Nathan should be prepared for the first shot.

"Nathan . . . ," I began.

And yet to open up the topic would be to undo all the stitches we had made to our marriage. Sex would be out in the open, and love, and heartbreak, and humiliation and desire and all of it, all the working apparatus of the human heart clicking in its springs and gears before us. I needed to speak, but it was not time for that. It was too late for that. It was time to let things remain as they were.

"I want to make sure you have everything," I said.

This happens at good-byes, when everything must be said, but anything at all would break the spell, would unravel what had been knitting together over the hours. So I watched him, and went through the items in his duffel that, with Mrs. Green's advice, I had bought him: a bristle clothes brush with a saddle-stitched handle, capeskin gloves, a hurricane pipe that would not go out in wind, a hurricane lighter, pair after pair of warm English socks, a pigskin writing case, and something called a "camp-lite": a travel light that could be covered by a mirror, for shaving in the dark, or reading in a tent, or flash-code signaling to faraway encampments. It was a foolish set of items, looking back. But it was all our minds could fathom: a Swedish widow and a time traveler who did not know her history.

"I think I'm set," he told me, taking one last sip from his glass and setting it down.

For it was too late. He was leaving in a few days. For me, it was thirteen procedures. So I was leaving as well. He did not know it, but this was good-bye.

"We should get some sleep," he said. "It's another long day tomorrow, and I have to close things up."

"Of course."

"Alan will call. We'll know more tomorrow."

"I hope so."

He gave me a long look, and I saw something else churning in his mind, about to surface, but then of course the phone rang. He did not pick it up at first. The words were there still, too important to discard. Not with life here measured in minutes. I stood up. It rang again. I heard Fee stirring in his bedroom. Nathan stood there with his hand on the banister, lips pressed together.

I said, "It could be Alan."

He nodded. The phone rang again. "Or a patient. Why not lie down awhile? I'll be done soon."

I went into the bedroom and made myself into the woman I had first awakened to: in a cream nightgown and long, brushed hair. I heard the apartment door open and close; he had gone out again. I lay down on the bed. It was my last night here with him. I knew I would travel the instant my eyes closed; I felt the cold wind blowing through the cracks around that little door. In a few moments it would open; I would be blown through. But I willed myself to stay awake, and it was just over an hour before I heard him enter the house. Familiar sound of a hat and coat on a hook, the footsteps in the hall. But different, somehow. Unsure, unsteady.

I went into the hallway and saw the light under the bathroom door, and the sound of him stumbling in there. "Darling?" I shouted, and the stumbling stopped. "Darling, is that you? Is everything okay?"

"Fine!" he yelled. I saw my purse sitting where it always sat on our mirrored console, right below his hat on its hook. It seemed like a portrait of us, right there. The hat, the purse. A moon, a mountain. He said he was tired, and was running a bath, not to worry about him.

"Want me to come in?"

He said not to. Click of a lock, rush of sound. Only a husband would not know that the lock had not worked in a long time. I crept closer down the hallway, past the shelves of little glass and ceramic animals, the lambs all in their row. I put my ear against the smooth white paint of our

183

old door, the same in every age. The water was a tiger's roar, but beneath it anyone, anyone who cared, could have heard him. The desperate, almost inhuman noises of a broken heart.

We had been here before. In this same house, at this same hour. How clearly I recalled sitting in my chair, reading a book, while white bean soup simmered on the stove. His face when he came in, as if he had witnessed a murder. The beard all gleaming with droplets. The sound of him sobbing like a boy. Violins dervishing around him. And me, in my chair with my book and the big brass lamp casting a hoop of gold across my lap. Wanting to tell him that I was angry and hurt and grateful. How I did not go to him. All of this, all of it had happened before.

Did I have to suffer everything in threes?

I waited and listened, my cheek against cold paint. The water rushing, and my husband sobbing, and the absurd little animals on their shelves, shivering from the rush of pipes. One little centaur was moving almost imperceptibly toward its doom. The hallway of this world, which in the last few weeks I had gotten used to; the cut silhouettes of Fee as a baby, and as a boy; the moon over its mountain; the little tin of face cream I had bought (Primrose: "You're as old as your throat!"); umbrellas peering alertly from their stand; the views of kitchen and bed- room and living room; all the alien tableaux of my life. Who was I saving it for? How did I ever dream it would be perfected? Here was a man in pain, behind this badly locked door. In another world, I had sat in the other room and read my book until he'd done his piece, until he had come out and had his whiskey and his soup, and we never spoke about the great thing that had occurred. In another world, he had left me anyway. I stood in the hallway, ready to leave. The water would not stop. The sobbing would not stop. The centaur moved its last half inch and toppled to the floor, breaking back to horse and man.

This time, I went to him.

December 12, 1985

Slowly I awoke, with a long sigh, and looked around the bare white modern walls of my 1985 house. Felix, I thought. *Felix is in trouble. And Nathan . . .* Now it was my real life that seemed strange: no portrait of my mother-in-law, no postered bed, no gleaming chrome wastebasket or vanity strewn with lace and nylons. Just the white-black-red I had known for years. Somehow, even though I had picked out everything myself, it seemed so false. The stark photos, the red-lacquered lamp, the one black brushstroke on the eastern wall. Like a woman pretending to be an artist. Like a woman pretending she had no heart.

"I see you're back!"

When she opened her apartment door, Ruth burst into that old wicked smile. She wore large turquoise beads and a striped caftan. Apparently she had set Felix's bird free, for it stood on an ornamental pig, cocking its little head. She hugged me and began telling me how sad the other Gretas had been this time around.

"Which one?" I asked.

"Both of them. The one from nineteen eighteen wouldn't talk about it." She took my hand. "But the one from nineteen forty-one. She missed her son. She missed Nathan."

I pictured myself, the midcentury mother, sitting in this room with a cup of Ruth's tepid tea, spending even one day in a world shorn of everything that made her life: her husband, her child. What a nightmare it must be for her.

She smiled and let go of my hand, heading back to the couch, where she was folding laundry. "She missed him so much that she met up with him."

I shook my head. "I should have expected that. When?"

"Last week," she said, straightening the cushions. "They went out to lunch. I think it was at the Gate, they make such wonderful cocktails—"

"Oh God. With Nathan? Oh God."

A crease of irritation. "Of course with Nathan," she said. "She thinks of him as her husband. She's not a little peeved that you managed to lose him here, I'll have you know!"

I took a deep breath. "She's trying to change things. But she doesn't know . . ."

"It's nice to have you back, dear, at least for a

while," she said, beginning to pick up stray clothes. "I feel like I'm dealing with multiple personalities. I had a friend, Lisa, who at very inconvenient times would be overtaken by the warrior spirit Gida—"

"I'm getting too attached. I'm doing more than . . . inhabiting these women. I'm *becoming* them."

"Usually a vegetarian, she would suddenly demand red meat," Ruth finished, folding a pillowcase in quarters.

"I'm *becoming* Nathan's wife. Fee's mother. I'm *becoming* Leo's lover. Well, I was."

Ruth's expression filled with worry. "What do you mean?"

I smiled sadly for a moment. "It ended."

She frowned. "What happened?"

"She couldn't hurt him that way. And she didn't want to leave Nathan. What is Felix's bird doing out? You know he doesn't like that."

"Our Felix is dead, darling."

"He's in jail."

"Not again?"

I told her it was a different Felix, and that I was terrified for him. And I told her about Nathan, his mistress, and how he had left her, all over again. How this time, something was different. I was different . . .

She interrupted me: "Greta, I want you to tell me honestly." She clutched her turquoise beads in one hand, watching my expression intently.

188

"Why haven't you, any of you, mentioned what I'm like in those other worlds?"

"I told you, you're just the same, you're the only one who doesn't change. Turbans and parties and—"

"Not that one. In nineteen forty-one."

The cat began to knead my leg and, for a moment, I let her, until her claws got through and pricked me. I looked back at Ruth and she was smiling.

"I'm dead, aren't I?"

I hope you never have to tell someone that they are dead. That there are not endless possible worlds for them, endless possible selves. That, in at least one of them, they do not exist at all.

"They sent me to Dr. Cerletti," I began, looking at my lap, "because I had a nervous breakdown after the accident. We were both in the car, sideswiped by a taxi. I broke my arm, and you—"

"Were smashed to Nirvana."

"Yes," I said. "I'm so sorry, Ruth. It was losing you that sent me traveling." From somewhere on the street, a police siren came into earshot.

"I knew it," she told me. "From how all of you acted, especially this last one. Clutching me all the time, clinging to me like a child. I suppose that's how you act with Felix."

"I didn't know how to tell you. I guess I thought I wouldn't have to."

She stood and began to sort the underthings

189

again. "It's strange, it's like an afterlife, living here. Somewhere, I'm dead. Probably in so many worlds, most worlds. We're so breakable, and we never guess it."

"I'm sorry." So strange to tell the dead that you are sorry for their loss, when they are also the bereaved.

Her head jerked around. "It's so unlikely to be alive, isn't it? The right temperature, and gravity, the right atoms combining at the precise right moment, you'd think it would never happen." She stood looking at a painting with a hand to her cheek, then watched the cat making its way across the top of the sofa toward the bird. "Life, it's so unlikely," she said, then turned to me again. "It's so much better than we think it is, isn't it?"

I visited Dr. Cerletti's machine—"things are progressing, just six weeks left"—and slept that night, knowing I would not see Nathan leaving for war. I would go, as always, to 1918 until next week's procedure. Far away in 1941, Nathan would be shipping out, and I would not get a chance to say good-bye. The 1918 Greta would be there. Standing in the door and waving to a soldier husband, as she had done before.

Nathan. The night before, I had been in 1941 and heard my husband come home, sobbing. I thought of how I went to him. How I worked the tricky lock open and found Nathan naked on the floor, weeping beside the bathtub's waterfall, showing me just his military haircut. His face when he looked up—how strange that we can never predict what that face will look like, even of the one we love! Ill shaped, mutilated by sorrow: a different man. How his hands went out—no, please, no—as I knelt down and held him, kissing his forehead, and how his body relaxed as it accepted me, too weak to protest, too naked. "I know," I kept saying. Nathan murmured, no, no, but that was all he could say beneath his tears. "I know, I know, I know," I whispered over and over, smoothing his hair with my hand, because I did know, because I, too, had kept a lover, and another me had left him. Did it matter if our reasons were different? "You loved her." How he did not deny it. How somehow our betrayals felt equal now, vanquished by each other, so that here we were, holding each other beside the bathwater's thunder.

DECEMBER 13, 1918

The next morning, despite the cold, Ruth and I made our way to Washington Square, where some horses were out for exercise, shining like leather, and everything was draped in Christmas pine boughs that reminded one that this once had been the countryside of New Amsterdam. A band in uniforms was setting itself up far away, perhaps the Salvation Army, and a woman in a bright green shawl stood watching them, but all I could make out was an enormous drum strapped to a small young man.

I wore a hooded velvet cloak, and Ruth marched along beside me in her black Turkish lambswool coat and hat, playing with the tassels on the belt. "Do you think we should change our names? Anything German is going to leave a bad taste for a little while."

"Why won't Felix see me? I try to call and there's no answer."

"Maybe he needs some peace and quiet," she said. "Not that 'Wells' sounds German. But I'm thinking maybe I'll get rid of 'Ruth.' Would you mind calling me Aunt Lily?"

I saw a newspaper, taped to a wall. My eye was drawn to the obituaries; the flu epidemic was worsening. GOODWIN, HARRY, 33, suddenly, Wednesday night. KINGSTON, BYRON, 26, suddenly, at his home. I could not bear to read more; it could have been any morning of dread from 1985. Drum, drum, drum.

"I'm just trying to help him. He got arrested again. In nineteen forty-one."

She seemed concerned. "Felix? What for?"

I didn't know quite how to put it. So I simply said, "There's another war, Ruth."

She stared at me and that crease appeared between her brows. "Another war," she repeated. Then she blinked and I saw her mind shaking it off. She did not like to think of terrible things she could not control. "Remember to call me Lily," she said. "I was thinking maybe you could be Marguerite. And Felix could be George."

"Has Leo returned?"

"She won't answer his letters," she said. "I don't know what to do with her. She's so sad. I really wish you were here more often, you'd handle it better."

"But what about when Nathan comes back?"

She shrugged. I wanted to tell her how eager I was to see this third Nathan. Somehow, I imagined a version of my man hardened, perfected by war. But it seemed the wrong time to mention such a thing, with my other self so lonely for her lover.

We neared the arch. Here was something only Ruth and I knew. That there was a door in the marble. That a boy might take me inside. That anything, even a cold city, might have a hidden heart. *I'm sorry about Leo,* I wanted to tell the 1918 Greta, as I looked up at the arch. *I'm sorry I started it, just to have it hurt you. But perhaps there is still a way.* Perhaps it was another of love's false endings; she could reach her hand out and he would come, just like before. Maybe take one of those ads in the paper, in the personals, that I had read: "HOL. Why were you not over Sunday? 'Twas a lonesome day! PEARL." After all, the heart can hear only one sound . . .

I changed the topic again: "I keep trying to confront Felix, but he won't listen." I heard a little sigh from Ruth and turned to face her. "You know about him, don't you?"

Our eyes met for a tough moment, and I was treated to that intelligent gaze I recalled from being a child, when I would ask her to take me to the theater and she would examine me, carefully, presumably to gauge if I was ready. "He has a hard fate, dear. I don't know how you can help a man like him."

"Ruth, I knew him so well."

"It's Aunt Lily."

"He wasn't like this, he didn't try to hide it and marry a woman."

She retied the tassels at her belt. "Some of these men," she said, "they can live as they like down here. Downtown. If they have money, and courage. They can go to balls in Harlem and find little hidden saloons and things. You've met them at my parties, you know I take care of them. I protect them. They're brave people. But your brother won't settle for what those men have. He wants . . ."

"He wants a lover. He had one, in my time. His name was Alan."

"Alan."

So I had said it, and she had said it, and we understood each other at last. The drum came from the park in solemn ceremony. "You could follow him one night," she said plainly. "Then, when you talk with him, he won't be able to deny it. If that's really what you want."

I heard barking, and then I saw that there in the park, walking two great Irish wolfhounds, was Leo's friend Rufus, whose long underwear I knew so intimately hanging on the line, in the bedroom Leo and I had borrowed. He wore a ragged raccoon coat and a determined expression. The dogs bore him along like horses with a sleigh and he looked less surprised to see me than he was to be drawn by his two charges.

195

"Rufus!" I said loudly. "It's Greta, Leo's friend. We met on Armistice night."

"Yes!" he shouted with a painful smile. Perhaps he did not remember; we had all had a great deal to drink. But then he said my name: "Mrs. Michelson. I remember."

"Rufus, this is my aunt Miss Ruth Wells." She tsked me at forgetting her new name, but I ignored her. "Are these your dogs? They're handsome."

"A rich lady pays me to parade them." He nodded at my aunt.

"You could probably ride them," I said.

He didn't laugh. "Yes," he said. "Yes."

Ruth said, "I've seen you at the Hatter. You play the trumpet, I think."

I pushed the velvet hood back from my face and felt the chill. I tried my calmest smile. "Have you seen Leo? I haven't heard from him in a while. I hope he's found work; now that the war is over the theaters are reopened. He's such a talented actor."

A look as frozen as the arch above us. The dogs sniffed us up and down.

"I'm . . . I'm sorry," the young man stammered. "You hadn't seen him?"

So he knew. Well, of course Leo would have told him, as young men always get drunk and tell each other tales of women. I looked up at the flat gray sky. 'Twas a lonesome day.

I told him I had been away.

"I'm sorry," he repeated in a quiet voice.

I tried to cover as best I could. I shrugged and laughed, petting the dogs. "Well, I've been away. Perhaps you could do me a favor and take him a message?"

"No," he said, so frozen. All he could say was he was sorry, so sorry. And then he told me.

Across the park, the band began to play a song that was all drum, drum, drum.

When I got home that afternoon, I found Millie smiling brightly in the hallway like a gaslight at full blast. "Two letters came for you while you were out," she told me, blushing at some private secret. I took off my coat like an automaton, and held it out, spangled with damp, to encumber her little arms, and set my hat on a peg. Struggling, she pulled the letters out of her apron. Looking at me from under her brows, she said she thought perhaps one was from my aunt's young actor friend.

"It's not," I said dully, making my way to my bedroom.

But, she said, pardon, she had noticed the return address, and thought—

"It's not," I repeated firmly. "He caught influenza. He died two days ago."

At six o'clock in the morning, my husband went to war.

Or so I was later told. I was of course far away, in the 1918 world, going through the empty rooms and setting each one right. With Millie, I brushed and cleaned each object in the house, scrubbing every mark that I had made on this world. I had Millie down on her knees cleaning the wine stains from the carpet. We used vinegar and water on the windows, so that even in the winter light they shone. It was all I could think to do. For one thing could never happen: I could never meet my other self and give the bad news to her gently. Tell her that her lover was dead. I could only make her world as one makes the bed of the aggrieved.

Days before, when Rufus told me—"He seemed better Tuesday, but then the fever . . ."—Ruth supported me as I stood in the cold and stared at that young man and his awful news: "It was Wednesday night he left us." The frozen sky with its scratches for clouds and the barren trees of the park, and the drum sounding inside me. *No no,* my mind kept insisting, *he can't be dead. It's impossible, impossible. I was just about to write him!* As if others' lives lasted only until we were out of their stories. I turned to Ruth, whose face wrinkled in sorrow. "There, there, darling," she said. "It's terrible, just terrible. He was so young and sweet." And I saw my old aunt's eyes begin to tear up, she who had known so much of death. The dogs shuffled on the frozen ground, and the band across the park began to play.

Is it better to hear of death or witness it? For I had suffered both and could not tell you. To have a person vanish in your arms is too real for life, a blow to the bones, but to hear of it is to be utterly blind: reaching, stumbling about, hoping to touch the truth. Impossible, unbearable, what life has planned for each of us.

Millie had been right; the letters were from Leo. He must have sent them before his illness, or on the brink of it, lying in his flat with Rufus sitting nearby with cold compresses, the lamp sputtering above them. The first was a cold lover's letter saying he was soon to change addresses and that if she had anything of his she could send it to . . . and so on. "I am excited about a new play a friend has written" was how it ended. The second, which he must have written moments after the first had been sent, began with just these words: "Is it too late? Write me and I will come at once. Tell me it is not too late."

Dressed as a Union soldier, grinning up at me, hair shining in bolts of brilliantine, flowers in his hand.

I went and saw his grave, out in Brooklyn where the dead of New York have been kept for a long time. An enormous field of stones, attended by a number of stout men with caps pulled down against the cold, only their beards

199

showing. Irish accents, giving me directions. A rake leaning against a nearby tomb, snow scattered like ashes, and there: LEO BARROW. BORN 1893. It seemed inconceivable that someone so young could have been born so long ago. DIED 1918. BELOVED SON.

Tell me it is not too late. Nobody could have known it was.

Could I have loved him? Ruth asked me. Snow had gathered in the newly cut letters. I set down my flowers among those frostbitten there. I thought of those sharp eyes beneath his mobile eyebrows, his wide lips in a tense, ironic smile. And at last came to the image I had pushed away all this time: Of him in my arms, in bed, on our one night together. The clothes hanging from their lines above us, glowing. Long lashes closed, hair swept wildly above him, the light catching the down of his ear. Watching as he began to breathe more slowly, slumbering as sunrise came. I lay there and could not tell which was more golden: the sky outside the window, or his flushed, sleeping face.

You didn't love him, I told myself at the cemetery, as one berates a careless child whom only luck has saved from danger. I turned and walked down the long snow-dusted slope toward the river. *But she did.*

Should I stay here? Should I leave the jar untouched, and like my other self, lock the door to this world until I had things right? Until I made a place for her grief? But I could not do it. It was not my world, and there was so much to be done in the others.

And so I cleaned. I wanted it to be ready for her, the other Greta, when she returned, and found her life fallen to dust. But I was also preparing it for another.

Over halfway through. Fourteen procedures. Eleven to go.

It was already dark, very late and unexpected, when the doorbell rang and I found him standing there. *I don't know what your other Nathans are like.* Narrow face, a scar on the chin. He was clean and shaven; they had taken them all from Grand Central Station and put them up at fine hotels, where their clothes were cleaned and mended, their bodies washed and deloused. *But remember, you haven't met this one.* I pushed the letters into the pocket of my dress and smiled. His shoulders were darkened with rain. He had no umbrella, of course, and did not care.

"Nathan," I said. He put his hand to my face.

Six o'clock in the evening: my husband back from war.

Part Three

DECEMBER TO END

DECEMBER 15, 1918

Name the woman in history who loved a man three times?

"Where is my girl?" this Nathan said to me those first few mornings of 1918. I would walk in with coffee and oatmeal, he would put on his glasses, and an attempt at a smile would creep over that long narrow face, marked now with a scar. Everything was reversed from 1941, when I was the invalid being brought coffee by this man. Now it was my turn to play nursemaid. So much was gone of the man I had said good-bye to in another world, but so much had returned of my old Nathan. The red-brown beard he was growing, streaked with gray; that Nordic face, lined with worry at the eyes; the heart shape of his hairline. The surprise in ordinary things: "Make me a steak tonight, Greta, I haven't had a steak since last Christmas," he might say, and I would tell him to make a list of what he missed the most. He dutifully did so, and showed me. At the top of it: *my wife*. He could be distant

205

and pensive like my first Nathan. He could be careful and attentive like my second. Like both, he checked his breast pocket for his wallet almost twenty times a day! But he was not the first or second. *I don't know what your other Nathans are like.* It was dangerous to see him that way.

One new thing: He did not smile. He could not; there was a piece of shrapnel in his jaw.

"We have our life back," he told me one morning as he stood in hat and coat in the doorway. The fuzz of the beard he was growing. He had dressed, this morning, ready to return to the clinic.

"We do," I said, not knowing, of course, what that life had been.

He frowned. "I didn't know if you'd even be here when I got back."

I cocked my head as I picked up my coffee cup. "Of course I am."

He lowered his gaze. "I didn't know if I'd be back."

I smiled dolefully.

"Sorry to be so dour," he said, shrugging and then coming to kiss me. Dour. He said it the wrong way, the way my old Nathan had corrected long ago. Like a cat come home from the rain.

He brought home flowers from street vendors, and soberly presented them to me. What trick of life was this? There was no "I leave it to you."

It was left to us, a married couple, to make the best of a world destroyed.

I wondered, but never asked, about the woman here, the details of their thwarted affair. Was she the same one as in the other worlds? And what had stopped him, in this one?

"I missed New York," he would say at night, so tired from his day; he had resumed his work at the clinic. "God, I missed it."

"Has it changed?"

"Yes, of course. But not the things I missed. The subway and the smell or the luncheon special at Hoover's." He closed his eyes to think of it. "And Ruth."

"Don't tell me you missed Ruth!"

He shrugged. "Yes, I even missed your crazy aunt Ruth."

And there was pain: When he sat to eat his dinner, he would wince. It was one of the things we never spoke of.

"It is bad today?" I would ask. He would close his eyes and say nothing. I would wait a long time in silence.

"I think I need to sleep," he would say, and I would nod. Something stern in his voice that I did not recognize.

"I need to sleep." It was the first thing he said when he walked in that door in 1918, returned from war, and what he said most evenings after dinner; the strong, scarred face would crinkle, his mouth would tighten, and I would see his mind retreat into itself like a snail into its shell. "I need to sleep," he would state, and I would know then that I was not his companion but his wife, his nurse, and would lead him to the bedroom where he let me undress him while he stared at the photographs on the wall.

"I love you, Greta," he would whisper in his half sleep. "I love you so much, Greta." He repeated it so distinctly that I felt it was what he said every night in his foxhole, to calm himself before the booming curtain of sleep covered the world where his nightmares began.

He needed to sleep. And yet—it was a war within him. He murmured things in sleep that I could not recognize; perhaps it was not English. The least sound from the street would send him shouting. Sometimes I woke to find him staring at me, but not in the tender way of a lover in the morning. No, it was the way you would stare at a ghost.

I think his nights were more like mine than I imagined. He, too, traveled to another world. He, too, awakened elsewhere, perhaps with another woman at his side. Or else in a hospital cot, grabbing a few moments before he was called to surgery again. Or else in a trench, half of his body in rainwater, watching the fireworks of war. You could say that his was different; his was all in his mind. But what does that even mean? What in the world is not "all in your mind"?

And one night: I undressed for my new Nathan in our canopied bed, and as he buttoned up his pajamas, winked at me in my envelope chemise, there was a honeymoon feeling about it. Of course there was; so worn from war, he had not yet made love to me. I was shy as a bride, lying on the bed. I was lonely, and needed to be touched. A replacement for the soldier who had left, a version of him who longed to do nothing but be home with me and watch my awkward knitting. He took my hand a bit more passionately than my old Nathan, and touched me a bit more roughly, something fiery in his eye. Different. For just as my forties Nathan had differed from his eighties self, here again I was faced with someone who looked and smelled and smiled and kissed like my old love. But who was not really him. A new start. The man I knew best in the world—I took him in my arms for the first time.

We sat around the living room card table, which was covered with white lace. There was my aunt Ruth, setting out the rows for solitaire, dressed in a violet silk gown sewn all over with trembling beads, her white bob falling into her eyes as she concentrated. There was Felix, across from her, in a gray suit and white shirt with a new collar. And there, in the corner, with a pipe in his mouth, all in deep blue, was Nathan. The silver-brown beard beginning to cover his scar; he was slowly becoming the Nathan I recognized from my world. White flowers were spread around the table with a glass vase in the middle—roses, foxgloves, other things I never learned the names of—and to Felix's amusement I was trying to arrange them. There they were: each lost in another world. To war, to prison, to death. Sitting in the living room as winter sunlight came in brightly through each window, as Brahms played on the phonograph. There was "tea" in our cups, from Ruth's supply of brandy.

"We're not supposed to play Brahms," Ruth said without looking up. "Especially being German. The *Times* said it 'emboldens the spirit.' I suppose the wrong spirit."

Nathan cocked his head. "Well, I'm the returning soldier. And I like Brahms."

Felix said, "I hear they're burning Beethoven in the alleys!" then looked over at my husband. I knew he feared Nathan resented him for not fighting in the war.

Nathan said, Well, Beethoven, that's a different matter . . .

Ruth suspended her game: "I went to a concert last week! A bunch of old krauts, stupidly playing German music. And a group of soldiers broke in and demanded they play 'The Star-Spangled Banner.' Bravo for them."

Did they play it? Nathan asked, and she said, Of course. They were Americans.

Here was my family, home again. Once again, I was tempted to reach over to Felix and grab him. Instead, I just watched his mustache twitch in his pink face, his eyebrows rise as he oversaw me snipping the stems of the white roses. "You've lost your touch, bubs," he said, shaking his head. "The stem should be one-third longer than the vase."

"What do you know about it?"

"That's what Ingrid says. She's interested in decorating. She says I decorate like a bachelor."

Ruth's eyes met mine quietly. I thought of the conversation we'd had, walking beneath *Washington Arch. He has a hard fate, dear. I don't know how you can help a man like him.*

I felt Nathan approach me and found him leaning down to kiss me. Here: the familiar feel of whiskers on my cheek, now absent in both my other worlds. The familiar scent of my Nathan. "I need some sleep," he whispered. "I'll see you a bit later." I asked if he needed anything, but he just kissed my cheek, touched my hair, and nodded to my family. As he turned, I saw his expression change; working his wounded jaw, frowning. Different, I reminded myself.

The only sound was the Brahms and my aunt placing a few cards down on the table. We heard the bedroom door shut. She glanced up and, this time, she and Felix shared a look. What had they talked about when I was not around? She said, "Does he still have nightmares?"

"Yes," I said. "And headaches."

Felix smiled at me as I cut a flower to his liking. "I'm glad he's back. I know it's been hard here without him."

Ruth said, "New York is completely different with the boys home. It's like a sudden spring. When the tulips jump up all at once, and you can't think how you bore life without them."

A glassy bell sound began to come from outside somewhere.

"Have you cheated yet?" Felix asked her, and she looked startled. "At your game?"

The bell kept ringing. "Ruth," I said, "is that your telephone downstairs?"

"Oh yes! I never recognize it. I always think someone's dropped a hammer down the stairs." Ruth stood up. "I'll be back, little ones. Don't drink all the brandy. It has to last." She came to kiss me, laughing. "It's going to be all right," she whispered. "You'll see. I have faith." And trailing clouds of netting, she was gone.

I turned back to red-haired Felix in his tight gray suit. It was Millie's day off, and we were alone with Ruth's booze in our cups, and his face was flushed with it and something on his mind. I leaned into the table, but pulled back; my breasts felt sore. I put a rose into the vase, followed by a long bell-like flower. Another rose, a fern.

"It must be nice to have Nathan home," he said at last.

"He's just getting used to things again. To me again. And I'm getting used to him."

He sat with his hands on the table cluttered with stems and said, "I'm sorry, Greta," and put his hand on mine. I sat and looked at his flushed face and the real sorrow in it.

"What do you mean?"

"I knew," he said. "I heard. About your friend."

The dusting of snow and fresh flowers on such a simple marker.

"How did you . . . ?" I began, and his eyes went to the door. I could not imagine Ruth telling my secrets so easily, but perhaps she had.

I pulled my hand away and went back to the flowers. "He died," I said, trying not to cry.

"That's what I'd heard. I just wanted you to know that I'm sorry. It must have broken your heart."

Flower in my hand, I looked up and saw his plain serious face so pink against the bright new collar. Had I ever broken down in front of him? In some scene I missed, had 1918 Greta stumbled into his bachelor rooms and fallen on the floor, her silk skirts spread wide, and wept onto his knees over the death of her lover? Sobbed and sobbed while he stroked her hair and said nothing but *There now, there now*? It seemed entirely possible. It was no less than what he had done in the lonely years before Alan.

"I'm doing better," I said, holding out the rose between us. "Dr. Cerletti is helping me."

"I said some things to you at Ruth's party," he said, lifting his head as if he had rehearsed saying this. I assumed he meant the Armistice party, though God knows there might have been others I missed. "I was drunk and they were careless things to say. Now I feel awfully bad about it." This seemed an almost miraculous change of character. Was it Leo's death that caused such sympathy? Or something else, something he recognized deep in his own life? It seemed impossible, in this world, that a man like Felix could bear to look that closely at himself. He leaned forward, and I saw his eyes go to the rose, which shook in my hand, releasing a single petal to the table, before they came up to rest on mine: "Did he love you?"

But your brother isn't like those men. He wants . . .

Why was he asking me this?

"I think he did."

"I know how hard that must have been for him. Someone married." He sat there stiffly, a sideways twist to his mouth, as he waited for my response. He looked so deeply sad, one would think it was his loss. How badly I wanted to grasp his hand and have it all out, as I had in 1941. But I could not find the right words for this world; it did not seem made for blunt conversation. I was not equipped for its rules and subtleties, and felt too tender to endure it if my brother turned in rage. So I said nothing. It was only after a long silence that he spoke, very quietly, looking at the table, saying, "If only we just loved who we're supposed to love."

"Felix—," I began.

He stood up, smiling. "I have to go. Ingrid's father is in town. He wants to get very, very drunk."

I put down the rose and the scissors and stood up, as well, but he motioned for me to sit. Here it was, the moment to speak of things. "Felix!" I said.

"I'll find you tomorrow," he said, and kissed my cheek. He pulled back, drawing his jacket around him. He glanced at the fire, which had died to a glow. Before he left, he turned and said, all smiles, "I'm getting married in a month!"

I put the rose into the vase and caught my breath, finishing the arrangement as neatly as I could. Something glimpsed in him, something of the old Felix I knew. It was there. But I had not possessed the nerve to chase it. I had to find another chance.

You could follow him one night.

• • •

Bloomingdale's in 1918 was full of postwar bounty, and the windows cried: PARIS SAYS FLOWERS FOR HAPPINESS! Girls in fresh white blouses smiled above sparkling counters, each with a penny in hand in case they found a thief among the browsing women; they were to tap on the glass to summon the store detective. High above them, a miniature gondola set rode by: baskets that salesgirls filled with money, sending them off on to the cashier's cage for change; how glorious the things that are gone forever! Ladies in long black dresses approached with scents from France—"A salute to our soldiers, madam?" But I shook my head; my ears had been stoppered to their song. My business was three floors above, in men's attire.

And there I was, as the elevator boy called out the floors: "Evening wear! Travel wear! Hats, gloves, and ribbons!" I had followed my brother from his home that night, to an evening visit to Bloomingdale's. I had come in disguise: wrapped in mink, with a matching mink toque, from which flowed a honeycomb-patterned veil and, beneath it, my influenza mask. I was not the only person wearing one: The lift boy himself was masked as if for surgery; you could see the yellow mark where his chewing tobacco had stained it. "Men's attire! Hats, cloaks, shoes, and sundries!" He pulled on his lever, undid the gate, and the doors opened onto that other world of men.

It did not sparkle or shine, like ladies' below. It spread, in a dull light that mimicked an April sky: a field of wool and leather and oxblood and gray. Instead of our bright novelties, it was a show of subtle choices: a shawl collar, a notched collar, French cuffs, or plain cuffs. An unaided eye would not have noticed the differences. But I put myself behind a screen, examining the gloves laid out like a botanist's display of leaves. For the men were the same as the clothes. Only a careful eye would notice. And there, among them, was my brother.

Like all the other shoppers that night, for some reason he wore evening clothes. He stood with his red mustache before a suited headless mannequin, about his size, with a careless smile on his face, his hands in his pockets. He removed his own jacket. Then, slowly, almost lovingly, he reached out to unbutton the dummy's jacket, pausing just a moment, as if asking permission, before he lifted the coat from its shoulders. The dummy wore just his shirtsleeves as my brother put the jacket on himself. Then, again with that sweet smile, he reached up to take hold of the mannequin's bow tie until the knot released and the ends fell on the dummy's bare shirt. With one practiced finger he unbuttoned the collar. He could not see me; the screen was pierced

217

mahogany. But I could see him, and the other men in the shop, who looked around seemingly aimlessly, picking up silk and percale and broadcloth as if considering the material. Only a careful eye would notice. That each one of them, though holding, for instance, a long white scarf up to the light to check the quality, had his eyes all the time on my brother, undressing his lover.

There was the sound of a tap; Felix's head turned, and I noticed, for the first time, a young man at a counter, with a length of measuring tape around his neck. He was perhaps nineteen or twenty, clean shaven, with slick brown hair and a pink scar on his chin. Felix turned to study the tailor poised at his counter, while the latter, fastened suddenly to the ground, taking root in it like a plant, was contemplating with a look of amazement the jacketed form of my brother.

Again, I thought of what time would wash away. Like the gondola that brought the money back and forth, simply because no one considered the salesgirls bright enough for change. A ritual constructed carefully over the years, as desperately, lovingly made as those chapels carved from stone high in the Javanese cliffs. The feeling, not just of desire, but also hope, that lingered here. Not very long from now it would be gone—raided or dispersed or replaced —but for now, it suited the moment in which it was born. Simply because no one considered it possible to state the heart's desire.

The tailor stood aside, and Felix walked past him, unbuttoning his cuffs, to a fitting room where I assumed measurements would be taken. Or whatever actually occurred; I nearly laughed. The men in the room shifted and ruffled their feathers in envy or desire, and two began to talk. But I smiled and shook my head to think again of Felix, of all people, participating in the dumb show. A fitting room, in Bloomingdale's. And the skinny tailor—he wasn't even my brother's type!

As I left, I noticed a decoration I had not seen on exiting the elevator; it was hidden by a rack of coats that had now been rolled onto the floor. I thought I would let Felix have his fun—hadn't I always?—and that the moment to confront him was later. I had a strange, romantic idea that perhaps I might put in motion. With Ruth's help. Yes, a way to perfect this world. I made my way past the scarves and gloves and terrified men who now noticed me, like a policeman invading their private, shaded grove. I stood at the elevator, waiting. And looked at the screen, on which had been painted a spring scene: two enormous bumblebees, facing each other, perched on the same bright flower.

DECEMBER 19, 1941

"Felix is coming home," Alan told me on the phone that morning. "They're releasing him on probation."

"Oh my God, how did you do it?"

Even through the wire, I could hear his smile. "I pulled every string I could."

The excitement in my voice had brought little Fee running down the hall; surely he thought any great news had to do with him. "Your uncle's coming home!" I told him, and he jumped up and down.

Alan: "There's still some red tape to get through. Tomorrow, maybe even today. I'll bring him straight to you."

"Thank you, Alan. Thank you."

I hung up and lifted Fee into the air, kissing him as he laughed and laughed.

I had to distract myself from the anxiety of waiting for Felix, so I tended the house, and cooked the oatmeal and ironed the sheets. There were no further calls from Alan. I just watched

Fee playing with his tin soldiers, and asking questions too hard to answer. That is how Mrs. Green and I found ourselves explaining to my son the concept of war.

It was like explaining the act of love, which lacks all internal logic except to those engaged, to whom logic is superfluous, because the only motivation is passion. The conversation was nonsense on my end and pure reason on his:

"There are bad guys, the Germans," I said, "who are trying to take what isn't theirs, and our country is trying to stop them and make them put it back."

"The bad guys are Germans?" he asked without looking up from his soldiers, engaged in a battle that he refused to connect with the present one. "Are we the bad guys?"

I had to explain, with Mrs. Green's assistance, that we were Americans, and were fighting on the side of America. The French shot the Russians with little explosions in his mouth (it was a Napoleonic set). Cease-fire. And then:

"Mrs. Green, are you a bad guy?"

This because she was not American. At which point Mrs. Green foolishly explained that Sweden was neutral, and did not care who won, at which point he burst into tears and asked, didn't she want the good guys to win?

It was only later we inserted his father into the war, which surprisingly did not elicit an outburst, but merely made him nod like a god above the battle scene. I opened my mouth, beginning to explain about his uncle, but closed it in time. Mrs. Green gazed at me curiously. It was something we had never discussed. So we sat and watched Fee play with his soldiers, his father now among them.

Later that day, we were out on the street, my son and Mrs. Green and I, making our way through another version of my city at war. It was all I could think of to divert myself from the news about Felix; some part of me believed it still might not happen. We were on a mission for blackout curtains so that Fee could have his Christmas lights. You must picture us: me padded like a linebacker in a woolen dress that felt as if it had the clothes hanger attached, Mrs. Green in a big-bully coat, and poor Fee struggling along in his stiff woolen matched set. I found it hard to believe nobody stared at us. But we matched the street we walked on, everyone in their own costumes: firemen in overalls, shopgirls in trumpet-shaped tops and blue alligator pumps, Italian street vendors selling hot sweet potatoes, and of course boys and men everywhere in brand-new uniforms from the boxes, still unironed, making their way with big duffel bags toward a train away from home. Very little else about the city seemed to have changed since

Pearl Harbor; I suppose I imagined everyone would stay inside, but that is impossible in Manhattan. Instead, you had to look for details: for instance the sign on pay phones: WHEN YOU HEAR AN AIR-RAID WARNING, DO NOT USE THIS TELEPHONE! and, down one alley beside a five-and-ten-cent store, a small bonfire of items "made in Japan." In another time, they were burning records of Beethoven and Brahms. Around it goes.

The fabric store, in contrast to the street scene, showed every sign of panic. Every bolt of cloth that could possibly cover a window had been brought out and labeled at thirty-nine cents. Mrs. Green somehow knew exactly what to choose, which turned out, to my surprise, to be not black at all but plain gray coated-cotton cloth. She grabbed a bolt and threw it on the measuring table, where a plump girl with pinned-back black hair and too much makeup cut her yardage; I paid out of my silly Lucite-handled purse. We had to disentangle Fee from where a "giant witch spider," as he put it, had ensnared him in her black lace web. I bought him a quarter yard and he wore it like a scarf. Mrs. Green seemed appalled. It was not until we were halfway home that the air-raid sirens began to sound.

First, nobody really knew what to do. Most people kept going about their daily lives. One man, wearing a black triangular armband, stepped into the street and yelled, "I am your civilian air warden! Enter the nearest building and lie down!" at which people merely stared at his preposterous command and kept walking. A policeman managed to stop traffic, but could not convince the passengers of a bus that they all had to disembark immediately. Not a single passenger would leave his seat. Brandishing his gun, he yelled, "But I'm the police! I'm the police!" and finally walked away in despair, asking nobody in particular: "What am I supposed to do? Shoot the poor louses?" But by then we had already rushed into a store with a crowd of other ladies, burdened by shopping, and I held Fee against my coat like any animal mother with her young. I put my hand to his face and from his wet cheeks I knew that he was crying.

After a few minutes, the terrible noise stopped and I could hear my son's loud sobbing. "Oh, baby," I heard myself saying, stroking his head, "hush now, hush now." I looked across the room and found some solace in another mother, consoling her own frightened son—no, it was a mirror, and just my unfamiliar self with Fee. We exchanged shocked stares with the tailor, and then, to add to the comedy, a young man emerged from the curtain wearing nothing but garters and boxers, saying, "Hey, are we supposed to lie down or something?"

"No," said Mrs. Green. "We are simply meant to wait indoors until the all clear."

He grinned. "Well, thanks, ma'am. So . . . can I go back in there?"

I heard her take a deep breath and then, to my surprise, she said, "No, not until the all clear."

"All right then," he said, smiling shyly, "if you ladies don't mind." He took a homburg from a shelf and placed it on his head, then crossed his arms and waited with the rest of us, nodding at each lady in turn. No one told him he was allowed to get dressed, especially not the stunned shopkeeper, who sat winding his watch. So we stood, we housewives with our bags of blackout cloth, and simply admired his form. Mrs. Green would not meet my eye. I wish she would have; I was so delighted to discover she had a sense of humor.

And then it came: three short bursts, repeated over and over. The young man tipped his hat to us, and the ladies all gathered their things, and I gathered Fee. There was a general bustle among the ladies that prevented us from leaving, as everyone expanded to grab bags and loosened shoes and gloves and coats scattered, somehow, everywhere, like autumn trees that have changed their minds, sticking every leaf back where it came from. I lingered a little, looking at Christmas tiepins for Nathan, knowing it was silly; he would be in uniform for years. What he needed was something to take blood out of khaki. And something to keep the horror out. "I need a bouquet," Felix used to say to florists, "that says, 'I will keep the sadness out.' Can you do that?" And sometimes they could.

"Here we are," Mrs. Green said when we were home, hoisting her pile of fabric. "Wipe your feet, Fee." Outside in Patchin Place, someone had not tied the cord properly to a flagpole, and it whipped in the wind, and even from our hallway we could hear its metal buckle dinging against the pole.

I heard my son shout, "Uncle X!" and rounded the corner, pulling off my coat, to see my brother sitting in the parlor with his lawyer: Alan Tandy, Esq., in a striped blue tie and a face flushed red by the fire. And my brother, in just a shirt and slacks, a cotton jacket. Probably the clothes he was picked up in. Turning to see me.

"Felix!" I said, running to him, my hat falling to the floor. "You're free!"

He smiled at my embrace, but there was a change in him. Dark commas beneath his eyes. Thin and scared and quiet. I could not bear it. It is the case with twins; it feels unnatural for the image in the mirror to change without you.

"Greta," he said. His eyes as dull as his cuff links.

"Merry Christmas, Greta," Alan said, smiling.

"Thank God you're out. Are you all right?" I turned to my son, who clung to his uncle. "Fee, go to your room for your nap. The adults are going to talk. Mrs. Green, would you . . . ?" She smiled, looking over the cast of characters, and shuffled my complaining son out of the room. Felix produced a cup for me. Alan rose to greet me properly, scratchy in his tweed suit. There were formal embraces and words. I wondered what to say, what to do, with these men, nervously holding their steaming cups, these men and their lives. I had a notion we should all just make a run for it.

"Thank you for visiting me, it was the only fun I had," Felix said. Ding, ding went the flagpole.

"I never asked if they were feeding you," I said.

He took a drag from a cigarette and rubbed his eyes with his other hand. "I suppose it's unpatriotic to say that if it's going to be bread and water, German bread would be preferable. They thought I was a spy."

"You look terrible."

He managed a smile with his eyes closed. "Thanks, Greta. It wasn't torture. It was me and Italians and lots of krauts. Now they, *they* were spies. But Alan got me out."

"We had a bit of luck," Alan was saying. "And I've managed to get his record erased. I knew the police. I knew the judge."

"Thank you," I said gravely. The loud voice of the wind was battling with the windows.

Alan took a deep breath. He smoothed his short gray hair and said, "But we can't erase his name in the paper."

A look of fear from Felix again.

"You mean where you were found," I said.

Ding, ding went the flagpole in the silence. The windowpanes shook violently. Not one of us moved from our places, looking, searching each other.

Alan broke the quiet: "We'll think of something. Greta and I, we'll take care of you." He looked directly at Felix and I saw him put his other hand around his cup. Perhaps to stop himself from touching my brother, to comfort him. Surely he had done that already, on the way home from the prison. Gripping his hand under a coat where the driver could not see.

I heard Mrs. Green discreetly coughing in the hallway to let us know she had reentered. Their gaze flew apart, and very soon Alan was saying his good-byes, back to the cordial businessman I knew. I tried to picture what he might be like in 1919, in his waistcoat and tails and pocket watch. The door clicked closed.

"Ingrid is staying in Washington," Felix told me, looking at the door. "With her father. It looks bad, that I was on a list. And what was in the paper."

"She took your son."

"I've lost my job," he said, looking back at me with shadowed eyes.

"Felix!"

He puffed nervously on his cigarette. "They gave no reason. They don't need to. No one will have me now."

"Felix," I said, startling him by violently grabbing the arms of his chair. It was not an easy thing to do in that stiff dress. "Felix, you can't live alone."

He leaned against his free hand, and blew his smoke into the air. "Greta. Alan was in the bar with me. He knows the police, but he couldn't help me."

"Move in with me and Fee," I said. "He needs a man around."

"I'm not a man!" he said, shouting now. "Didn't you read the paper? I'm a sex criminal."

"It's going to be all right."

"When is it going to be all right?" I said nothing as I stepped away from him. "I'm sorry, you shouldn't have to see this. Or hear any of this. It must disgust you."

"I'm not who you think I am," I told him.

He looked up and I saw there a little spark of hope.

"I told you before."

He swallowed and winced visibly at some thought I could not imagine. In a quieter voice, he asked, "When is it going to be all right? For someone like me?"

Bright reflected sun came in the room, afternoon sun, hitting the chandelier and sending prismatic lights briefly around the room, across my brother's face and body. I realized I had not yet seen a time. But you can't tell a person something like that. You can't tell a person that you have seen many possible worlds, where people thrive or fail, but there is no world for him. In a moment, the beautiful effect was gone. At the front door, I heard Dr. Cerletti's voice. Time for my procedure.

"Move in with us," was all I could say before Mrs. Green let the good doctor in.

DECEMBER 24, 1985

It was Christmas Eve, and I found myself on the roof with Ruth, wrapped in her old furs, passing a joint back and forth. Say what you will about the eighties, at least the pot was easier to come by. We were both in black, our faces red from weeping; we had just come from a funeral.

"I can't bear it," Ruth said to the 1985 sky. "I think from now on I'm going only to wakes."

It was Alan who had died.

His memorial service was held in the Metropolitan Temple and we listened to men between two gorgeous urns of roses speaking about his life. Gay funerals are always good for flowers. I had stopped going to funerals, and this was the first I had attended since Felix's, almost a year before. I noticed a change, an awful change: Whereas in early services, the old friends of the dead gathered and spoke of memories, always of the man as young and strong and smiling and virile, these eulogies were now given by young men who had known the dead only briefly, six or seven months. Young men of twenty or twenty-one. There in their new beards, dressed in tight handsome suits, weeping endlessly. One thin boy stood up and sang a spiritual I knew well, "In the Garden," in a high uneven voice with his eyes on the stained-glass image of an ever-burning lamp. Of course it was because these were the new friends, the only ones left alive: the young. Gathered around the grave of an older man they had so recently befriended. And would even they be taken by the fire? I could not bear it. With Alan's young lover singing "In the Garden," just as Alan had sung it for Felix. We quietly walked out of the service. There was nobody to disapprove; nobody knew us there.

"Do you remember when we first met Alan?" Ruth asked me, pulling her head up high as she took a drag. The sky was hard and luminous as wax. Somewhere in it was the sun, but damned if I could tell you where. "Felix brought him to a brunch at my house. So big and handsome. He was wearing a wedding ring."

"That can't be right," I said, taking the roach from her. "He'd left his wife a year before."

"Maybe it was the line a wedding ring leaves behind." She sighed. "Is it awful to admit now that I found him terribly sexy? I think I was envious of Felix."

"I remember how worried he looked. As if we might hate him, maybe because he was older.

232

And all I was thinking was: 'Oh thank God, at last.' "

She put her hand on my arm and looked away. "You're going to get me crying again."

I told her about a moment Felix described to me. They had been together only a few weeks, and were lying in bed one morning. And Alan started crying. And Felix said, What's going on? What did I do to make you unhappy? And Alan, so careful with words. He just kept crying, turned away and didn't say anything. That big man crying in bed in the morning. Felix asked him again, Why are you unhappy? And Alan just said, beginning to laugh through his tears, shaking his head: "I'm not unhappy." The morning light on their shoulders. "I'm not *unhappy*." And Felix knew what he meant.

"He was terribly sexy," Ruth said, and took a deep, sad breath. I saw she was crying again. "I miss them so much."

"I wish you could travel with me. And see them. It doesn't make today any easier, though."

She gripped my arm tighter. "I miss you, too, Greta. It's not easy for me, you changing all the time. You're all I've got now."

"I'm sorry," I said, though I imagined Ruth might secretly enjoy her time with 1918 Greta, a new "project" for her to take on. If things went wrong, and we were trapped in the wrong worlds again, she might not be a bad companion for my aunt. I said, "There are only eight procedures left. Then it'll be over."

"Tell me about Alan," she said, sniffling. "Make me feel like he's alive."

"Things are bad in nineteen forty-one. Felix just got out of prison, you know, but he lost his wife, his son. His job. I don't understand it, I try to fix these worlds, and they're full of traps. But at least he has Alan, in a way."

"Is he the same cowboy we knew?"

I laughed. "Oh, he's all business. No cowboy shirts! But I've seen them together. He's . . . not unhappy. He's not unhappy with Felix."

"What about that other world?"

"I haven't seen Alan there." I leaned over and handed her the joint. "You know, it's almost a year since Felix died. I'm having a memorial for him. I want to have it here on the roof." She took the joint from me with a frown. "I invited Nathan."

"You talked to Nathan?"

"I left a message on his machine," I said, then added: "He has as much right to be there as anyone."

"I understand. You want to see him. Now that she's seen him, the forties version of you. Don't worry about her, she's just trying to understand what went wrong. I don't think she told him she's not the woman he left. I don't think she'd do that." She pulled her fur closer about her

234

and poked her chin out to take another toke.

"I don't know what I'd do if he came. I'd be so anxious. I don't know what I'd say," I said, then laughed: "I'm making people come dressed as Felix. That's what he asked for."

"That's ridiculous," she pronounced in a long exhale of smoke. I managed to smile at the idea of this woman finding anyone else ridiculous.

We sat there in silence for a very long time. Everywhere around us, smoke and steam trailed into the air: from cones on the streets, from chimneys, high towers, boats on the rivers. Layers of soot blue and gray. I had something to tell her.

"She's looking for Leo, you know," Ruth began suddenly. "The nineteen eighteen Greta."

I nestled in my soft coat. "What do you mean?"

"She went to the library, to the city directory, to look for a Leo Barrow. I was hopeless, that library is baffling to me. It breaks my heart to see her. I can hear her crying upstairs. I haven't seen you so sad since Felix died."

"Leo was very, very sweet. And witty. So different from Nathan. I can see why she fell in love with him. It makes a difference to be some-one's first love."

"I'm curious to meet him. But she couldn't find him. In any of the boroughs."

"He grew up in northern Massachusetts. He could still be there in this world. I wish she

235

could find him, but what would I do with him later? I mean, when all this is over."

"It's funny. You're all the same, you're all Greta. You're all trying to make things better, whatever that means to you. For you, it's Felix you want to save. For another, it's Nathan. For this one, it's Leo she wants to resurrect. I understand. Don't we all have someone we'd like to save from the wreckage?"

I looked down on the Village below us, the water towers like minarets rising from the taller buildings. The smoke and steam and lights beginning to come on in the gloom.

I said, "I remember Alan carrying Felix into the ocean, both of them screaming their heads off."

"I remember Felix was so worried about moving in with him," Ruth said. "Moving out of Patchin Place."

"I remember how Alan loved that awful mustache."

"I'm old," she said, in a kind of defeat I did not recognize in her. "I'm supposed to lose my old friends. Why are the young ones dying?"

Below, the cold city: leafless trees in the parks, and red brake lights all down the black-and-white avenues like a badly colorized movie. Somewhere a radio pounded music for street dancers, that new incomprehensible music of shouted rhymes. It was all drum, drum, drum. I had to tell her.

"Ruth, I'm in terrible trouble."

"You mean with Nathan? I thought you fixed things. He left the girl, you said you thought it would be different this time. I have faith."

"Not then. In nineteen eighteen."

"Your new Nathan. It's the young man she loved, isn't it? There is time to set things right."

Layers of soot blue and gray in the sky: a tarnished silver tray.

"Ruth, I think she's pregnant."

It was Dr. Cerletti who gave me the clue, on my last visit, though he did not realize it, preoccupied as he was with the circlet he crowned me with, the jarred lightning he put into my hands, the blue spark from my finger. Usually, he told me, I convulsed in an upright position. This time, however, I fainted. When I came to, I was lying on the bed with my wrist in his hand.

"How are you feeling? Is something different today?"

"I don't know."

"How are your female issues?" he asked quietly.

Then it occurred to me. I had missed a month at the beginning of the treatment, but my cycle had seemed to reset itself. It was hard, with everything else, to keep track of when my period was expected in all of these worlds. But every woman knows. Fainting, hunger, my sore breasts. I knew at that moment, lying in my canopy bed with the doctor's face wrinkled in concern. I knew. I could sense it.

"Normal," I said. "Everything is normal."

He looked deeply at me for a moment. Then he smiled, uncrowned me, and closed his little wooden box. He told me to rest for a while, and then left me alone in the afternoon light.

A child. Not just borrowed Fee, racing my shoes around the living room carpet, but a child in my body. I was like Cerletti's magic jar, sitting in my box of green velvet: latent, quiet, but charged with something that would change my world. And in eight months, there would come the spark.

For it was not that night with Nathan a week before that started this, but a night a month before in moonlit Massachusetts. What would happen when I gave birth not in nine months but in eight? Or even a few weeks from now, when I would show far earlier than a good wife should? And when the child came out looking very little like a certain Dr. Michelson, and with large brown eyes . . .

I stood up, dizzy, and went to find Ruth. I told her, and she took my hands and asked me hard questions. Then she gave me an address on the Lower East Side. "I know women who have saved their marriages there," she told me. It was dark, but hours before Nathan would be home. I dressed myself in a long cloak and went out into the rainy night.

It was a nightmare scene: skeletal horses sat with feed bags over their noses, patted by skeletal owners who watched me stepping over cobblestones in my silk skirts. I wore a veil, to keep my anonymity, but still, a woman unchaperoned must have been a strange sight at that time of night. Perhaps they took me for a streetwalker. I came to the door and saw just a stained-glass oval and a knocker shaped like a lily. From within, I could hear a woman talking. At first I thought it was someone on the telephone, but then I heard a slight whimpering. A light beside me came on; the window was heavily shaded. From there, I heard the sound of retching. The woman's voice grew stern. Suddenly there was a boy beside me: "Lady, got a penny? Got a penny?" He said it mechanically, as if a penny would set him in motion for my entertainment. Grubby and torn, grimacing with need. He knew so much more than I did about what happened behind that door. "Here, go away, go away," I said, handing him whatever change I found in my little purse. I felt a light rain beginning, and thought how it would never clean this place. A ragged little hansom was coming by, and without thinking I hailed it and climbed inside. I told the driver Patchin Place, and realized I was shouting. Off we went as the rain grew gray and luxurious. I did not go to that place again.

I did not tell Nathan.

December 26, 1918

I returned to 1918 and, as Millie and I cleaned the house, I knew I had to decide what to do. For one version of me, after the lightning had stopped, would end up here, with a child. One of us would have to explain it to her husband. When I sent Millie out shopping, I stood before the mirror and felt my belly and my breasts. I was not showing yet; I had time. There were ways to make things all right. It was only the difference of a month, these things were hard to tell. Leo was dead; there was no point in Nathan knowing anything about him. I had not considered, however, that this Village was a smaller town than the one I had come from. And, in small towns, there are no secrets.

When Nathan came home from the clinic, I heard the sound of two men in the hall instead of one. Jangling keys, unsteady footsteps, low laughter; I surmised he had brought a tipsy buddy home.

"Greta!" came my husband's drunken voice. To

see him try his crooked smile, to see him anything other than shaking with grief and memory, what a joy it was. Even with the whiskey so strong on his breath. Beside him, a little walrus of a man in a beaver-fur hat. He kissed my hand. "Greta, you remember Dr. Ingall." I said of course I did, and retired to the kitchen where my chicken à la king was waiting.

I could see it was a comfort to Nathan to be in the company of men once more and not just me and Millie and Ruth, chattering away while his skull ached with metal shards and memories. We talked about Nathan's plans, and my brother's wedding coming up in two weeks. Perhaps it was the drink, or my feminine presence, that made Dr. Ingall so at home that, without meaning to, he set off a little dynamite in our dining room.

He was thanking Nathan for his service, admiring him, explaining how his own bad leg had kept him from helping the men overseas. It was then he mentioned a notion I had read about in the paper: that our soldiers were, in fact, returning to their daily life, better than before. That was the phrase everybody used: "better than before." Dr. Ingall's lips were glistening with butter when he dropped his theory into our conversation as one does when speaking of a political opinion you assume everybody shares, simply because your world is as small, for instance, as the West Village.

"I think I don't understand how my men are better than before," Nathan said in a friendly way. His hand was always at his chin, touching his new beard.

"Oh, I'm sure you would know, Nathan," the man said, bowing his head. "But surely they have seen bravery that we could never experience. Wounded comrades who insisted their friends get help before accepting treatment. Selflessness and sacrifice. Things they never would have known. The best of the human spirit."

"I suppose that's true."

"And," the man said, emboldened by Nathan's words and by drink, "I've heard there's nothing brash or boastful about a man who's actually been on the front lines. That they're gentle and humble and kind. Not what we think of as a soldier, but what we want in a man."

Nathan's own spirit seemed to mirror this. He said, "Yes, that's so."

"So they will return to their lives, and leave the war behind. It will have touched them but not changed them."

"You are so right. But I wonder about Henry Bitter."

"Who's that? Don't know the name."

"No, no," Nathan said, putting down his fork and looking away from us and out the window, where city lights shone. "When we debarked at Grand Central Station, they took us to a midtown hotel and we were showered, and deloused with kerosene, and our throat cultures taken for diphtheria. They gave us socks, pajamas, slippers, and a handkerchief. There was a boy next to me who couldn't hold his handkerchief, so I put it in his pajama pocket. He had a wide smile. He was from Dubuque, Iowa. Both his hands had been blown off by a grenade, and he was blind. That didn't worry him. He was worried about how to break the news to his family; he hoped they wouldn't learn through the newspaper. So I got the Red Cross girl to take a message that he dictated and I wrote it down. I remember it perfectly." Then his eyes were on us again. "Would you like to hear it?"

There was no possible answer to that.

"It said, 'Arrived safely in New York. Feeling fine. Met with accident in Divisional School November sixteenth. Both hands amputated. Eyes affected. Undergoing treatment. Tell Donna I'll understand if she won't have me. Tell me how all you are doing. Henry.' "

"Ah," said the doctor friend.

" 'Feeling fine.' 'Eyes affected,' " Nathan repeated firmly. " 'Tell me how all you are doing. Henry.' "

"That's a sad lot. And a gentle thought for others."

"It is."

"And so?"

I looked at my husband, that stranger, full of

the strength and fury I remembered so well from our early days, when he would pound a table with philosophy and politics, whose studies got him out of Vietnam. I looked at this man, who did not escape war, saying: "And so tell me, how exactly is Henry Bitter from Dubuque, Iowa, better than before?"

After Dr. Ingall left, we moved to the living room as Millie did the dishes. We could hear a little Irish tune coming from the doorway, and the fumble of china and glass in the sink. We drank soda water from a chain-mail siphon; it would never have occurred to him to share his whiskey with me. Nathan took the siphon again to force the water into his glass and, without turning, he said to me, "I heard you had a friend who died."

The song went on from the other room and there was something in its lyrics about a lass and a lad.

"Who do you mean?"

"An actor friend."

"Yes," I said. "It was very sad."

A hive of bees loose in my brain. How did he find out? Millie, surely. A maid can be paid for anything. How much did he know, how much did the other Greta let Millie see? I thought of a night of booze and celebration, Ruth at my door, a parrot on her shoulder. I sighed and looked up at Nathan. He held out the siphon for me. I'm sure he could not control the violence of it shooting loudly into my glass; it was the nature of it, but a little terror went through me.

Nathan's whiskered face was as calm as when he talked about his patients. "Were you there when he died?"

I found myself adjusting my skirts, just to make a little noise. "No, you know it all happens so fast. I heard about it days later."

Nathan sat back in his chair and sipped his drink. He watched me without any emotion in his eyes.

I went on: "It's nothing compared to what you've been through."

"Yes," he said, with the glass in his hand.

And I will never forget what I saw there in his face, just before he stood up to get ready for bed. Something I did not recognize. Was it something that war had hammered into him, and loss, and the heat and pressure of this time we lived in? Or was this the difference among my Nathans? Before he left the room, something bright shone in his eye. I thought at first it was the aftershock of war, but now I know it was not. It was an aspect only solitude and hunger and pride can force out of men, even the best of men, as Nathan was, in his way. It had always been dormant in the Nathan I'd known, a smaller part of him. But here: bright in his eye like the gleam of a gold tooth. It was pure pain.

DECEMBER 27, 1941

I awoke to the chiming sounds of 1941 quite shaken by the events of the previous evening, and talking with Mrs. Green about my husband's upcoming visit, I tried to separate the man who showed his pain from the man returning home. They were different men, in different worlds. And yet, somehow, just as a new lover can unwittingly summon up the hurt done by another— with careless words or gestures—I blamed each Nathan for the crimes the others committed. I had always said my Nathan was kind but could be cold when angered. It had not occurred to me that worlds could separate him: into a kind Nathan, in 1941, whose passionate mistakes could not disguise his love for me, and a cold Nathan, in 1918, whose own affair was a mirror to his jealous rage. Each had harmed me in degrees; each loved and quarreled with me in different portions, and yet, in my mind, they were all one man. They were still the Nathan I loved.

Of course, by that logic, I should be all one

woman. The one who had forgotten him in my brother's dying; the one who was all mother and no wife; the one who carried another man's child. I had committed only one of these crimes. And yet, by this thinking, I should have been tried for them all—like conspirators who all hang together.

Nathan was still processing soldiers at Fort Dix, and they were letting him come home for one night to say good-bye before leaving for Europe. His visit was still a week away, and Fee and his uncle X were readying the house for his arrival—for Felix had indeed moved in with us, onto a little couch Mrs. Green had carried into Fee's room. The visit happened to coincide with my and Felix's birthday and so it took on the aspect less of the homecoming of a weary army doctor than of a springtime party. The kitchen smelled of failed attempts at cakes and cookies until Mrs. Green, monitor of our ration book, put a stop to it and announced that she would make the celebratory food. After that, the Felixes were left only to decorate themselves, and secretly plotted in their room with Mrs. Green's sewing machine humming, the door posted NO TRESPASING! FELIXES ONLY! (BY ORDER HOME DEFENSE). I stayed away except to correct the spelling with a curve of lipstick, and in there I could hear them giggling away.

I checked my appointment book and saw a note at six fifteen: *Every day at six fifteen, the*

33rd Street bridge. What could it possibly mean?

Alan's absence from our merry midwinter scene alarmed me, as if his death in 1986 had somehow carried through to the other worlds. It turned out, as Felix whispered hurriedly before dinner, that Alan was on the West Coast for business, and would be all week. *Not back in time for the wedding?* I thought, and then of course remembered that there was no wedding, not here, not for my twin brother perched on a ladder to tack the letters H-O-M-E to the ceiling. Instead, his wife was filing for divorce, and taking the newborn son with her to D.C. for good. "Good," I had said, then immediately saw my brother's fallen face. "Oh, I'm so sorry," I said, touching his arm. "I'm so sorry, your son." He smiled ruefully. "You'll see him again," I said, and by saying it I felt I had cursed it never to happen. In those times, we both knew, sons went to the mothers. And were rarely seen again.

But it was Alan I mourned for.

What is it, the missing of people? It kills, and kills, and kills us. We think back on a weekend at the beach, and cooking lobsters and splitting their shells, and making margaritas with lemons instead of limes and the car breaking down, walking all the way back down the sandy road to find a house with a phone, laughing and laughing in the drunken heat of the afternoon—a wonderful time, one of the best times!—and think, "Where are they all now, all my young friends?" Dead, of course; and the memory changes. It deepens and alters and grows happier and sadder all at once, but why should it? We were happy then, they were happy; shouldn't the moment be set? Yet it is not; every moment is changeable. How strange, for the present to change the past! In just this way, I lived in these worlds knowing something like the future: a sense of how things could be. Isn't this the time traveler's curse? I did not see what was to come, but I saw the possibilities. And the pain of seeing life and happiness in people I knew to be dead in other times, it was like that sad sense of the past, when the glass warps how we perceive things. I could not ever be there with them, truly. Because I was both seeing them, and remembering them. Alan with his lawyer's voice; Alan telling his donkey story. Alan in his business suit beside three phones; Alan in his swimsuit, carrying a screaming Felix into the sea; Alan in an urn. The possibilities. Is there any greater pain to know what could be, and yet be powerless to make it be?

Every day at six fifteen, the 33rd Street bridge. I slipped away from home. I had to follow it, had to know.

I got out at Times Square and was thrown into a mass of sailors in their winter coats and whites, faces burned red from the Atlantic sun, walking tipsily either from a day of drinking or from so many months at sea. They shouted at every passing girl, and a few gave me long leering looks. I pulled my seal jacket around me and flashed my ring; it did no good; I suppose they had heard about married ladies. I suppose that they were right. I headed west and knew it was a poor decision as soon as I passed Eighth; I didn't know what it was like in 1941, but in my time it was Hell's Kitchen, built along the train tracks and full of derelicts, addicts, and whores. The streets smelled, unmistakably, of bread and sugar and ginger: a nearby cookie factory. I felt conspicuous in my jacket, my jewelry, my doctor's wife's hairdo and dress and shoes. In my old life, I would have taken a New York stride and held my head high. In 1919, I would have been hauled off the street. Here, I did not know what would become of me. But I hurried to the Thirties, to where a small iron bridge rose over the train tracks, then back to the avenues. I climbed the stairs to the top.

And here I stood, waiting. It was nearly six fifteen. I looked across the bridge—how did I not expect the obvious?

At first just the silhouette of cap and scarf against the lights, among the few others crossing the bridge or loitering there. But I knew instantly who it was. Head high and confident, arms wrapped around himself against the cold. Another world, another Leo. My child's father, returned from the dead.

There Leo stood, in a gabardine jacket and bright red scarf, the same shaved and polished face, smiling as widely as ever. As if simply existing was no great miracle. My heels made a clanging noise as I made my way to the middle of the bridge, hung with railroad lanterns that glowed in the wet air. Servicemen were gathered at the curved railing, a few wandering navy boys, and Leo. I stopped at a distance, watching his head move back and forth as he took in the scene around him. A hand went to his hair to smooth it down; I knew no gesture could ever tame it. I had gone and seen his fresh grave carved with the twenty-five years of his life. And yet, there he stood.

The soldiers were gathered nearby, making a great deal of noise, so he left his post and began to walk toward me; my pulse quickened immediately. He was still in shadow and then passed into the light and I saw the face I had last known in a coldwater flat, hung with clothes glowing like lanterns. Wide handsome face, his chin already blue with a new beard, large brown eyes, long lashes gold in the bridge lights. He walked on, and I saw in this world that he had no limp to hide, no dance when his lame leg tripped him.

He thrust his hands in his pockets and grinned, looking around him, and then he looked right at me.

He nodded, and walked on by.

Just that look: appraising, with the flutter of a smile, the way young men look at dozens of women every day. Just that look and nothing else. I watched him as he went by. So we were strangers in this world.

He took his place against the railing again, looking south as the soldiers bickered grandly from the other end of the bridge. Waiting for something, but not waiting for me. The boy who surely grew up here and not up north, a poor boy from Hell's Kitchen. The Greta of 1918 must have learned his rituals, and knew he came here every night at six fifteen, as the others had, to witness something that had nothing to do with Mrs. Nathan Michelson.

I felt how much she missed him.

I read in her diary how their time in the cabin ended:

Greta and Leo had gone on a walk in the woods he knew so well, where he stopped and showed her where, hidden in the trees, a few boards were nailed to the trunk of an old bare oak—nothing more—the last remains of a hideout from his youth. He stood for a long time in memory before the scene. It was colder without the falling snow, and her fur did not warm her enough, but she bore it. It was, after all, the last day, and she would not turn back, knowing it would be their final walk together in that place. She thought Leo was lost in childhood; instead, she realized he must have been building up the will to ask her.

"Should I fight for you?"

She did not think about it more than an instant. Shivering in her fur, feeling the cold like an ice coat beneath her own coat, working its way up against her skin. She found herself saying, "No. Don't fight for me."

But who on earth would say no? Who on earth would not long to be fought for? Is this not the very heart of human existence, to be worth fighting for, worth losing everything for? That was surely what Leo proposed. But no, she said. No, don't fight for me. She horrified herself by saying it so plainly. But it was what she had to say, to save him from a deeper heartbreak. Now it was done. Now she would bear the pain for both of them, probably for always, and he would go and have a life without her.

"Don't fight for me, Leo."

He said nothing in response. He just turned his back on her and walked alone back to the cabin. It was quite cold.

A mistake, made in another world. And here: It could be righted. There was so little time—only six procedures left—and here we all were: with me grasping for Felix, for Alan, before my world killed them again: another bringing Nathan once more into my life, to understand him, to have him in all worlds: and this one: She was trying to pull Leo back through the ether. Each of us: to fix the mistakes we'd made. To say the right words, do the right actions, before the porthole closed. For the first time it occurred to me: Perhaps the Greta from 1918 no longer wanted her world. She wanted one where the snow did not fall on Leo Barrow's grave.

I thought of the clothes hanging in that apartment, how the light had made them glow. Like the lanterns of a pleasure garden, with dancing couples and music playing from a sleepy band. Here, it was the swaying railroad lamps and the pillar of steam rising from beside the bridge. The soldiers jostling for another swig from the bottle. The brick warehouses stacked around us so that we stood in a kind of cove, a hidden place. The place where boys might come with nothing else to do, and no money, making the best of what they found around them. The lights of midtown had been dimmed for weeks now, to hide Manhattan's silhouette from German ships, and only the vague red glow of Times Square burned there like the embers of a fire.

A bell went off somewhere, and the soldiers began to group as if something was about to happen, but Leo just stood there. I watched as he pulled his collar around his throat. How well I knew those hands. How strange to think that they did not know me.

How many more times would I have it? The chance to meet someone anew, begin with everything I had done right and wrong, clear all mistakes and start fresh with life? This Leo had not met any other Greta. He was untouched; no electric hand had reached through the dimensions yet to grab him. This one was, for the moment, mine alone. Mine to greet for the first time, see smile for the first time. Sense, perhaps, something stirring inside him that even he was not aware of, as he could not possibly know he had loved me terribly before, and died, and been brought back to life to love me again.

I pictured how he would look if I approached him. An eyebrow raised, that smile making a dimple in his cheek. His voice so low for a young man:

"Good evening, ma'am, what's your name?"

"I'm Greta Wells."

A dark look in his eye. "Leo."

There he stood. I took a few steps toward him, watching him from behind: stoop shouldered against the cold, hat jammed onto his head, patches on his elbows, eyes looking right and left. A sudden wind made all the lanterns swing in time and a soldier's hat went off, with a shout, from his head and over the side of the bridge. Leo laughed.

There before me: the scarf unwound, the neck pink with warmth and bare to the wind. The soldiers laughing at the rail. Somewhere a key hidden under a rock. But which is worse: To start an affair, knowing how it will go? Or to walk away, knowing it could have been his great love, and leave to someone else a first crack at his heart, which would be broken now in another place, but broken all the same? He looked back at me and caught my eye. The light on his ear, the way it glowed with a child's softness; everything was returning, could return. For her. *Should I fight for you?* Is there something worse in life than to make someone love you just because you need it, just because you can?

Then, from nowhere, he stood bolt upright. From the soldiers I heard a shout: "Here it comes!"

And from the depths of the train yard, lit by the shaded lights of the train itself, and by the moon, and every ambient light even on that dim night, great clouds of steam rose up like the arrival of a genie from a lamp, billowing soft and warm around us. He was laughing. I saw him as a boy, in the depths of the Depression, running from the sweet smell of the factory with his friends, cookies in their pockets stolen from the loading dock. I saw his childhood there on the streets, playing stickball in short pants, filing down to the public baths with a towel in one hand, a bar of soap in the other, singing "Over There!" with obscene lyrics in a chorus of boys, his jobs as a corner newspaper boy, or handing out playbills, which he would duly dump in the sewer and spend his working hours skinny-dipping in the trash-strewn Hudson. I saw again how close it was, his boyhood. Still on the horizon, where his adult life was so far away it frightened him. Leo as a boy, his features even more outsize, grown up here and not in that cabin up north, where life might have been easier. I saw all the boys charging up the stairs and waiting for this moment, just at sunset, when the old six fifteen came clanging by and they could jump up and down, crumbs in their mouths, and imagine—as the only freedom they knew, in days when nothing was theirs except what they invented—that they could walk on clouds of gold.

And that is where I left him.

January 2, 1986

It was a new year.

"Dr. Cerletti, how does it end?"

"What do you mean, Miss Wells?"

"Six procedures from now. When we finish, do we consider another round?"

"Your progress has been remarkable. There's no reason for me to believe we'll continue. In fact, I don't think it would be wise. You'll continue seeing Dr. Gilleo, of course."

"But how does it end?"

"I don't know what you mean. You're yourself again. Or on your way."

As I left Dr. Cerletti's office, I saw an elderly woman sitting there where I once had sat, on my first day. High lace collar, bright green shawl, her hands clutching her purse as she stared at the sign for ECT. I paused for a moment. There was something familiar, constant about her. I recalled a park, a median strip, an army band. Could it be? Our eyes linked and, for a moment,

I imagined that she and I shared the same blue bolt of lightning, the same strange story.

Could it be she traveled as well? Nothing seemed impossible anymore. After all, there was nothing special about me, nothing unique; our fate is made, so often, merely by the place where we are standing. The piano falls an inch to our right; we are kept safe. And not because we are special, and the other person is not. But perhaps: because our sorrow is so great, that like a star its gravity can bend the world a little, shift things ever so slightly. Could wear a little hole in the universe. The sorrow of a woman like me, and that frail old woman in the lobby.

"Mrs. Arnold?" came the nurse's voice and our gaze broke. I watched her make her slow way into his office, and who knows? Maybe that very night she fell through the void and woke in a world where she was young again? Or married again? Or all alone? I saw the door close behind her; I heard my doctor's murmuring voice. And as I made my way back to my home, I considered that I could not ask someone how it would end. I could not wait and see. There was no time for that. It was up to me—and the other Gretas—to decide.

And act.

January 3, 1919

"Where the *hell* did you get Chablis, Ruth?" Felix asked with delight.

"I have a diplomat friend," Ruth replied to my brother, winking, "who stockpiled in nineteen hundred. We all have to stockpile before they vote it away." Aunt Ruth stood in quite tall boots, wearing a sleeveless, beaded-bodice gown in Peking blue. As if to make up for the simplicity of her dress, she had done her white hair up in strands of pearls, like a wedding cake. "Does my other self have so many pearls?" she asked me mischievously.

It had taken only a few days to arrange the party, in Ruth's place, decorated with candles and Bolsheviks and some stunned-looking society people eying the bohemians through monocles. I could not shake the image of Nathan's face that night, the hardness in it, but was relieved to see it brighten the next day when I asked him where we could go that he missed. "Central Park," he said, looking up from bed at the prospect. "We could take a long walk. Or the Woolworth Building." The only trouble came before the party. I found Nathan putting on his coat; he had been called back for a late night at the clinic, and objected to my being seen at a party without him.

"I know, darling, I know," I said. "But it isn't for me. It's for Felix. He wants me to introduce him to a publisher."

"What publishers do you know?" he asked, then said, "I know you're used to parties."

"I'll just be gone a moment."

"Things have to change, Greta. To how they were."

"Things will change, you know they will. We both will have to learn."

And at the inclusion of himself in this sentence, he assented to my visit to the party. He took his top hat and looked into my eyes. As long as it was just a moment. And I went down to join the party, aware that I had committed some marital crime.

"It's vile," my brother was saying after downing a glass of Ruth's wine. We stood together in the room, hovering beside the odd Promethean lamp as Ruth's pearls jangled in her headdress. I stared out at the carpet, its central figure of a maiden.

"I know," my aunt said, sighing as she looked at her glass. "It tastes like wartime butter."

"I'll have another," Felix said. He had his glass

refilled, raised it to me. I watched as he walked off to another side of the room, where a famous man was shouting about the League of Nations, and how it was an abomination against the people's cause. From beside me, a bald astronomer was talking about Halley's comet. "I was the only one of your aunt's friends who knew we would pass through the tail, but it's harmless, you know," he said to me, winking. "Of course she wouldn't listen. Threw an end of the world party anyway."

"The effects," she pronounced gravely, "are not yet known."

The astronomer toasted us and moved toward the political discussion. I watched Felix pollinating the room like a bee in clover.

"He's not here yet," I said to Ruth. "I'm worried."

She shook her head tipsily. "He'll come. I told you I telephoned him and explained I needed him to do my will. I'm afraid I sounded like I was loaded with money. It's a dirty trick you're playing, Greta."

I told her she didn't understand about love.

"Oh me," she said, giggling. "Oh no, not me!"

It took a little doing on my part, once again visiting the library and going through the city directory, working with the operator until I found the correct number, then forcing Ruth to dial it. Her pretext was preposterous—that she was leaving the country the next day, and could only be found at this party—but she assured me it would work. What a romantic girl I had become! For I had experienced firsthand the sensation of an old love revived, again and again, like a drunk forcing a bar pianist to play the same song over and over, and knew both the ecstasy of rebeginnings and the confusion of how differently, unexpectedly it could go. And yet I wanted to bring this gift, this curse, to Felix. For my brother, I would provide it, in a setting of candles and bad wine and avant-garde attitudes. I would, at last, make something perfect in the world.

Who had I invited to my party in 1919? It was Alan, of course. I would bring him back to life.

I listened to Ruth talking about Bolshevism, but in my mind I was picturing how it would go. He would arrive in a black coat and a top hat, handing them gently to the maid, looking around the room with the nervous smile of someone stepping from shore onto a tipping boat. Ruth would approach, in her mermaid headdress of pearls, and hand him a glass of Chablis, murmuring to him about business, and then she would introduce him to me ("Enchanted, madam," he would say with no recognition, though we had shared the hardest scene of our lives together), and then gesture across the room to where Felix stood. There would be five paces between them, the length of the figured carpet, and Felix would look up and there it would be. Who else had ever seen it, knowing what they saw? We can imagine, introducing two friends, that something electric arcs between them; we can even pretend, later, at their wedding perhaps, that we saw it and knew it and noted it in the diary in our mind, but it isn't so. Even lovers can't know; an angel in their mind flies back and rewrites the past to make it perfect, for the stumble of hope and doubt on meeting does not fit the rules of romance. Yet this was different. I was like the one who alone knows, of all the audience, that a celebrity is about to appear upon the stage. Not Alan, entering in his coat and hat. And not Felix, standing to stare, so handsome in his evening clothes. But the third, rising like the figure from the carpet to float between them. It had happened before, was happening in another time, and I alone knew that here it would happen again. The little terror stiffening their bodies; the hot metal in their veins, not unlike the jolt from my magic jar. Terrified, bewildered, charged with wonder. That would happen here, any moment. And I alone would see it.

"Ruth," I whispered, and she turned back toward me, motioning for a little man with a hearing aid to leave her. "Ruth, I think Nathan suspects."

"What do you mean?"

"He said he knows my friend died."

"That doesn't mean anything," she said. "And I'm sure he had his ways to get through that war."

"Ruth, I want to ask you. Is he different? He seems so grim. Is he . . . harder than he was before?"

She blinked at me and her headdress jingled as she shook her head no.

I remembered that my other self had been afraid of this Nathan, what he might do. I pictured young Leo under my window. I saw a bit of my other self's heart.

Ruth spoke quietly: "You see why I couldn't blame her."

"The other Nathans aren't like him," I said. "Not really."

"And how about the other Ruth?"

I looked at her sparkling face. "You didn't say 'Ruths.' "

"Yes, darling, my Greta told me. I'm like Felix. There's a world where I'm dead."

"I'm sorry," I said, as I had said once before to a different woman. "You know, I miss you there. I don't have an ally, just a servant, and she doesn't know."

"It's not like anything else in the world, to know you're dead somewhere. I guess I always thought of myself as a weed, the kind that would grow anywhere, between the cracks of any time. But I'm not. I'm a rare, delicate flower," she said, laughing. "Me and Felix. And Leo. The right temperature, and air, and soil, or else we wither."

"Don't say that. It was an accident. I'm so sorry." I felt a touch on my shoulder.

"I have to go," I heard my brother say.

I turned and saw Felix already putting his arms into his overcoat. There was perspiration on his brow and a reddish flush, perhaps the poor Chablis. I said, "No, you can't. You have to stay, just a minute."

"Greta, I have to go," he said, and there was something desperate in his eyes; he would not look at me, but seemed consumed by something inside him.

I took his sleeve. "No, I want you to meet someone, please stay!"

He shook his head, gave me a forced smile, and kissed my cheek. "I have to go, I'll see you later, enjoy the Bolsheviks," he said, and without saying good-bye to Ruth (who was talking to a man who had just arrived, his back to me) he took his hat and almost ran out the door. It had all happened so quickly; my plan, carefully built over the past few days, washed away like a castle on the beach. I would have to do it again. There was so little time, not even two weeks left before the wedding itself, and of course not much longer before my own passage would crumble and be blocked forever. Perhaps tomorrow I could arrange another dinner, something he couldn't leave; I could still force this flower to bloom.

"Greta," Ruth said, her hand on my arm, "I want to introduce you to someone."

"Ruth, it's a disaster," I whispered.

She gave me a tense smile from beneath her mermaid tiara. "Greta, this is Mr. Tandy."

And there he was: Alan, another man returned from the dead.

He was altered, in this world, as we all were altered. Silvered beard trimmed neatly to a point, pince-nez sitting on his nose like an insect; stouter, grander, in a white tie and dark suit, smiling more easily than I imagined. I recognized him, under there. Manly and careful, of few words, the Iowa farmboy grown to prominence, his eyes trying to say things his lips could not. Alan, I thought. Alan, you're dead now. Your ashes sat between roses, and a young man sang for you and I could not bear it. Save him for me. You don't know how close we are to never existing at all.

I noticed his eyes, cracked green glaze, glancing at the doorway through which my brother had just gone. I saw the thoughts working there, the blood rushing from his face, and all at once I understood. How stupid I was! To think that nothing moved in the world without me, that it was all a chess game for me to ponder, when in fact the pieces were alive, and moved all on their own accord, for they were not figments of my mind but people.

"Wonderful to meet you, Mr. Tandy, I'm sorry you just missed my brother." I looked to Ruth, whose face widened with alarm.

He sputtered out a few polite words, but the color had not returned to his face.

"Felix *left?*" Ruth asked, and I shot her a meaningful look. We should have guessed.

"That's a shame," Alan said, pulling an awkward smile out of some private reserve.

I said, "He was looking forward to meeting you again."

Ruth acted like an actress whose supporting cast has begun to improvise. "You've . . . you've met him before?"

Alan said, "Through . . . through my wife . . ."

But I did not hear the rest of the conversation, for I was already out the door.

I found his glossy top hat decorating a fireplug, and my brother leaning against a house. He had not gotten very far, and had predictably headed west, as he did on his brooding walks around the Village in my 1985 world. He had a long cigarette going, arms crossed, fur collar bristling with streetlight, and he stared at the fireplug as he had at the dressmaker's dummy, this time with an expression of vindictive rage. The night sky over Washington Square was aglow with a street fire, and shouts could be heard.

"I was at Bloomingdale's the other day," I said

loudly, and his head jerked with surprise. I walked forward, hands in the pockets of my coat, warm in the chill night air. "I was there, in the men's department."

He said nothing to me. A couple walked by, the woman almost completely shrouded by a hood, the man staggering drunkenly. Felix just smoked as they passed us. Both of us knew the next few minutes would unravel everything our lives had been.

I asked, "Is that where you met Alan?"

A puff from the cigarette; nothing else, no glance at anything but the fireplug, the hat. My brother leaning against a building, staring at the New York night. The smoke trailing from his mouth.

"When did he leave you?" I asked him. For now it was all so apparent, with Felix taking a deep, angry breath and staring out at a shining black horse carrying a policeman on his way. Then, saying nothing, he looked at me.

I can picture them in Bloomingdale's, staring across the gloves at each other. A meeting in a bar, a hotel room carefully arranged. But different, this time. Strong and wary Alan, in his beard and pince-nez, worrying and worrying in that room, drawing every shade, hushing his young lover. Telling him it cannot go on. Felix different as well, framed in an oval mirror: terrified, fascinated, in love. And then meeting him again:

more darkened rooms, and promises, and did Alan weep? Not unhappy? Secret visits to Alan's Long Island house. Easy days, no chance of being caught. Reckless midnights on the beach—silver-haired Alan carrying my long-limbed brother into the ocean. And I can picture another scene out in that house, shuttered against a December storm, when Felix arrived by mistake one weekend when the family was there, and the maid let him in, and they all had to endure a long supper of pressed duck before Alan took him aside and whispered this was danger, this was folly, this could not go on. Closing his eyes so he would not look at the man he loved. He was so sorry. It was best forgotten. A dark driveway, and a silhouette of Alan in his study, head in his hands. Felix in a carriage that took him the cold four hours back into Manhattan, and time to think over all the ways in which he might kill himself.

I saw that when he looked at me at last. In his eye: a gun, a rope, a bottle of poison.

"You don't have to marry," I said loudly.

"She's the best thing I have," he told me, standing very tall and his bright hair on fire in the streetlight. "I'm sorry. I know you can't understand the things you've seen."

"I understand you completely," I said. "This is the brother I know."

"I want you to forget all this."

I repeated something he told me: "If only we just loved who we're supposed to love."

The glow on the clouds grew brighter in the distance. Fire trucks were making their way down the avenue, and from the south one could hear shouts and the rusty working of a water pump. A rush of action, and then we were left alone again on the street.

"The tourists are ruining everything," he said, dropping the cigarette and smiling grimly. "We've made a mistake, you and I. Ruth was wrong about everything."

I wrapped my coat around me; it was too cold for this. "I love you, Felix."

"That party. All her parties," he said, staring at the top hat. "All her talk about life. Living each day." Shouts and cries from far away, shadows on the low clouds.

I walked toward him in the freezing air. "You told me you understood. About loving someone married."

"Living each day. It only works if there's no tomorrow," he said to the hat. He spread his arms wide. "Well, it's tomorrow."

A New York wind blew down the corridor of the street and the hat toppled from the fireplug. Felix stepped forward to retrieve it.

"We have both made mistakes," he said. "I need to fix mine."

"Was mine a mistake?"

He picked up the hat and brushed it off, staring at it as if some answer were contained there.

"What does your husband know? What will he do?" he said, speaking with pity now. "It's tomorrow, Greta."

A cheer from an invisible crowd, a dimming of the fire glow. Another police horse came clopping by, black and polished.

He put the hat on his head and stood up tall. "I can save myself, Greta. I can marry and be happy."

"I've seen enough to know that isn't true."

In the sky, the fire was dying, flame by flame. My brother's face was full of heartache. "Greta, Greta, it's a lie," he said wearily. "You can't just *love* people. You can't just wander out there and *love anyone*."

"Yes, you can!" I said rashly. "That's exactly what you do!"

At that he stared at me with the purest sorrow, then turned and ran away down toward the fire, leaving me alone in Greenwich Village on a winter's night.

When I returned home, I opened the door to the overwhelming scent of camphor. It was only after a moment that I could make out the silhouette of a top-hatted man against the gaslight in the hall-way. Like a chess piece, like a king. We stood there for a moment and I heard the faint tinkling of my beaded dress, but I did not think much of the silence; my head was full of my conversation with Felix, and the growing life I carried within me. "Greta," I heard, and there came the light of a match into a pipe bowl. "Nathan?" I said, for it was his face, though somehow behind the face it was not him. "Nathan, I thought you were working late at the clinic."

There was no sound except the crackle of tobacco in his pipe. The camphor odor from his clinic was almost unbearable. I closed the door behind me to keep the alley cat from coming in. I turned and saw that he had not moved in the dim light.

"Nathan?" I repeated.

"Did you know," he said at last, just a shadow and the glow of embers, "that it got so bad, before the Meuse-Argonne offensive, that half my cases were influenza?" I recognized the break in his voice. Had he been crying?

My eyes searched the darkness. "You've had too much to drink."

"I swore I'd never tell you what I saw," he said, shifting position. "I wanted to keep you . . . safe. That's what we fought for."

"I will never know what you went through."

"But you need to know, Greta. There was a man from a submarine just come over from the States. He had a minor case, and was ready to fight in two days, but he couldn't fight. He was already shell shocked, before he ever saw the war. The nurse told me his sub had gotten the flu the day they left Long Island. He woke up the next morning and the man in the hammock beside him was dead."

"My God," I said. I stood and watched his broken shadow.

"You know submarines are on orders not to dump garbage? But they had to. There were too many, piled in the dining room. The stench. And this man was taught how to wrap the bodies with iron to weight them down, and kneel on the canvas to get the air out. Then it was someone else's turn to send them into the sea. Almost everyone who was on burial duty got sick and died."

"I'm sorry, Nathan." We can hardly guess the burdens people carry.

"I know what he did. I did it, too. You sit by their bed, and you take down a letter, a last letter. 'Dear folks. Am down with flu. Feeling better, home soon. Love to everyone.' They look up at you and ask, 'Will I die?' and you say, No, no, hold on tight, you'll be fine. They smile and fall asleep. Dead by sundown."

"I'm sorry." And what I meant was: *I am sorry about how things turned out, here in this world.*

"When the sub arrived in France, they had two hundred bodies in the dining room. They had buried only a hundred. We had twice that piled in our hospital." I was silent. I watched his profile, bent over with the memory.

"Do you know," he said softly, "what I do for you?"

"I know, I know," I said, my hand to the wall. "You don't need to tell me more."

"You don't know," came his voice from that shadow, as if he had not heard me, and then to my relief he stepped at last into the gaslight, where I saw that below his long, bearded Norwegian face hung his gauze mask: the source of the camphor smell. His face was flushed with sweat. Was he drunk? Ill? Then he took my arm and said, "Come with me."

I had been here before. After the tense, quiet ride in the cab, the sound of freezing rain hitting the roof and the sight of people scurrying across the black-enameled streets, after we had burst through the doors into the dark hush of the room. I had been here so many times, so many times. Not this clinic, but one surely just like it smelling of incense to cover sickness. I never wanted to see it again.

I had seen those rows of beds lining a long room, separated by white pleated screens, and beside each patient the small little altars of things that loved ones had brought and which the nurses, quietly visiting the patients in hats and soft-soled shoes, removed and threw into incinerators the next morning. I had seen the men too thin for words, eyes wide open at night, staring at the ceiling with one arm dangling from the sweated sheets. I had seen the holiday cards still on display at the nurses' station, from patients who were grateful for their recovery. Some of them long dead. I had seen twins, identical beds, identical fevers; the New Hampshire chauffeur, hired by a hospital that would not take a patient, arriving late at night with a skeletal man; the choirs that came with masks and sang outside the windows; the wreath at the station that read KEVIN WAS THE SWEETEST. How could he guess that I had been here, in another world?

"It's gotten worse," you whispered to me. "They told us it had ended over here, but it's gotten worse again. Fifty more cases today. In Brooklyn the gravediggers are dying of it."

I tried to think of what to say. What you wanted me to say. "I've seen it. I know all about it. Let's go."

"Greta," you said. "I want you to see with your eyes what I do for you."

But that wasn't really why you wanted to bring me, was it? It wasn't to learn your life. I saw it in your eye.

I loved you, Nathan, once. Twice, even. Isn't that enough for anyone? I loved how you tapped your foot along with music because you couldn't help it, and made me get up and dance with you.

And the way you laughed till you cried, and the little tears gathered in the corners of your eyes before they fell and glistened in your beard. Your grumpy insomniac stalking of the bedroom. The way you found things on the street and put ads in the *Village Voice*: "Found: a child's necklace, three pink bears, broken." No one ever called to claim them. But somehow it set your heart at rest. "Found: pair owl eyeglasses, red, one rhinestone at the corner." It was not just first love in which nothing is impossible. It was also whatever comes after. Love, I suppose. That must be what we call everything that comes after. I loved you all those years, most of my life, it felt like. I never thought you had it in you. But in a different time: a different man. I never took you for a murderer.

"I'm no fool," you said quietly. "I'm no fool, Greta."

"There's no one," I said. "He died."

"No, he didn't," you said. "He's right here." And I knew you meant the baby.

How did you know? Cerletti, perhaps, or your own doctor's instincts. Or something I had done, something I had said that gave everything away. The other Gretas were leading this life along with me. Who knows what they had told you?

I was too weak with shock and shame to fight you, Nathan. I understood what you meant to do, and in some awful way I felt I deserved it, but who deserves death for what they have done? Who deserves to be pulled into a plague, not only to be infected, but to infect the child living inside me, to erase us both with one easy gesture that nobody would ever call murder?

But you stopped just short of the beds. The nurses turned with their blank masked faces to stare at us, hearing the struggle of a wife with her husband. You stopped and began to breathe heavily, then took a step backward, looking around you, turning, at last, to look at me. Now I know you did not really know what you were doing. It was the fever already at work.

"Oh God," you whispered, your eyes wide in alarm. It was the first time I had seen it, the face I remembered, staring at me in that darkened clinic. You put your arm around me and rushed me back toward the door. "Oh God, let's get out of here."

Back home, I felt how hot with shame you were. Breathing heavily, sweating even in the chill of the winter evening. Flushed and tired and astounded at what you had nearly done. You were shaking with it. "I lost myself," you whispered to me, "I lost myself, I'm sorry." What did it even mean, to lose oneself? Who are we then? Shambling, empty creatures, for that one moment: out of time. But even then you could not do it. Not even in that misshapen form, in that misshapen age. Holding your face and sobbing, there in the hall. "I love you, Greta," you said. So we had made it, almost. You had passed through the other side of hate.

I felt your grief that night you nearly tried to kill me, Nathan. I felt your hands, and heard what you said. Your skin was hot as red iron.

You took the guest bedroom for the night. I could not sleep, confused by that strange evening, and our strange lives together. And it was not even a few hours before I called Dr. Cerletti. You had thrown the sheets to the floor, and lay there burning with fever.

He survived, my husband. A few days later, I heard Dr. Cerletti at the door, and Millie's voice as she answered. I felt the baby growing inside me, building in secret like the war machine of a walled city. Twenty procedures done, only four procedures after tonight. There were things I had to do. Before the other Gretas came. One particular action I knew only I could take. I found the bald doctor coming out of Nathan's sickroom. "Your husband's fever has broken. He will make it. You can see him now."

I found Nathan lying in the bed, propped up by pillows, his face white and clean, his breath still suffering slightly from the fading illness as, above him, the hired nurse put a comb to his greasy, sweated hair. It seemed to me he winced in pain at every movement of the comb, catching the coarse hair I knew so well. But he bore it like a dentist's drill. Only when she was done did he turn and see me there in the doorway. And his eyes, which brightened suddenly, went from my face to my belly, where, unconsciously, I had begun to rest my hand.

I gestured to the nurse, who paused before departing, wiping the comb on her apron. I sat in the chair beside him and touched his hair. On the table: a glass of water, whose optical effect made its immersed spoon split in two.

"I heard you're feeling better."

He nodded, his eyes on my face. "You shouldn't be here. I might still be contagious."

"The doctor said you wouldn't be."

"What do doctors know?" He gave a broken expression. "Greta," he said. "I'm so sorry. It was . . . the fever."

I took his hand and he squeezed it hard. He said he loved me, lying pale and exhausted in the bed. He said it over and over and over.

"I love you, too, Nathan. I've loved you for so long."

"So you'll stay? You'll be my wife. We'll raise your . . . child."

I held his gaze as firmly as I held his hand. "No," I said, smiling sadly. "No, I can't be your wife anymore."

He looked at me as if the words I'd said were

still perhaps a figment of his fever, like the slight ringing in his ears, or the shutters that opened and closed on parts of his vision, or his trembling hand, which I held very still. I sat and held his gaze and let him understand. The magic effect of sunlight on a passing carriage, reflecting around the room, across his face, so blank with shock. He began to cry, just as the other two Nathans had cried. He had not known, not expected this. I went and held him, his head against my chest.

"Something, there's something I could say," he said, trying to sit up. "That would turn this."

"There's nothing to say. Just rest."

"Pretend I've said it, Greta."

I kissed his forehead and stood up, flattening the starch of my black dress. "Nathan," I asked. "Who am I to you?"

His exhausted face could make no sense of this, and he tried to sit up and failed.

"When you think about me," I asked. "When you remember me after, who will I be to you?"

"You're my wife, Greta."

"Yes," I said. "Yes, I thought so."

"I don't understand. Who am I to you?"

I stood with my hand on the doorknob and saw the flush of emotion reddening his neck, a sign of his new health, and his new grief, which he would have to bear. "Nathan, I thought you knew. You were my first love." And so I closed the door and told the nurse he needed rest, and walked down the hall to where the doctor waited with the jar.

Why is it impossible to be a woman? Men will never understand, men who are always themselves, day after day, shouting opinions and drinking freely and flirting and whoring and weeping and being forgiven for it all. When has a woman ever been forgiven? Can you even imagine it? For I have seen the plane of being, and nowhere upon it is the woman tracing her life as she always dreamed of it. Always there are the boundaries, the rules, the questions—*wouldn't you prefer to be back home, little lady?*—that break the spell of living. What a fantasy to live within that spell, the enchantment of speaking one's mind, and doing one's will, and waking in the bed of one's choosing. I say this simply as a woman rattling the cage to be free. And what do I mean by free? Just to walk down the street. Just to buy a newspaper without a single eye deciding my place. A shrew, a wife, or a whore. Those seemed to be my choices. I ask any man reading this, how could you decide whether to be a villain, a worker, or a plaything? A man would refuse to choose; a man would have that right. But I had only three worlds to choose from, and which of them was happiness? All I wanted was love. A simple thing, a timeless thing. When men want love they sing for it, or smile for it, or pay for it. And what do women do? They choose. And their lives are struck like bronze medallions. So tell me, gentlemen, tell me the time and place where it was easy to be a woman?

January 9, 1942

I can so easily imagine that scene in 1919: my husband standing with his suitcase in the hall, staring at me across the long distance that separated us. I see myself at the bedroom door, all in hyacinth silk. The war scar white in his beard the only change in the face I knew so well, a face that in another scene of leaving had looked at me from a car window. In another world, it all might have gone differently. Pocket watch in his pocket, a crease of pain in the corner of each eye. Once again, the flash of light on his glasses might be the last I ever saw of him.

In another world, he would have tried to say the right thing. Even with love lying dead on the operating table, yet still the right thing might bring it back to life. But who has ever found the right thing to say? Who, in the history of love, has ever found it, and said it perfectly to the woman standing there? In another world, he might have come close. But my Nathan, in 1919, was too battle worn and proud to say he was sorry again. I imagine all he said was, "Good-bye."

For I was not there, and can only imagine it. It was the midcentury Greta he said it to, who might have begged him to stay had she not loved a better version of that man. And I was in her life, the one who stood outside the door in 1942 at Patchin Place, with my son, weathering the cold in our hats and mittens, watching the iron gate for half an hour before—at last!—a shape in an army coat and duffel came and undid the latch and stepped into our little cobbled road and I let my son free to run to him. I watched the clean-shaven man drop the duffel and pick up the boy, shouting ridiculous nonsense before he turned to grin at me. You, Nathan, all over again. My husband home from war.

There almost has to be a heaven, so there can be a place where all things meet. Where time folds in, a lifted tablecloth after the meal, and gathers all the scattered crumbs of life. A son and a brother, a husband, all sitting by the coal fire while from another room comes the scent of Mrs. Green making split-pea soup, a smell so rich it is almost as if we are eating it. Nathan costumed in drab, creased and pinned and necktied with his glasses sitting a handbreadth above his smile. The sagging sign above him done in silver, WELCOME HOME DADDY, and his son misbehaving wildly, almost delirious with joy, his collar now firmly in his father's grip, a wife amazed to see him alive again, no hatred anywhere, nothing but the grand relief of being home and shouldn't there be a dog here with its head on his polished shoe? Shouldn't there be a grandmother knitting scarves from reused yarn? Shouldn't there be a white-frosted cake—oh there it is! HAPPY BIRTHDAY, TWINS.

"Looks like it's England for me, though that could change any minute," Nathan was saying, one cheek glowing red from the warmth of the fireplace, the creases white around his eye. "Guess I'll have to learn the language." With a wink.

What a different man from the one I had left in 1919. He stroked his son's fine hair and smiled and told us stories of bad food and bad behavior, the underfed Okie boys who showed up more Adam's apple than soldier, and the funny old lady who sang to them from her fire escape as the soldiers stepped out of Grand Central. "Over There" was what she sang. As he talked, and petted Fee, he looked across the room and smiled at me and, as the poet said, that smile would make a stone love.

Felix, beside me, leaned over and whispered: "Happy birthday, Sis, I have something to show you." He bent his head to the right. There, in those red hairs, only an expert could have picked out the weeds of white. He turned back and his mouth gaped in alarm. "Old! We're getting old!" I told him that was nothing; my hairdresser had been plucking mine out for years, and I kept the smile on my face as it occurred to me that this Felix was changing, aging as I watched. The brother I remembered had never seen a wrinkle, never known a gray hair. This Felix, along with me, would have to grow old. How I wished I could stay to see it. For there were only four procedures left.

Downstairs, the next day, making the beds after Cerletti had given me my procedure, I felt as if I was closing up a house for the summer, closing up a life. Everything was cycling one last time, three more shocks after this, which meant I would return to this world one more time before taking my final dose. I knew that each object I touched might be the last I would ever see of it. The people as well. But how do you say good-bye to someone who does not know it is good-bye, will never know? To stand with Mrs. Green and fold a quilt with her, approaching close enough to her at last to smell the nutmeg and cigarette in her hair, how could I tell her: *You were my only friend in this age?* To wonder, if I looked for her in my modern time, would I find her anywhere at all? Would she be back in Sweden, or France? Would she even be alive?

"Mrs. Green," I said, turning to her as she picked up a pair of Fee's knickers to mend, "what is your given name?"

She did not look up, but kept sewing her maidenly stitches, so small and perfect even without the use of the machine, which was being repaired. "Karin," she replied.

"And what happened to your husband?"

The room waited for four, five, six stitches before she said, "I never had a husband, madam." She looked up at me but nothing was furrowed or marked on her face at all. She simply added: "I found it easier to say so, long ago."

I went through all the possible stories in my mind, as one does at moments like this, when a human being one has known breaks the bonds of expectation, expands almost infinitely beyond them, then contracts again into the small woman in the parlor, making stitches with a thread not quite the right color. We are so much more than we assume.

"I will still call you Mrs. Green, if you don't mind."

"As you wish, madam," she said, nodding and going back to the knickers, adding only, and this time more quietly: "Yes. Thank you." Then: "Your brother took Felix out to the toy store and your husband had to stop by the clinic. It might be a good time to take a lie-down."

"Thank you," I said. "Thank you," and I said it

the second time as one double-ties a knot, to ensure that it will stay.

That night, his last before he left for England, Nathan removed my cast. "You're married to a doctor, after all," he said. "And it's time to come off."

Sitting beside me, he began at my elbow: I felt the cold metal of the shears against my skin. The rasp of his gentle cutting was the only sound in the room. Only once did the shears grab at my skin, causing me to gasp, and he stopped, took my hand, and paused for a moment.

As I sat and watched him, and felt him with those shears so close to my tender skin, I wanted to ask, *How often do you think of her?* With his gaze so intent on his work, wiping bits of plaster from his cheek where they had stuck. *How often do you mistake someone on the street for her, and your heart starts pounding?* The silver circles the light made in his military hair. But must we always ask those things? Does it always bring us closer? Or was this itself the closeness: the prick of the shears, the careful adjustment, the tear of the plaster, the trust and concentration? There, haloed in the light, biting his lip and changing his position so as not to hurt me if he could avoid it. My blood beating so close to the sharp metal. Was this the marriage? To hold still, to do our best.

Only when he reached my thumb, and with a great crack was able to tear the whole thing loose, did he place my naked arm on a fresh towel and begin to clean it with a sponge. I flexed my fingers, amazed. As if it were not my arm at all. I looked up at my husband, who sat flushed and beaming at his work. "There," he said. "As good as new."

And on the walk we took, later, around the old neighborhood, something came into my head and I took his hand in my now unbroken one, thrilling at the freedom and lightness of my new arm. "Wait," I said. "Come here. I want to see something."

"Well, what's this?" he said, looking amused.

"I just want to see." I pulled him along with me toward the arch, now with its statues complete. There was a couple beneath it saying a prolonged good-bye. I walked to the side and saw, there, just what I had hoped for. The same white stone. "I wonder . . . ," I said, and picked it up. And it was there.

I turned to him, laughing, the key in my hand.

Only in brief flashes does it come to us that we may never see someone again. It is an absurd thought; a car crash or heart attack or rare disease may take anyone, and the last may be that matinee you sneaked to together, or the tipsy lunch, or the silly phone argument that one more meeting would dilute; equally, the melodramatic moments in hospitals and airports and apartment doorways are no assurance of an ending. They are just the preparation for one. And it is doubly true with lovers, for with them it is not just the person who might vanish, but the beating heart itself. With people, the end is rarely in our minds; it takes a man with a scythe to remind us. With lovers, though, the end is always there. It is a death as certain as the real death, and those of us in love, as at the bedside, begin to prepare ourselves. We might say it isn't working, or I can't give you what you need, and yet a day later there he is in your arms, and who can help it? There is the good-bye, and the good-bye, and the good-bye, and which will stick? Who can ever say, this is the last? Only one is true, but all of them feel true, and the tears we shed are equal every time.

"Nobody comes up here," I said to Nathan as he looked at me in amazement. "Nobody even knows it exists."

JANUARY 15, 1986

Only two procedures left after this one. *How does it end?* I lay on Cerletti's table, letting the electricity trickle out of me. Tomorrow I would be in 1919, then a week later in 1942, and there would be one last bolt of lightning before I awakened, at last, back home. We would all be home, for good. What would I do in mine, with Felix gone again? How would I talk to Nathan, now that another Greta had put us in touch? Was anything better than it had been before? Well, each world was changed. Each one worth loving. But did we still each love our own?

I smiled at my doctor. Tomorrow, Felix's wedding. But today: Felix's memorial.

Ruth had warned me no one would come dressed as Felix, but what an assortment came to my house that day! Felix in the awful plaid shirt Alan threw out long ago. Felix in a swimsuit and tank top and towel. Felix in a Cub Scout uniform. As a cowboy, on our last Halloween. And in the white linen shirt he wore at their "wedding." And with his arm in a cast that time he fell off his bicycle. There they all were, dressed as Felix, drinking from my plastic cups and looking at the spread of photographs that covered my dining room table.

Even Ruth had been unable to resist, in her way; she wore a long white beaded gown. She explained with irritation: "Oh, I'm sure he wore this at some point. He was always borrowing my clothes." Then she turned to a black man in tennis whites and asked if the plural was Felixes or Felices? "You know," she said, "like dominatrices?"

In the mail, among the condolence cards, a simple letter. Why did I recognize the handwriting?

Ms. Wells,
*   Thank you for your interest in my father's property in Massachusetts. Feel free to give a call and come up anytime, I'm always around. There is a regular train. I look forward to meeting you.*
*   Leo Barrow*

Here, again, in honor of my brother: the dead brought back to life. I stared at the signature and thought, *Greta, you devil, what the hell are you up to?*

I found a knife and dinged it against an empty

glass, and watched the whole crowd turn to look at me. In blond wigs or baseball caps or towels done up as turbans. "Thank you all for coming!" I shouted as the talking faded away. "Thank you! It was a year ago today we lost my brother. He was a ridiculous person. He was the kind of person who insisted on a costume party, no matter the occasion!" A laugh from the crowd. "Thank you for indulging him. He loved life, he hated to leave it. He would tell you, 'I understood nothing . . .'"

Later, as the wine warmed the crowd, people changed out of costumes and became more comfortable. It was the closest approach of Halley's comet since its last time around, almost eighty years before, at the time of Mark Twain's death, and even New Yorkers were curious. We moved some chairs, and brought up blankets from Ruth's flat, but it was bitterly cold up there and the blankets went only so far. People found their coats and hats and scarves. Despite the cold, or perhaps because of it, there was a jolly camp-out air to things and one man had found my barbecue and a broken wooden crate and created a bonfire in miniature. I was not feeling well; I assumed it was the wine.

And then I heard Ruth whisper in my ear: "Darling, he's come." I turned around to the skyline: indigo New York against lavender New

Jersey. And a silhouetted man cautiously approaching.

"Hello, Nathan."

"And so," he said, after we had embraced and stood a foot apart again with our glasses of punch.

"And so," I said, smiling.

Taller, somehow, than he had been lying in his sickbed reaching for me. Taller, brighter, stronger; he had not suffered as that other Nathan had suffered; he had not heard stories of death in submarines, or trenches. My Nathan, calm and kind and tough as ever, bearded and bespectacled in a brown jacket and plaid shirt, a scarf printed with frogs that his new wife must have given him. As a costume, he held a little birdcage with a stuffed canary. Felix and his bird. He had the wary expression of a man who has been called to a meeting whose purpose he has not yet been informed of, and I thought that perhaps we might start instantly on the conversation that was loading itself up within our heads, cocking, aiming—when he stood sideways and put the safety back on, so to speak, by remarking very blandly: "I have missed your aunt." I set myself sideways as well, and the old foolish lover in me knew him well enough to know he meant what he said, and yet could not help imagining that he was really saying he missed me.

"Don't tell me you missed Ruth!"

He shrugged. "Yes, I even missed your crazy aunt Ruth."

"She doesn't miss you," I said, trying to tease this out. "She says you always broke things."

"I don't have anyone in my life as interesting as Ruth anymore," he said. "I remember that summer she came to Alan's house and gave us each a bottle of Incest Repellent." Grinning, hands in his pockets, shaking his head. "*Incest* Repellent!"

I laughed. "You got used to her."

So this was why. Here, a moment like this. Laughing and comfortable with each other. The sensation like wandering lost in streets and alleys late at night, down passages that seem farther and farther from your destination, until at last you turn a corner and see the green wooden fence you know so well, and think, with great relief: *I'm home!*

There he was before me: the real Nathan. Of course no more real than any of the others, no more original, but this transport back to a world I knew could not persuade me of it. Because this was the man I loved. That old gesture, checking his breast pocket for his wallet. This was the man I loved, not any other. Yet even still, something had changed forever. Not that I didn't love him as always, and still felt the reverberations of our embrace as a gong shivers for an hour after it has made its bellow. But that, after everything I'd seen and done, I knew. That even with the spider of old love remaking its broken web between us, here on the roof. Even with his eyes looking into mine. Even so—that I would never have him back.

"Well, I will be careful with her punch this time. You look well, Greta," he said. It was the thing a lover says to the woman he left long ago. Meaning: You look like you are no longer in pain. We moved an inch apart.

"I've had a wild ride this year," I told him, laughing.

He smiled, again warily, unsure if the joke was on him. I touched his chest: "No, no," I said. "No, no, Nathan, not because of you. It's something . . . I can't explain it to you. I've seen myself from all sides."

"That's a rare thing to do."

"I've seen you, too. I understand things, I think." What I wanted to say was: *I understand that it wasn't that you didn't want to be with me anymore, but you didn't want to be yourself anymore, the one you were with me*. But all I said was: "You look well, too."

And it seemed as if that might be all. We smiled our kind smiles, and he touched my cheek, I'm sure because it felt safe to do so. Now that the danger had passed. There were shouts at the edge of the roof—Aunt Ruth with her hand

297

to the telescope as if to a lorgnette—and we looked. Pinpoint stars and the little brushstroke of the comet hanging there. Come around again.

And suddenly I turned to him and said: "Nathan, there's nothing to lose, so I'm going to say everything. I never thought before how unlikely it was. With all the possible ways it could have gone. To have what we did, at least. Ten years."

He had nothing to say to that, perhaps not wanting to stop me, perhaps also not wanting to encourage me. I reached out and put my hand on his shoulder and then, impulsively, I kissed him lightly on the mouth. I felt his tense worried lips, dry from the cold, and smelled, extraordinarily, the pipe-smoke scent I knew from another world, and the soapy odor from another, and beneath it all the unchanging Nathan I had held in every world but this one. I pulled back and squeezed his shoulder.

I smiled and said, "Who else has been so lucky for so long?"

Those separate men, the different men he was, in different worlds. Perhaps it's because I knew Nathan so well, and knew his moods; of him thinking beside me: so quiet! Of him silencing the alarm so I could sleep another hour: so kind! Of him reading some infuriating news in the paper: so angry! I could roll them all into one ball and put it in my brain as one person. Even before my travels, I had met and lived with these different men: the quiet one, the kind one, the angry one. Just as Nathan had lived with those same men himself. For others are not the only ones forced to face our other selves; above all, we must face them. On my last visit to 1942, Felix showed me a photograph of the two of us. It had been taken the week before. And while I knew it was not me, I could not tell which one it was. Perhaps one day they will invent a camera to capture the fleeting self—not the soul, but the self—and we can truly see which one we were, on any particular day, and mark the shifting lives we lead that we pretend belong to one person alone. Why is it so impossible to believe: that we are as many headed as monsters, as many armed as gods, as many hearted as the angels?

JANUARY 16, 1919

What a beautiful day for a wedding. Morning had awakened like a girl in a tantrum who will wear nothing but her party dress, and an unseasonal warmth spread over things, leaving darkened stains where ice had coated the sidewalks, baffling old ladies who handed their minks to their maids. Gray-coated crowds filed into the Metropolitan Temple, and one could enjoy the variety of ladies' hats and men's top hats, one of which belonged to the famed senator about to lose his daughter. And one young woman, all in lilac silk, standing on the steps, arms crossed, staring up at the church.

For it stunned me, standing there, in the church, beside the groom's door, that no one had stepped forward to stop this wedding. Neither of my other selves, not the free-love Greta nor the mothering one, had said a word. Two-thirds of me had chosen silence. Even Ruth had done nothing. It was a new kind of madness to think that I alone knew how unhappy this new bride would be, the stifling pact that would be made within that church, all with the sun cruelly shining. It had happened before; my brother had married this same woman, and had a child with her, and had he not been German it would all have been handled as it had been before: with money, connections, and a father-in-law's stern words behind closed doors. Yet somehow this was what everybody wanted. Families, Ingrid, even Felix himself. Was I the only one who wanted something else?

And I pictured him: Just behind this door, my brother in his fastidious suit, staring at the mirror. Taking a jolt of whiskey, adjusting his boutonniere, and grinning at his bachelor self, about to vanish at a word from the magician at the altar.

Do we have the right to ruin others' lives? It seems so easy to believe that if we swooped in like an angel, we would not hesitate to change things: tell the secrets, right the wrongs, and bring lovers together. But I could not promise happiness to Felix. I could not say, Oh, give up your life, there are men waiting everywhere to love you! You won't be blackmailed or robbed or killed for what you are! Even his faithful Alan could not bear the burden, here. At least, in a wife, he would have a companion. A son, as before. Someone on whom he could project his hopes, so that one day there would be a version of him whose life went right. For, as I stood before that white-painted door and thought of ruining everything, I knew that not all lives are equal, that the time we live in affects the person we are, more than I had ever thought. Some have a harder chance. Some get no chance at all. With great sadness, I saw so many people born in the wrong time to be happy.

The ushers were pushing people to their seats, and already one was walking down the hall to summon the groom. A young man in a curled mustache and dove gray suit, he smiled at me and tipped his hat. He said something else to me, but I was already back outside the church, hearing the organ sounds bleating from within, watching the unusual weather awakening the city as if from a deep sleep. Grimly I crumpled the program in my fist. I was feeling ill, anyway. So I was already outside the church and on the street when the gunshot rang out.

It was only when I ran home that my heart stopped beating out of my chest. For there he was, sitting on the floor and staring at the fire. My brother. Again: alive.

"I got the gun from a soldier," he told me.

The ushers had burst through the door to find the groom's quarters empty: just a mirror shattered by a bullet, and a window thrown wide open to the day. In the mud below: the distinct boot prints of a man who had made his choice.

I looked cautiously around the room, searching for the weapon. He looked so thin, and with his gaunt pink face, his mustache, his unruly hair, at last I saw my dead beloved brother before me. He said, "I had it sitting on the little dressing table. And I thought, it would be so easy." He spoke in the low drone of a teacher taking roll, his eyes fixed wide on the flames. He did not seem to be aware of me at all, he was so numbed by what had happened. "It would be so easy."

"Thank God you're here," I said quietly, my eyes looking everywhere around the room. Light fell in a long perfect diamond across my brother's body, like a coverlet, patterned with the shadows of branches. "Felix, where did you put that gun?"

"I wasn't afraid," he said. A lock of his red hair had fallen and caught in his eyebrow, but he did not shake his head to release it. "I liked the idea of everyone hearing the gunshot. I especially liked the idea of the senator hearing it. Isn't that crazy?"

"Felix, where's the gun?"

"I'm not myself these days. Isn't that what you told me once?" He took a deep breath. "It's in the church. I left it there."

I sighed with some relief. I looked around for water; I could feel a headache, and a flash of vertigo overcame me, forcing me to sit in a chair.

I was not feeling well at all. The sound of a police van clanged along West Tenth, and with it the noise of young boys running after it.

"I met him in September. And he left me in December," he said plainly to the fire. "It wasn't very much time."

I watched him lying there so bleached of emotion. Something had shaken it loose inside him, the thing he feared, and now I saw how still he lay so that it would not rattle and wake him again. I suppose it was holding that gun in his hand. Standing in his wedding suit before the long mirror and watching himself aim it at his head, as if it were the hand of another person. Fascinated by the image. And then something—who knows what?—moving that arm to aim the gun directly at the man before him. The suited, brushed, and polished man he had made himself become. Reflecting the world as neatly as that mirror. What does it take to pull a trigger like that? What does it take to open fire on that man, the one who they would have us be?

"It wasn't much time," he continued. "But it was enough to wreck everything." Then he put a hand to his forehead. "Oh my God, I just walked out of my wedding . . ."

"I'm here now," I said, walking quickly over to him and touching his arm. The dizziness came back. "I'm here."

At last he looked over at me. "I think I've gone

crazy, Greta. You have, too. Look at what I just did. Look at what I almost did. I don't know what . . ." He could not finish the sentence. He froze there in the coal-heated air, shivering, staring and staring at the fireplace as he began to breathe heavily. I saw it came to him in waves, the real vision of what he was. And that it frightened, disgusted him.

A cloud went over the sun, and the light vanished from his body, and I thought of how this was the last time I would visit this world, this Felix: I had seen Dr. Cerletti already that day. Tomorrow, I would shoot forward. Then one last spark before the end. I always assumed it would take me home. How could I not sense something else at work?

"What do you need to hear, Felix?"

"That it's going to be all right," he said, trying to breathe easily.

"Felix," I said, sitting down beside him now and putting my hand on his knee. "It is going to be all right."

"Is it?"

Back it came: the diamond of light, falling over us both, keeping us warm for now. This was the last time, I thought, that I would see this Felix. I thought of all those mourners dressed in their Felix drag, the swimsuit, the cowboy, the torn plaid shirt. The blond wig, the stuffed bear, the birdcage. I thought of pressing that spoon between his lips. "You're alive. It's going to be all right. Life's better than you think it is."

That night in 1919, I put Felix to sleep in my bed beside me, and lay there for a long time listening to my brother's breathing. How I would miss that sound. And so I stayed awake as long as I could, seeing his fox face pale in the dim room, breathing fitfully on his pillow. I was so tired, so hot and weary. I assumed it was the struggle of the day. Images began to swim before my eyes, more than blue sparks and stars. A tightness in my throat like drowning. Was it just the sadness of leaving him? And my unborn child? I tried to calm myself, focus on the lights behind my eyes. I do not know how long it was before I fell asleep.

And for the second time in my travels, something went wrong.

January 17, 1986

Had I already been awake for some time? I seemed to be in the middle of a conversation in a blurred setting, and began breathing heavily because I felt my body collapse under a wave of pain. A cold cloth on my forehead as I tried to catch my breath. Drowned, nearly drowned. And now who knows where?

". . . Don't tell anyone," I found myself saying. "Don't let them know."

"Know what, dear?" It was Ruth, it had to be Ruth.

Heart like a stone outside my chest, weighing me down. Had I read that somewhere? Or was it happening?

"I forget. I forget. What am I doing here?" The cloth was removed and I could see, at last, my red-black-white room toppling sideways in my seasick brain. Ruth was leaning over me with a grim expression and, beside her, Felix's canary cage, covered by a towel. Perhaps she had brought him here to keep me company. I put a

307

hand to my face and it was burning; I could feel the creases left by the sweated pillow. It was 1986, not 1942. A brief moment of clarity: "I'm not supposed to be here . . ."

"You've come down with something. Doctor says it's the flu," she said. "It's time to take your aspirin again." Two white pills and a glass of water held before me; they seemed as impossible to swallow as a glass of vodka. Nausea billowed inside me and as I leaned over the bed I saw there was already a bucket there, prepared for me.

"I'm not supposed to be here . . ."

"Oh, Greta, oh, poor baby, poor baby. It'll be over soon. Five days, the doctor said." She wiped my face and I sobbed for a moment, overcome with the shock of a body gone bad, in which no good place could be found to rest. Everywhere —my head, my muscles, my blood—had turned against me. Someone had missed a procedure. Just like before, someone had missed and so two of us traveled, and mixed up our places in these worlds. But there was no time left.

"Ruth, something's gone wrong. I should be in nineteen forty-two . . ."

"Just rest."

"Something's gone wrong . . ." The cloth covered my eyes again, and pinpricks of stars appeared in my bruised brain.

JANUARY 18, 1919

Washed ashore and moaning, a bell constantly tolling of pain, I found myself alone and in near darkness; a green flame seemed to glimmer from the door, then was eclipsed by someone passing. I could hear whispers and the rasp of a match so loud I felt it scratch along my skull. I moaned again; the pain was not gone, and I widened my eyes in amazement that it could persevere. I could feel my illness pulling me back again, arms of thick watery darkness, and before I went under this time I saw, at the door, a man standing there in a gauze mask. "Get back," I heard in a whisper, "she's in quarantine, I've given her medicine, let her rest." My husband's voice. The man remained a moment, and movement in the hallway sent a gaslight glow across his face. Above the mask, I saw in my brother's eyes the same fatal concern I had once seen in Alan's. *Felix,* I wanted to say. *Don't let me die here. You will be all alone, and they won't treat you well.* The flu, we had the flu. All of us.

"Can she hear us?" "No, she's too far gone, we can only wait." "And the baby?"

Then they closed the door on my room. And again I traveled.

JANUARY 19, 1942

A vague memory of awakening, that third day of my sickness. I watched the darkness melt away and where the desk had sat, a three-mirrored vanity appeared, blooming with reflected light, and I saw in its mirrors even before he appeared: my brother, Felix, in yet another form.

He was in the middle of speaking: ". . . to Los Angeles, there's a chance there, you look bad again, Greta, I'll call . . ."

And he melted like a pat of butter in a hot pan, before the blackness of my fever.

JANUARY 20, 1986

And again, in that white room of my own world, where a vase of white roses shivered in the light. I heard Ruth's voice in my fever, talking to somebody. The photographs moved and watched where I was pinned to my bed. The roses said to me: "I will keep the sadness out." Ink drowned the scene, fringed with hot, throbbing pain.

I was dying. I felt it, and knew it. Nathan thought he had killed her, his wife, but his knife slipped and got me instead, and I remember thinking that it was right that I should die. The others had husbands and children. Who did I have? If someone had to die, let it be me.

In those awful days, as I went from one world to the next, my belly waxed and waned like the moon, filling with my unborn child, and from the door or chair or bedside Nathans came and went, in glasses and hats and beards, and strangers, and Ruths, always the same, but mostly I remember the paper-doll chain of Felixes smiling down at me.

JANUARY 21, 1919

Tell me who awoke that morning? Who felt the sickness draining from her, the bells fading at last, the sheets cold with someone else's sweat and fever, who blinked her eyes and looked around as one does stepping from a long sea voyage onto solid ground, everything still rocking slightly but safe, familiar, home? Who tried to sit up, breathing steadily, and found it hard going but not impossible? With the long gold spear of sun thrown on the floor? A chair beside her, a bookmarked book resting there, a glass of water on the table, white sediment at the bottom, and an unfolded piece of paper beside it? A sudden thought—a hand to her full belly, sensing a life there? What woman was it who cried? Surely not the one who had been there before. Surely not me. For I was dead, I had to be.

In came Millie in a mask, carrying an empty tray, looking startled, then backing away again and gone. A noise I could not make out and Felix rushing in.

"You're awake! You're better? The fever's broken, how do you feel?"

"Alive."

He laughed. "Yes, yes, I think so."

"And my daughter." He looked at me in confusion, perhaps thinking it was the fever still. Somehow I knew. "My baby."

He put his hand to my belly and smiled, but I already knew my child was all right. I found myself laughing, then wincing in pain.

"You had us scared," he said, that red lock falling over his face again. "It was a rough time. All over the city, there were no beds, not even at Nathan's clinic. We thought it best to keep you here."

"Thank you," I said. "How long was it?"

He shrugged and watched my face carefully. "Almost a week."

"Nathan—"

"He's not here, Greta," he told me. "He wanted to move back in, to care for you. I wouldn't let him. We argued about it. You told me what happened, and I let him know I knew. And at last he left."

"What about the procedure?"

"Dr. Cerletti would not let us give it to you again. He said we could administer the last one when you felt better."

"But it's wrong, we're all in the wrong—"

Then the door opened on my aunt Ruth, all in

black with a black turban from which dangled jet beads. "She's alive! Oh, my dear dear girl, I've brought my last champagne."

I said, "Why are you in black?"

"This? Oh, it wasn't for you. I had lined up a bootlegger and he got himself shot on Delancey Street, and now what am I going to do next year? Oh, you've missed a lot, my dear."

"I've seen a lot."

She began to tell me about the wedding after-math. "This one. He caused an uproar. The senator exploded like a French '75 when he learned the groom had slipped out the side window!"

"Ruth—," I tried to interject, but she was far into her storytelling.

The wrong worlds. For if I was here, that meant 1919 was in my world, and 1942 was in her own. One had missed her procedure and switched us all around, the wrong way. How had it happened? Had 1919 gotten so sick in her own era that Cerletti would not shock her? One charge left, but then where did that leave us?

Could I live forever as a wife and mother in 1942? That was not the only question, of course: Could 1942 live in my world, with nobody but Ruth to comfort her? And more: Could 1919 live again in her world, in this world where I now lay in bed? My brain began to work: We could ask for another procedure, another shock, a charge, a jar, we could yet fix things . . .

Ruth was still talking: "We had to hide Felix in my dressing room when they came by, Pinkerton bullies. You can't drink this, you're still recovering, we'll drink it, shall we?" She popped the cork. "It was in the papers. An absolute scandal." She stood, very regal, and looked down on her nephew, sitting with his hands crossed in his chair. "I was very proud of him." She turned and shouted for Millie to bring two glasses. No, three, to hell with it, I could drink as much as I pleased. I was alive, after all. "It's not such a bad world, is it?" she asked of nobody in particular. "Flu and wounded soldiers and Pinkertons and Prohibition, I know, and growing old and losing everything. It's too easy to get down about it. But look at this . . ." Millie came in with the glasses and Ruth filled them sloppily and went on with her toast while my mind submerged into itself, worrying over how it would end now.

After Ruth was gone, Felix picked up his book, as if he, too, was about to leave. "Stay," I begged again. I wondered if I could hold him tight and bring him with me when I left. He must have heard it in my voice.

"Of course." He sat back down, the book on his lap.

"It's going to be okay," I said. He nodded his head gravely and looked out the window. I watched his throat tense as he swallowed some memory he did not want to share.

"Greta, I'm leaving."

I reached out a hand across the quilt. "No, stay just a minute."

He looked down at the book in his lap. "I mean I'm leaving New York," he said, and faced me resolutely. "I'm going to some small town where no one knows me, where Ingrid's father can't ruin me. I'm thinking of Canada."

"No one thinks of Canada."

A glance out the window, where the alley cat was making its way across the roofs. "Maybe I'll change my name." He laughed. "I'll be Mr. Alan Tandy, as a kind of revenge. Someplace I can start all over."

I looked at him in profile, the strong nose and slightly weak chin, the same mustache as the brother I'd lost, the same gray hairs as his 1940s self. A version of my own face. "Quit," I said to him loudly. "Give up. Start over. I see. I just have one question."

He took a deep breath. "Yes, Greta?"

"When you were a little boy," I asked, "is this the man you dreamed of becoming?"

A cloud of anger blotted out his peaceful expression. The alley cat paused and leaped from roof to roof, then glared across the way to us. I wonder what it saw from its perch? A red-haired man planning his escape, his twin sister come from another world one final time. Together in their child-hood home, each thinking that somehow, if they left it, life would be better. The silent exchange of expressions, the things that could not be said. The quiver of his lower lip, the former bridegroom, considering the awful question she had put to him.

He stood up from his chair and sat beside me on the bed. He spoke in a whispered tone. "When you were sick. In your fever," he said, leaning forward, controlling his emotion as best he could. "You told me about a dream you were having. Do you remember?"

"Tell me what I said."

He looked down at my hand, remembering whatever story I had told him in my madness. "It was in some future world, you said."

"Yes, I remember it."

"You said you missed me," he said. "And I wanted to know—"

"I did miss you."

"Did I die in your dream?"

From the other room I could hear his dreadful bird twittering away; Millie must have removed its cover now that I was well, and it was moved to sing at what it thought was morning. My brother's face was calm and bore only the few lines of age that the brother I had known would never bear. Another bedroom, another version of that face. The pills, the spoon, the pink elastic.

"Felix . . ."

We had prepared, Felix. A nurse friend had found us barbiturates and sleeping pills, and I went into the kitchen and found the Jell-O pack we had already bought. On the back, I remember, were instructions for quick hardening, which involved using ice cubes instead of cold water, and I shook heavily as I poured in all the drugs and waited for it to set in the refrigerator. I would go in and hold your hand while Alan whispered to you, and I would run back to check on the Jell-O; it took only an hour or so, but it seemed endless. I was so afraid your pain would increase every minute, and I knew that waiting for death would be the hardest part, though that would not be the hardest for us. When I came back in with the Jell-O, and Alan tried to feed it to you with a spoon, we found that the lesions in your throat were so painful that you were unable to swallow. "Come on, baby," Alan kept saying, "come on, baby, just swallow a little. Just try." I cannot describe what it was like to watch it fall from your mouth like a child. To watch your eyes rolling in your head. And your hands tremble with the pain and confusion. It was not something for humans to endure.

I want you to know it was not you there. I want you to know it is not how I think of you. I did not keep any photographs from that time because it was like watching a family home set on fire. You are always yourself. You are always stubborn and funny and handsome and strong and alive.

Alan and I had planned for every eventuality. And we knew what to do, how to help you. We managed to get enough of the Jell-O down your throat, because after a while you fell asleep, and once we heard your breathing roughen we took a large plastic bag and—Alan and I together— we put it over your head and held it tight with pink elastic from your sewing kit. Your breath clouded the bag until we could not see your face. I did not think it would ever end, any of the terror of that night, but we watched the bag contract over your features as you breathed your last oxygen. Like a mask. I know you didn't suffer then; I am sure you were sleeping as soundly as a child, and who knows what your last dreams were of? I like to think you dreamed of the summer house, and the three of us together. Or else our times out on the fire escape smoking weed until we giggled as the sun set. Or maybe —and wouldn't this be wonderful?—of our childhood by the lake, and our old dead dog Tramp coming from the water and shaking herself all over us so that we screamed. Golden afternoons, that's what I think. What else would anybody dream of? I held the elastic against your neck and stared at the mask of your face until Alan said, "His pulse is gone. It's over."

I turned away from him, saying nothing. How could I say it? But then I saw something that made me pause. As I was looking out at that view I might not see again, I watched as there, on the glass, a set of fingerprints appeared. One by one they materialized on the surface, lit by sunlight. Somehow I knew that Felix would not see them, for they were his own fingerprints, left there in another world. I pictured my brother standing by the window in 1942, touching the glass. The gesture of a trapped person. I thought I saw his breath cloud on its surface, then begin to fade. And I imagined that world I would be going to. Five glowing prints on the glass as he listened to another Greta. Tomorrow, it would be me. In an apron and a kerchief. And she would be in mine, where he was gone.

"No, in that world," I said, "you're perfect. Perfect."

The impossible, the unbearable, happens once to each of us.

He stood up, my twin brother, without saying a word, and went to the window and put his hand just where the fingerprints had been, breathed onto the glass just where I had seen his breath appear and fade.

"Stay," I said. "Stay with me and my child."

"No, Greta, I'm leaving. It's too much."

I closed my eyes and shook my head. "Don't ruin the Felix I know with self-pity. He wouldn't say these things."

"I'm not that Felix."

"Yes you are. I saw it on Halloween. I saw it in Hansel. What happened to him?"

"I shot him."

"So that's the end? We're giving up? At thirty-two, we're done? Well, let's find that gun of yours. Let's finish it off."

He listened to me with anger in his eyes, then walked from the window straight to the door, his fingers on the handle. "I'm going to let you rest. Have your procedure."

"Let me rest and I won't ever be back," I told him.

I looked at him frozen at the door to my room. How often in life do people make that awful sacrifice, that murder of possibilities? His hand resting on the carved brass doorknob. How often do they stay?

He looked at me as the bird sang on, welcoming its false morning, and what was in his mind? Did he know what I was saying, truly? Could he tell, from my voice, the way I gripped the bedsheets, that this was my last day? That the sister he would find tomorrow might be the old one, the one he had grown up with, in matching white lace, who knew him as the boy I never met, but who would never understand

323

him as a man? The sun died behind a cloud, and his face grayed out in the shadows, but I recognized the expression. Astonishment, fear. For here was someone who saw him down to his bones. And not just his brand of love, for who knows how that would go? In any age, for any of us? But the one person who knew the best of him.

Then I said something that made him take his fingers from the door handle and turn to face me. The sunlight came and went within the room, glowing and fading over us. The bird sang on in its dream.

"Stay," I said to him. "And I'll stay, too."

My brother walked from the door to stand by the window and stare out upon our little Patchin Place. "They say it's going to snow tomorrow," was all he said to me, and I saw that I could keep this promise if I wished. Snow, coating that world, and his waking face lit bright from it. I have never been so jealous of tomorrow. Nineteen forty-two Greta, awakening to a husband before he left for war, to the shouts of her son. And 1919 Greta, in my world: seeking out her young man Leo. We were not in the wrong places at all.

"Go," I said. "Get some sleep."

"I don't want to leave you here alone."

"I'll be fine. We'll talk tomorrow." I added: "I'll still be here."

The look in his eyes said: Will you? but he just smiled, tapped his hand on the door, and closed it behind him. Silence floated down upon the room. I looked at my world, the other world I first had entered. I spread my arms out on the coverlet and watched the patterns of light.

The gate creaking at Patchin Place: some neighbor coming home from work. Horns of ships at sea. Horses on Tenth Street, the clop and whinny of a still unfamiliar world. I could hardly believe my luck, or that it took so long for me to recognize it: The world I had missed all along was the one I hadn't seen. Ruth to bedevil me every day. My brother to bring back to life, now in the ordinary ways. And a child to raise, together. What is a perfect world except for one that needs you?

I stood up, unsteadily, and took the wooden box down from the shelf. The hinge opened neatly and showed my jar and crown. I lifted out the jar and set it on the little table, the wire leading to where the circlet remained in its velvet—it was perfectly safe to touch that way. I looked around, thinking, then took the porcelain chopsticks from their place before the fan. Gently, sitting in a chair, I used the chopsticks to disengage the wire from the life; now the jar stood alone, but still full of charge. I paused a moment, staring at the shining object before me. A hammer raised above the machine that brought me here.

I will never know if I did the right thing. And yet—my other selves, were you also standing before the electrical machines? Did you also shake your heads, refusing this last lightning bolt? Because I know you, 1942 Greta. I know where your heart resided.

I can see you so clearly, ironing the sheets of your forties apartment. Wiping your forehead on your arm, the heat an inch from your face. Hair done up in a cloth, beauty put aside. Don't iron too perfectly; don't do everything that is asked, or expected. Put your son to bed and read him *Peter Pan*. Write a letter to Nathan in England. Douse it in enough perfume to last the journey. Write to Felix in California and tell him you're feeding his bird; my dear Greta, it may not be in you to fathom his heart, but who gets to say? It will be tempting to forget, once it is all over, with your husband and son and house again, to think of it all as a blot of madness in an ordinary life, and iron the sheets and black out the windows. Believe me: It will not work. No one has an ordinary life. Remember awakening those strange mornings, the fearful thrilling sensation. Do not dilute yourself in petty days. Greta: Mark your hour on earth.

Felix, I remember what you told me by my sickbed in 1942. I remember awakening to hear you speaking of Los Angeles, and I said, I'm sorry, I wasn't following, California? "Alan's found a job and a place out there. He thinks he can find me work, they've lost so many screenwriters to the draft, it's a chance. What do you think?" Up came your worried face. But I knew that, outside that door, your bags were already packed to go; you could no more stay here with me, in our little house with Fee, than you could move into the Empire State Building. Alan had beckoned you to another life, away from snow and hatred—or so it seemed—and don't we come when they beckon? Don't we step onto the plane and feel the stomach clutch on the takeoff of a possible mistake? Of course we do. Who wants to be the kind of person who doesn't? Who even wants to know such people? "Go," I whispered to you. How you gripped your hat and nodded.

A son to raise, I guess, that's what you left your sister. A son, a husband overseas who'd been won back, a taciturn housemaid and friend. Don't think she didn't cry. But don't think the stove alarm didn't go off, signaling that the corn bread was ready; and the mail didn't arrive with new reminders for old bills; and a lightbulb didn't crack and blacken in the study; and she didn't step barefoot on a tin soldier bayoneting her tender instep. Don't think she didn't have her own life to lead, and tomatoes to can, and bins to empty, and sugar to ration, and pants to let out, and *Fibber McGee and Molly* on the radio, and air raids in the skies, and boys to discipline, and meatballs to simmer, and all the lovely minutes and hours of Mrs. Michelson of Patchin Place.

And what to tell you, Greta, in my strange cold world, in its strange cold war? To have chosen this, to have traded a beaded, silken world for one of wire and steel; I hope you won't regret it. You will find things missing. Prussia. Palestine. Persia. Your brother. Your husband. Your unborn child. Alone, perhaps for the first time, a woman alone. I have never met you—and will never meet you!—but I have a sense you're suited for it. More suited than I ever was. I see you in a long white coat striding up Sixth Avenue, your camera bag under your arm, in sunglasses and a wide-brimmed hat. How strange to sense that my life has always been wrong somehow, like a machine with an ill-made motor, when the solution was so simple: Replace the missing part! Replace the person living it! And see how smoothly it all goes: the coat, the stride, the glasses, up Sixth Avenue and away. I know the heart that churns there; I have felt the wake it leaves. You may awaken some day, months from now, and realize your daughter has been born.

The web between us will have dried and blown away, but something will remind you. Will you cry to miss it? Will you mark it somehow?

How clearly I can see you on that summer day: stepping out of a pollen-dusted rental car. Out the window: a small dirt road, a long stone wall. How strange to see it all again, this time uncovered from the snow that hid it, like furniture in a summer house. The sound of your slamming door is an insult to the quiet all around, the low-tide noise of a million insects. A bird sits on the fence, looking back and forth, back and forth. All for this: someone stepping from the cabin, wiping his hands on his jeans, saying, "You must be the New York woman who called about the property."

"Yes, I'm Greta Wells."

The bird looks back and forth, back and forth. A handshake—and will the air warp slightly at this fresh impossibility?

"Leo," he will say, that same awkward grin, raising a dimple on his wide handsome face. A lifted eyebrow, a chin already blue with a new beard. Back from the dead. You cannot say: *You have a little girl.* Just nod when he says he could show you around. Out in the woods, you wonder, is there an old treehouse? You cannot say: *Hello, love of my life.*

He turns, blue shirt and jeans; you follow. Nothing changes, nothing is lost.

For we are the same woman. How could we not make the same choice? My hand trembled slightly as I stood on the stone hearth, lifted the jar over my head, and then—crack!—it shattered in a bright blue bolt of electricity.

I felt it in three brains.

And then it was over. I looked at the broken glass around me. Dorothy, dewitched. Alice, unrabbited. Wendy, never neverlanded.

I understood nothing, Felix, I thought as I held myself steady against the wall. *But it was a great show.*

Standing in that room, the room in which I first awakened. The passage back to my world in shards upon the floor. Pale lilac wallpaper, ball and thistle. Gold-framed painting, sooted gaslight back plates, long green heavy drapes pulled nearly closed, and the great oval looking glass before me. I sat back on the bed and looked at that reflected woman, who not long before was a stranger. Long waves of red hair, flushed narrow face, a yellow nightgown over a pregnant belly. The woman I dreamed of becoming?

I heard a sound in the distance.

I turned and almost saw it, on some distant sunset-gold roof: a hammer pounding a wooden stake, not unknown at that hour, but how strange the effect on me. The hammer, and after it the faint sound of another, but this one not from my world. And after that: another. The worlds were echoing, one last time. A workman's hammer, a wooden bowl, a shutting door—whatever they were, each beat in sequence from its time, almost the way the lost memory of a sound will ring out, unprovoked, from the past when the mind hears its twin in the present. Thud . . . thud . . . thud. I sat and listened to them pounding through my body. Thud . . . thud . . . thud. The universe threaded itself together at that moment. Thud . . . thud . . . thud. And we all sat and listened, sat in that exact position, with that exact sound. Thud . . . thud . . . thud. One last time, the drum was sounding, the drum that no one else could hear. Then it occurred to me: It was no drum. It was my three hearts beating.

And I knew, as the sound faded away and the whip of a carriage outside took its place, the noise of children on the sidewalk, that it would be the last I would ever feel them. The other Gretas. I was once again on my own.

I lay back on the bed and watched the strip of light cast through the drapes onto the floor. Tomorrow there would be a house to run, a maid to order, a husbandless life to lead, a brother to quarrel with and bully. Tomorrow there would be Ruth's phonograph playing too loudly down-stairs. A dress to mend. A job to find. A daughter growing to meet the world I made for her.

But for now there was this: that gold spear of sunlight, glowing with the last of the day. The burnt electric smell of spent enchantments. Ruth's glass where she left it on the vanity, a little champagne sparkling at the bottom, and Felix's gloves, which he must already be missing.

"Stay," I had said, and that is what I had done. I pictured already a daughter in this room, pink as a shrimp, bundled in blankets and warmed by the fire, Ruth bringing elaborate outfits that the child would never wear except for her delight. Felix measuring her height on the landing as she grew. First too tall, then too pale, then from nowhere another girl would arrive: slender and beautiful with long black hair and shining eyes and I would think: It's Leo. Her father, reaching through time at last. She would meet some man and marry him, wearing Ruth's diamond brooch, and follow him to England. Felix and I would see her to the boat, and watch as it tore away from its streamers and good-byes. "There she goes," my brother would say to me, all gray hair and glasses, and I would fall into his arms weeping. I pictured us both, much older, Ruth long dead, in this room when I would ask why he never moved into a flat with a man he had been with for many years, and Felix lighting his pipe by the window and saying, "We promised to stay, didn't we? We promised, bubs." And I knew, already, that I would never tell him the strange story of my life.

For is my story really so unusual? To wake each morning as if things had gone differently—the dead come back, the lost returned, the beloved in our arms—is it any more magic than the ordinary madness of hope?

But we do wake, each of us, to find things have gone differently. The love we thought had killed us has not killed us after all, and the dream we had for ourselves has shifted elsewhere, like a planet our starship is set for; we have but to lift our heads and right ourselves, move toward it once again and start the day. We will not get there in our lifetime, and some would say: What's the point? A journey to stars that none will see but our children's children? To see the shape of life, is all we answer.

I lay there and watched for a long time as the bar of gold shortened on the floor and dissolved into a glow. The glass, the gloves in shadow now. I pulled the drapes aside and saw, out the window, the setting sun, coldly lighting the world. And there: the first few flakes of snow. Another promise kept. I settled myself into bed and watched the snow begin to fall. Time for sleep. And so, as always: tomorrow.

Center Point Large Print
600 Brooks Road / PO Box 1
Thorndike ME 04986-0001 USA

(207) 568-3717

US & Canada:
1 800 929-9108
www.centerpointlargeprint.com